THE HISTORY OF ARCADIA

LILY
The Silent

THE RELUCTANT QUEEN

THE HISTORY OF ARCADIA

Lily
the Silent

Tod Davies
§

ILLUSTRATIONS BY
Mike Madrid

EXTERMINATING ANGEL
PRESS

Portions of this book first appeared, some in different form, on the
Exterminating Angel Press online magazine at
www.exterminatingangel.com
Exterminating Angel Press
"Creative Solutions for Practical Idealists"
Visit www.exterminatingangel.com to join the conversation
info@exterminatingangel.com

Exterminating Angel Press book design by Mike Madrid
Layout and typesetting by John Sutherland

ISBN: 978-1-935259-18-3
eBook ISBN: 978-1-935259-19-0
Library of Congress Control Number: 2012935087
Distributed by Consortium Book Sales & Distribution
(800) 283-3572
www.cbsd.com

Printed in The United States of America

CONTENTS

"The 'devil' is always that which wants us to settle for less than we deserve, for panaceas, handouts, temporary safety; and for women, the devil has most often taken the form of love rather than of power, gold, or learning."

—Adrienne Rich,
"On Lies, Secrets, and Silence"

§

"To the ignorant nothing is profound."

—Mervyn Peake,
"Gormenghast"

In memory of my godparents

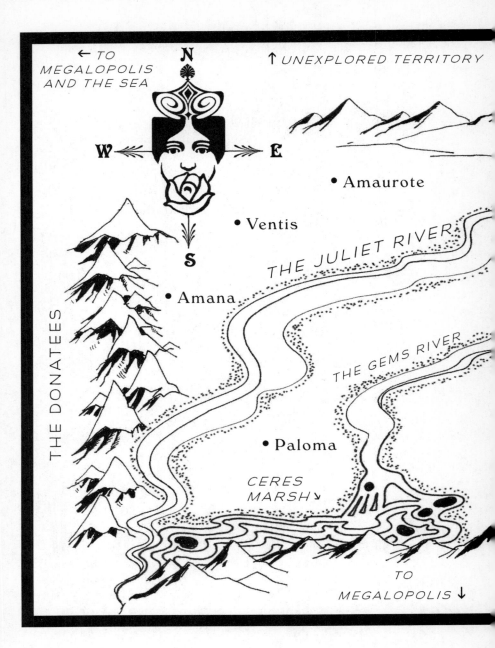

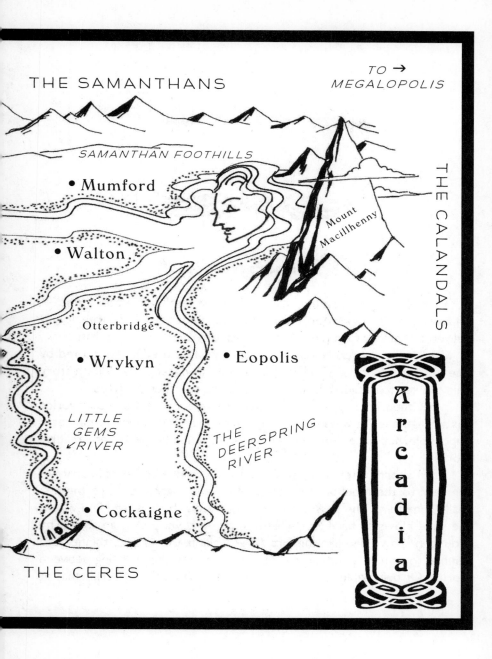

Editor's Note

One winter's day some time ago—I almost said 'Once upon a time'—, on a walk in a snowy wood, I found a parcel under an old fir tree. It was delivered there by Owl, from Arcadia, a land in another world than ours.

This was the Arcadian fairy tale, Snotty Saves the Day, footnoted by one of their scientists, who had discovered this deceptively childish story held the key to Arcadia's history…and maybe to other truths as well.

Since then, I'm happy to say that communication between our worlds has strengthened in ways I never could have imagined before. It may seem impossible, but since then we have received a number of other Arcadian works.

Then shortly after that day in the forest, I moved, at least for part of the year, to the mountains of Colorado. Going over the range there is really something. The passes are at 12,000 feet, above a tree line where the wind blows so hard that whatever grows is warped at an angle. The mountain lakes shine like mirrors. As you climb, the air gets thinner and thinner, so thin, in fact, that you get the strong feeling of being between worlds. Of being able to see through a now transparent scrim that at lower elevations is permanently opaque. That you can actually see through to another world.

As it turns out, you can. I did, anyway.

That was where I met Sophia, who is called, in Arcadia, Sophia the Great Queen. Sophia the Wise. Climbing in the mountains one day, alone, all of a sudden, a voice called out to me, quite loud. Startled, I turned. And there she was, transparent, but there all the same. And she was laughing.

Sophia doesn't sound the way you'd think a Great Queen would. Her voice is raucous, even booming, and she has a loud, shouting laugh that punctuates many of the things she says. Even though I can only see her outline, and the landscape shows through her, I know that she's tall, though a little hunched over, and slender, though with a little bit of a stomach that she says is the result of her fondness for a certain kind of Arcadian wine. She has red hair well streaked with white, and a rather large nose and mouth. I think her skin tends toward the brown, though that's harder to tell when you're looking through a person.

It was Sophia who passed over to me the bulk of this book, which is the story of her mother, Lily, as a young woman; the girl she calls "a reluctant queen, the way I am a reluctant queen." The tale came to me from her in bits and pieces, some in sheaves of paper that managed, on good days, to make it through to me, some verbally from Sophia herself, with me scribbling frantically, hoping to get it all down before the coming of the first snowfall.

Then, as suddenly as she appeared, she stopped coming. I went to look for her two times more, but she didn't come again. The Legend of Lily the Silent, by Wilder the Arcadian Bard, I found lying on a piece of bark, floating at the edge of a mountain lake, that last time I waited for her, in vain.

I'm still thinking hard about what Sophia said the last time we met, her voice and figure fading more than usual on what was one of the final brilliantly sunny autumn days in the year. That day, she tried to tell me why she thought her world could talk to mine. "What our worlds have in common," she said, "is the story of the garden." But before I could ask her what she meant, the air crackled and she was gone. I came back, anxious to find her, as I said, two times more. Then the weather changed, and the snow fell, and the pass was inaccessible for many months to come, over the long winter in the mountains.

Which garden? Which story? I'll have to wait for answers to my questions till the spring, if she comes again. She promised me she would. It troubles me, though, that she would just disappear like that. It doesn't seem like her. I'm left wondering what could have gone wrong. She had so much more to say, I know that. But until I can find her again, or her world can find ours in some other way, I have this new part of the history of Arcadia to wonder at and ponder over, both in the form of a legend told by a bard, and a story told by a daughter about her mother. The story of Lily the Silent, the first queen of Arcadia.

The Editor

The Legend of Lily the Silent
FIRST QUEEN OF ARCADIA

As told by
WILDER THE BARD

rcadia, best of lands, lies between the four mountain ranges that protect it, in the best of times, from the Great Empire: To the east, the Calandals. Mt. Macillhenny, the tallest mountain in Arcadia, is in this range, and it is a dry, windswept place, hard to farm, but peopled by settlers who know the secrets of making and doing. To the west, the Donatees, the most impassable of the mountains, snow capped all year 'round, the place of Resistance, where game of all kind abounds. To the north, the Samanthans, rising up from the golden Samanthan foothills, mysterious, never crossed until the days of the Lizard Princess, not even by the technicians of Megalopolis, protecting Arcadia to the north from Monsters, Creatures, and the Restless Sea.

To the south rise the Ceres, the sacred mountains. The site and heart of Arcadia, of which no more, to my hearers, needs to be said.

Arcadia provides in unfailing plenty everything that is suited to the use of human beings. It has towns of individual grace and beauty, where women and men can live in comfort and safety, without envy of their fellows. It has rivers that run full and fresh, teeming with

1

fish and other life, the Juliet River, and its tributaries, the Gems and the Deerspring. It has green fields that cradle the towns, growing every kind of food to be traded and sold in its playful markets, no one market more than a morning's walk one from the other. It has forests made of every kind of tree growing each at its own favored place, trees that spread, mysterious and benign, about Arcadia on all sides, evergreen and elegant silver in winter, pale copper green and chartreuse in spring, emerald in summer, and golden, ruby, and velvet bronze in the fall. In three seasons there grow everywhere flowers of all colors and scents, in such profusion that the bees, ignoring categories, make honey of a hundred indescribable flavors. The vines of the Samanthan foothills, which reap the harvest of the southern sun, make our fine wines, those to the east productive of a deep gold wine and one, popular in summer, of a pale rose, while the vines closer to the west produce what we call Queen's Wine, from it having been, always, the favorite of our queen, Sophia the Wise, a burgundy red drink that smells of strawberries, tasting of violets, mountain truffles, and fresh hay.

The people of Arcadia have grown up from two strains: those who have inhabited the towns since Before the Time of Records, and those who came over the mountains with Lily the Silent, at the time of the Great Deluge, in the days before she became Arcadia's first queen. And these are every kind of peoples that the Great Empire of Megalopolis had conquered and enslaved, and so now our people are of every conceivable kind and color, as our forests hold every kind of tree, and our fields every kind of flower.

In the early days, the time between Before the Time of Records and the Great Megalopolitan Invasion, Arcadia was a magistracy, arranged so that each neighborhood in each town elected its own leader, who then joined with the general council of her town in choosing one representative to attend the twice yearly councils of Arcadia. But this system, rational and humane as it appears to us, its inheritors, even now, could not survive the Evil Times that come when the Warlike threaten the Peaceful.

It was in such Evil Times that Lily, she who would become Lily the Silent, first queen of Arcadia, lived, and began the journey that made her queen.

The birth of Lily is unknown, being in the time Before the Records. Of her birth many different stories have been told, each one holding in common only that they speak of a great mystery. Little is known of her origins. No one knows the name of her father. No one knows her past. It was her silence about these that gave her the name Lily the Silent.

Mae the magistrate was her mother. Her stepfather was Alan, son of Maud the Freedom Fighter, whose exploits we all know through the twice told tales of our forebears, always spoken, never written, by tradition and preference, passed down at many a winter hearth, and never before collected into words on a page. Until now. Now by me, Wilder the Bard, tasked with the setting down of the History of Arcadia by our queen, Sophia the Wise. The stories of Maud the Freedom Fighter are those best known by every Arcadian child. I have no need to sing of them here, when they sing, brave and sweet, in every fellow Arcadian's heart.

Mae, Alan, and Lily lived in an Arcadian garden house on the hill of Harmony Street, in Cockaigne, in the days before the Great

3

Invasion.

Mae was a refined and prudent woman, a magistrate, as I've said, and a leader. Alan was a good man, a good husband and father, peaceful in times of peace, never offering to strike a first blow, but fierce in defense.

Mae and Alan raised Lily as an Arcadian child, that is, quiet and content, loving her land and her neighbors and her family, in the way of Arcadia. She was a beautiful girl, the most famously beautiful, not just in Cockaigne, but in the other towns, too. Her hair was as black as water-splashed rock in morning shadow, and her skin was as cream colored as good strong coffee and milk. Her eyes were large, slanted and oddly colored: red brown when she was calm, but striking sparks of green when she was not.

All the boys were in love with her. But she would have none of them. For Lily, from the beginning, there was only one great love, and that love she gave away to lead the Great Migration and become our queen.

Lily often visited her stepgrandmother, the great Freedom Fighter Maud, whose story we know from the tale of the Dog Husband and other nursery fare. Maud lived in a tiny, solitary, well built house at the edge of the forests of the Ceres, where she had retired at the end of her legendary exploits, and where she entertained seldom, and then only the closest of her friends.

The closest of all Maud's friends was Death, and it was in the Tiny House in the Forest that Lily, as a young girl, met Death and was befriended by her.

And this must have happened close before the Great Invasion, when Megalopolis found itself in danger, and in the power of its magnificent panic, overran the Calandals and came into Arcadia with a pretense of Peace. And Lily knew this would happen, because Death had told her so. When Maud went away with Death, it was Lily who saw them walk, arm in arm, away.

Then Lily, and her dog, the famous Rex of our hearthside stories, were taken in slavery to Megalopolis to work in the Children's Mine. For Megalopolis had discovered a profit in forcing children to pay their own way, and not just their own way, but that of others, too. While she was there, she should have languished and perished with the hardness of it all, for the contented children of Arcadia do not make good slaves, as history has shown. But Lily had lived in the times Before the Records, and what happened there is dark to us, but whatever happened, it tempered her strength and stored it against just such a need as this. So she lived through these times, and many times to come, until she became our queen.

She was silent about this time later, as she was about many things. And I cannot say that I can find it in me to blame her, as there are many things the wise cannot say. Or even those who are on their way to becoming Wise.

Now it happened that, then, in Megalopolis, there lived a young man who was blessed with everything it was in Megalopolis' gift to give. He was handsome and rich. He was the darling of all the women. Not a one would have resisted a look from his eyes, which, it was said, were the color of the blue sky over a snowy mountain on a sun filled winter's day. Not a one failed to dream of pulling tenderly at his golden hair. Not a one didn't long to caress and be caressed by him.

He was the son of a rich man, and, as they call them in Megalopolis, a rich man's wife. Livia, well known to Arcadian children as a witch, a witch who had long ruled Megalopolis in secret, through the magic spells she worked on men. The name of her son was Conor Barr. He was engaged since childhood to wed the beautiful Rowena, as rich as her long blonde hair, as untouchable and cold and brilliant as a frosty night's star. But on seeing a portrait of Lily, he would have no one else, and, leaving Rowena behind, rode into the mountains to take Lily and her dog from the Children's Mine. All marveled at this, that a son of those who were like kings would take, even as a concubine, a lowly slave.

But his mother, Livia, smiled. And no one knew why.

At this time, and in secret, the Glorious Empire of Megalopolis was dying. Few knew it, though all felt it. This was a time that comes to the Great when they have forgotten the Small, and the earth rots under their feet. So it was, then, with Megalopolis, and it was this that was the reason why the raging Empire reached out farther and farther and farther still for slaves and treasure and food and water, in hopes that it could hold off its ordained end. And hold its end off it did, with the goods, and the lands, and the foods, of others.

But the people of Megalopolis, the masses, felt the ground shift under their feet. This made them uneasy, and hard to drive. And so it was that the rulers of Megalopolis built a Phony Moon, a second Moon in the sky, at first as a pleasure ground for even the very lowest of their country to amuse themselves, and then as a haven for those who could afford to flee to the Cold City. They did this not just to save themselves from their own folly, but also to hide the Real Moon. For when the common people could see the Real Moon, they could see the angels there, those beings who made it a way station on their flights across the heavens. When nothing but the Real Moon was in the night sky, the people could watch the angels' shadows fly across its pale light. Then the people were reverent and silent, and thought again of the old days, when the land did not shiver and quake under their feet. And when there had been the promise of justice for all.

It was to the Phony Moon that Livia took the beautiful Lily and the dog Rex. And Lily, the darling of every festivity given on that Phony Moon (and there were many such, that final season before the Great Disaster), danced and sang, and dallied with Conor Barr, who, for all his charm and riches, was as beneath her as the Earth is beneath the Real Moon.

Lily knew this was so, that Conor Barr was handsome and courteous and fair. But that he was also vain, and boastful, and pleasure loving, and weak. She knew that he was weaker than she. But she loved him, and only him, and knowing his faults did nothing to erode her love, but strengthened it, in the way of love, against a darker day.

That darker day was not slow in coming.

On the seventh night that Lily danced, with the cream of Megalopolis, on the Phony Moon, Livia led her away. The witch led the girl across the Crystal Bridge to the Real Moon. The rulers of Megalopolis met there, in secret, in fear of their promised end, and in defiance of the auguries that told them of it, auguries that appeared thick and fast, as the days turned. They met around an Angel who had been captured in her flight, bound and tortured. They demanded that she tell the remedy for the disasters Megalopolis had brought to Earth. But rather than tell, the Angel died. And the rulers cursed the Angel, but read again the Great Book of Megalopolis, in which was told everything that had happened and that would happen. No one knows where the Great Book of Megalopolis came from, whose gift it was to the Empire, but the Great Book was there, on the Real Moon, and it told of what was to come, though in hidden words. And the scientists of Megalopolis said this was not possible under the Sun, that these hidden words were meaningless, that those who studied them were fools.

But on the Real Moon, what is possible is just that which cannot happen only under the Sun. On the Real Moon, what is Foolish under the Sun, is there Wise. The scientists of Megalopolis had forgotten that, though what Bards there were then (and there were very few, and those poor and hungry, as I know) did not.

What the Great Book said was that the salvation of Megalopolis, if salvation there could be, lay at the bottom of the Great Ocean that lapped at the Empire on its three sides, those borders other than the impassable mountain ranges of Arcadia. It had happened that the salvation of Megalopolis, the Key, had been dropped by an Angel (whether or not it was this poor broken one, no one could tell, since an Angel can only be told from another Angel by those who have eyes to see) into the sea. And the only person who could retrieve it, at the risk of her own life, was Lily.

"And if she fails, the sacrifice to the Great Ocean will be enough to stave off disaster for a little while. It will buy us time," said the chieftain who had taken for himself the right to sit in judgment on the poor, there on the Real Moon. And who was there strong enough to gainsay him? His name was Alaistair, and he was an old man, puissant and terrible, and canny, too...almost as canny as he himself thought. Which was canny enough.

He was canny enough to know that what the scientists of Megalopolis told him was not enough, it would not save him or his or the vast country he robbed for his power, no, their magic did not reach that far. What magic was needed now was the magic they said was dead, that they said had never been. They were wrong, he knew. That magic was on the Real Moon, and Alastair was canny enough to know this, and to know what had to be done. Lily must be sacrificed if Megalopolis was to continue as the grandest empire our world had ever known.

This Livia knew. This was the reason she welcomed Lily, even though the family of Rowena Pomfret was a powerful one, enraged by the insult to their daughter. She welcomed Lily because to sacrifice her to the Ocean would bring her, Livia, more power still. For Livia loved Power. She knew nothing of Love. And this made her the highest of the high among the high of Megalopolis.

Livia rejoiced to see the dead Angel, for Angels had ever been her bane. She had been taught they did not exist, and this had made it difficult for her to see her Enemy until it was almost too late.

But now it was, she thought, too late for the Angel. And Livia grinned a hideous grin.

Lily saw the dead Angel, and saw she was not dead. Since Lily knew Death, she knew this. No one else there, among the richest of the rich of Megalopolis, knew Death; they feared Her and ran from

Her and were pledged to be Her Enemies. So they could not see what Lily saw. What Lily saw was this: The Angel had been waiting for her, in her poor tortured body, which she now fled to take up her place in Lily. Lily felt the Angel move into her heart. It was like the falling of a white feather into the place meant for it away from the wind. So she knew what had to be done. She accepted that she would sacrifice herself and walk into the sea to save Megalopolis. And two young girls of Megalopolis, Phoebe (she who was born on the Real Moon), and Kim (she who was later called Kim the Kind) would not let her go alone, but braved Death in the sea to comfort her with their company.

They braved Death, but because Lily knew Death, Death welcomed them there and led them deeper into the Sea.

While they did this, Rex the dog took a long, hard journey across the Calandals to his fate, as the Empire scorched the beautiful land of Arcadia. And what happened to him there, happened to the Grayling clan of the Calandal Mountains. But that is a dark tale, and a dangerous one for Arcadia, with dangers yet to come, and the full story yet to be told in its time and place.

The Three went deeper and deeper into the Sea. And there were many adventures there, and they had many favors from those they found there. They met Manaan, who the scientists of Megalopolis say exists  only in song. He led them to the Mermaids' Table. It was beside it that the Tree stands, that Tree of Tales from which every experience grows, with its branches more numerous than the stars reflected in the Sea, and its stories also. Lily and Phoebe and Kim had favors from Manaan and the Mermaids, who swim, restless, until the day when the Sea is unafraid to meet the Land, and who give those they love many gifts denied by those who live by the Sea.

It was there they found the Key.

And Phoebe, born on the Real Moon, knew herself when they found the Key. She stayed with the Mermaids below from that day on, for she knew then who she really was. For Phoebe had known Lily in another time and in another world, when her name had been Melia, and her form much different then, and she saw that now, and knew that her work in this world was done.

When Lily and Kim came out of the sea, and journeyed across the dead marshes of Megalopolis to return to the City, they were met by the Procession of the Dead, led by Death herself. In this procession were many that they had loved and lost, their families, and the dog, Rex. But they journeyed on.

Next, on that Road, they were met by a brilliant festival, a wedding parade, a celebration of the marriage of Conor Barr and the snow white Rowena, made that day. Conor did not see Lily, so dazzled was he by his bride, and by the herb his mother, Livia, had put in his marriage drink, and so Lily, his true beloved, walked slowly behind the cheering crowd and was the last to enter the banquet hall. But it was at this feast that the Fortune Teller announced the child of Conor Barr would be the Wisest Ruler of them all. And the crowd murmured and hoped: surely, this would stop the earth from moving under their feet?

But that night, the earth moved again and again. Only women and children heard what the earth said, and so began a long, slow walk to the mountains. Past the jeers of the crowd celebrating the wedding of Conor Barr and Rowena Pomfret, the women and children made their way, straining forward, not even stopping to pack much more than a wrap against winter and a bag of bread, toward the mountains, toward the Ceres, the most beautiful mountains of all, on the other side of which lay Arcadia, more beautiful still, even after the lootings of the Empire.

 And Conor had come from Rowena's bed in secret to lie with Lily, and in his vain folly, promised her the highest secret position in the land as his private love. But this, Lily, though she loved him, could not accept, not just because she was proud, but because Death warned her of what she must do. And Lily ever listened to Death.

Lily and Kim the Kind, who had braved the waves together, joined the refugees walking to the mountains. They climbed and climbed and reached high into the secret parts of the Ceres where winter came to meet them. The others thought of turning back, but, it is said, it was Lily who stopped them, and from an icy shelf high up in the sacred mountains, they looked down on Megalopolis to see an enormous wave lift from the sea and dash over the city, drowning all left there, all who had not had the money to flee to the Phony Moon that shone dimly above.

It is said that it was the magic Lily carried that enabled them to see this. But no one would say what happened that night, except in whispers to their children, much later, in safety finally, on the other side of the mountains, when that long cold winter was past. It is said that it was the magic Lily carried that kept them alive. But in this, as in so much else, Lily was silent.

The snow came early that winter, too early, for it was still harvest time. And the women and children were only halfway up the third tallest mountains in the world. It was not the tallest, for that is the Samanthans, and those no one had yet crossed. It was not the Donatees, for those could only be crossed by wily fighters, knowing every rock and crevice. It was the Ceres, but the Ceres could be terrible enough, as can all things beneficent and kind.

Towards dawn of that terrible night, the night they saw Megalopolis drown, there was a scream. Lily rose quickly from her bed made under a tree, and, shaking off the snow from her hair, hurried toward the sound. For Lily was the child of Mae the magistrate, and she could never hear anyone in pain or in need without hurrying to give aid.

A poor woman had mistaken her footing, stumbling in the dark into a ravine where she now lay dead. Her child, a girl, stood mute, looking at what had been her mother.

Lily wrapped the child in her own coat and led her away, and this was the child who later became Clare the Rider, and it was well done of Lily to have saved her that way, for Clare saved Lily's own child to come, many times. For Lily carried a child out of Megalopolis, though she told no one. One other young woman, who was Devindra Vale, later to become the Queen's closest counselor and friend, knew, for she was wise beyond her years, and recognized Lily for what she was. It was Clare the Rider and Devindra Vale who helped Lily keep the women and children who had fled Megalopolis safe, and it was they stood by her on the night of the birth of Sophia, in deep December, surrounded as they were by the warmth of mountain ponies, with a night owl on a branch above to announce the arrival of she who became Sophia the Wise. She was named that for her temperance, her prudence, her compassion, and her clear sight. Much of what she learned was at the time of the Lizard Princess, but about that I will tell another time.

The snows did not stop, that winter, and it took all the bravery and knowledge of the women to survive. Some say it took the magic of the Key. Whatever saved them, survive they did, and when spring came, though it was almost too late, they had, some of them, lived. Led by Lily and Devindra Vale, they went down over into Arcadia, the first and last ever to find the pass that led through the most hidden part of the Ceres Mountains, the pass that has never been found again.

There and then it was that all of Arcadia proclaimed Lily their queen. But she, silent, neither accepted nor rejected the crown when it was pressed upon her. Three times it was given her, and three times she was silent. "See, she takes the crown!" the crowd called out, but it was not so, Lily did not take the crown, it was given her, and from that day on she ruled with the idea that the crown should be given back.

But she was silent about this idea, as about much else, and no one knew. And many lies were told about her by many enemies, and many who should have seen were blind, and many who should have loved, hated.

For she had the Key, and through the Key, she knew what must be done, and it is ever so that people hate those who know what must be done. "Even though I wish it otherwise," she thought, "it is as it should be." Even she thought it was as it should be when, at the height of her reign, and the height of her sad beauty, a murderer entered the court where all were free to come to ask what they pleased, and he killed Lily the Silent in the seventh year of her reign.

This was Will the Murderer, who Chief Counselor Devindra Vale would not allow to be executed, and he lives still, as I, Wilder the Bard, well know.

As for the Key, Lily took it with her on the Road of the Dead, though poets say she dropped it there when she met her old friend, Death, and sailed away with her across the sea. And the poets further say that Death, because of her great love for Lily, gave her a great gift, a book of the type found on the Real Moon, but more beautiful and more cunningly wrought, that tells everything that will be.

And that Lily, in the Land of the Dead, turns over the pages of this book and sees what is done in her beautiful land of Arcadia, sees her daughter become the Great Queen, the Wisest Ruler of Them All, Sophia the Wise.

The End

· In the ·
year of
Sophia
the Wise
83

Lily the Silent
or THE RELUCTANT QUEEN
As told by SOPHIA THE WISE

One

My mother was a reluctant queen.

That much is clear from the stories I've heard about her, stories I have collected and coaxed from friends, loved ones, even enemies (I've certainly learned through my life that the fullest truths always come to you, if you're ready for them, from enemies). Early on in my own reign, once I had also become a reluctant queen, I began to get serious about my mother's legacy, and began a serious search for who she had truly been. By then, it was clear to the most advanced of Arcadian scientists that stories about ourselves, stories about our shared past, were the key to changing those selves, for good or bad. I knew, of course, that my mother Lily's short life as queen had been devoted to restoring to Arcadia the happiness and harmony it had known before the Great Megalopolitan Invasion. I knew she wanted that in a real, unsentimental way, and that she believed it could happen with all her heart.

I started collecting these bits and pieces of my mother's past when I was about twelve years old, five years after her death. When it was my turn to be queen, I began, with Wilder the Bard, to put together some kind of epic...well, maybe not an epic, but at least a tale, a foundation story for us Arcadians to tell ourselves and pass down to our children. I really think we have a need for that, we Arcadians. You can't have a community without a shared story.

Wilder and I have enjoyed ourselves. At least, I have, and the signs are that Wilder, no matter how much he moans, has a pretty good time, too. Discovering the different shapes and sizes and colors of stories about Lily, bringing my booty back to Wilder's room in the Tower for us to exclaim over (even if his exclaiming is a bit in spite of himself, dear, melancholic Wilder), laying them out, piecing them together, pacing back and forth declaiming them, laughing together (me always laughing harder than Wilder), and crying, of course (there was lots to cry about, Goddess knows)—these have been my deepest pleasures.

To every other ruler, of every kind, I give this free advice: find yourself a poet you can talk to about the story of your realm. Have lots of good talk, long into the winter night, by a real wood fire. Talk your way into your own people's story. Weave it in good faith for your own good, not just theirs. It's an unbelievably relaxing activity, particularly at the end of a day of listening to petitions and granting justice. Take my word for it.

Mind you, the fairy tale we stitched together of Lily's life and her death, that really is Wilder's work and not mine. In that project, I was the enthusiastic sous chef, as it were. The one who shopped for the ingredients, being careful to only pick out the choicest of the facts (and I really believe that the most beautiful are the truest, and the truest are the choicest, in spite of Aspern Grayling's arguments). I was the one who laid out all the bits and pieces for Wilder to work into a whole. I was there to comment and admire and exclaim...and sometimes suggest a little change here, a little addition there...a little more salt, Wilder, it does need just a bit, come on, don't be mean, you want to make that flavor pop if you want them to pay attention. And we want them to pay attention, don't we, Wilder? It's not so easy

17

to get them to follow us without that, Wilder, is it? We need good smells and tastes to coax them onto the right road, because it's so awfully easy to get off that road, isn't it, Wilder? Don't groan and put your head in your hands, Wilder, I didn't mean anything personal by that. But isn't it true? It's so easy to do evil, so hard to do good, to try to do good, to try to help others do the best good they can. It's so hard to stick up for Truth and Beauty and Kindness. It's so difficult, Wilder, I would say on those days where he would throw himself face down on the blue and red and green and gold carpet I'd given him specially, the one with the twining pattern that reminds you every time you walk on it (or lie on it, sulking) of the beauty of a true story. It is so difficult, he would mutter, pulling at the carpet's threads with those dirty fingernails of his. (And how did they get that way, with him always in his tower? I've always wondered. Never asked.)

"Difficult," he would mutter. "And think how easy it is, Snow, to... to...to do the other." Here he would groan again, and my heart would hurt a little to think I had hurt him, no matter how little I'd meant it. Then Wilder would shake his head. "To build up a good life, or even a story on which to rest a good life—that, Snow, is hard."

You'll see that Wilder the Bard, at least in private, never calls me 'Queen Sophia,' as does everyone else in the court, or 'Sophia the Wise,' as everyone does who views me from a desirable (to them, anyway) distance. Wilder doesn't even call me 'Sophy,' which has been my nickname since I was a little girl. Devindra, who was my mother's own Chief Counselor, and is mine as well, calls me Sophy. And Clare, my oldest friend. Of course, it was what my own nurse called me, my own dear Kim the Kind.

In our researches, long before I'd ever told Wilder about my most secret times alone with my mother, I did tell him of her private name for me. She called me 'Snow,' which was, she whispered, short for 'Snowflake,' and Wilder, delighted for some unknown reason with that, took it over for himself. I let him, of course. There's no lèse majesté involved in one artist acknowledging another as an equal. And I can tell you, one of the most exasperating aspects of being on stage as a Great Queen is that there aren't too many fruitful friendships on offer. You take what you can get.

Lily found it really hard, taking what you can get. She found it not just hard to be alone, as Goddess knows I do—alone in her particular courage and hopes, both of which were so much greater and more visionary than my own. Her loneliness was to her like a harsh and endless wind, pushing against her, no matter how determinedly she braved it, no matter how hard she tried to get past it uphill to her goal. It pushed her back two steps for every one and a half that she managed to win.

But she was a shrewd woman, and her judgment always led her to aim for the possible—which is amusing to me, who has discovered the many impossibilities of her life. Still, being a queen, she used to say, was the art of the possible.

I can still hear her voice, as she bent over me while I lay in that little trundle bed next to her own vast queen's bed: "Snow, always remember: you can't tell someone a truth they're not ready to hear. It's dangerous." And she reached out, smiled, and took my hand in hers. I held it, feeling cautiously, the way I always did, for her missing finger. When I felt the place that finger should have been, I knew, even in the dark, that my mother was with me. And I would sigh with happiness, with content, and listen to her advice with all my small child's heart.

She meant, if I remember that particular evening right, a loving correction of my babyish habit of impertinent frankness. I think that time I'd gotten in trouble for innocently commenting on how much I liked the Lord High Chancellor's characteristic stammer. Pompous old Michaeli took offense, even though it was obvious I meant the sound was beautiful to me, the way he called me, "P-p-ppr-pr-princess." It was, truly, my favorite version of my title. But, of course, he hated me for calling attention to what he thought of as a shameful defect, and I always wondered later if it wasn't a large part of the barrier that grew between us in later years. He was always so sensitive, Michaeli. They say he started out the owner of a sweet shop in Cockaigne, but that he came to prominence during the Invasion. Anyway, he was always careful of his dignity, much more careful than I ever have managed to be of my own, and I think he always disliked me for that. As a child I couldn't see the need for silence about the truth, about truths of any kind.

My mother had been right, though. Innocence was no excuse. You can't tell people what they don't want to hear, no matter how true it is. How much is that a fact about countries, as well as people!

Of course, that was one of the problems at the heart of my mother's short reign, people not wanting to hear what they all agreed was best forgotten. But she stood up to it as well as she could, because she was (she had learned to be) a brave woman.

She really was. I'm proud to say that about my own mother. She was brave to try to better a world that seemed so determined not to be better. And her goal was always love. Always, always, Love.

But Love was not enough. Is that only true of Arcadia? No. I don't believe that now. What was, and is, true for Arcadia, I know now, is true for all of the other worlds.

The Arcadia of my mother's childhood was a gentler one than it is now, a more hopeful community, untroubled by any thoughts of a guilty past, smugly confident that its modern version of traditional village ways would continue, if not forever, than at least long into a prosperous future.

Then, as now, Arcadia was what we call a 'necklace' of towns, each with its own governance and special features, divided by a fertile countryside of allotments and larger, mutually worked fields. The

whole of the queendom was surrounded on four sides by mountains: to the east, the Calandals, with their dry, high desert climate; to the north, the mysterious Samanthans; to the west, the impassable Donatees; and to the south, the Ceres Mountains, most beloved of all. The Juliet River runs in a rough diagonal across our valley, striking off into two smaller tributaries, the Gems and the Deerspring. All three of these fall, finally, into the marshlands at the foot of the eastern part of the Ceres. We have no port. We have no rivers, even, that run to the 'outside' world, which has historically meant Megalopolis on the eastern, southern, and western sides, and even now, in the days after the Great Flood, still means the Megalopolitan territories, its vast administrative region. This, of course, has always been both a blessing and a bane, a source of protection, but also of much hardship and loss.

Of the Arcadian towns, I won't have much to say in this story, so I'll just briefly list them here, both for the record, and for the great pleasure it gives me. 'New' Eopolis, known for its practical know-how. Wrykyn, home of St. Vitus's College, teasingly called 'abstemious Wrykyn' for the great care its inhabitants take to have a comfortable life! Flower-covered Amaurote. Market-mad Walton. Ventis, gathering place of thoughtful farmers. Amana, known as the center of Arcadian healing, both human and animal. Paloma, famous for its artistic, and frequently snobbish, leanings.

Mumford, called 'Learned Mumford,' the seat of Juliet College, the first college of the entire Otterbridge University system. The royal town. My own home.

And Cockaigne. Famous as the most beautiful of the many beautiful gems in the necklace of Arcadia. The pearl that is the pride of all the rest. And Lily, at fifteen, was the most beautiful girl in Cockaigne...

LILY WAS THE MOST BEAUTIFUL GIRL IN ALL OF ARCADIA

Two

...which made her the most beautiful girl in all of Arcadia. She was well-made—perfectly made, in fact; of compact height and slender build. Her hands and feet were particularly graceful: even the hand that was missing its smallest finger was so perfectly shaped, you almost thought four fingers was the proper number when you held it. Her nose was elegantly small—not like this beak of mine.

Her hair was glossy black. Not blue black, but a dark color that hinted of chestnut and teak and mahogany and ebony, like a deep forest at night. Her eyes, too, echoed those forest colors, being a dark reddish brown, but with emerald flashes emerging unexpectedly whenever she was deeply interested or involved. I've mentioned her nose, but her features in general were regular—so regular, in fact, that they gave the impression of being a reworking by an unknown artist of an earlier, less perfect draft. Her skin was the color of coffee and cream, half and half, blended by a skilled hand.

All the boys in Arcadia were mad for her, of course. But she would have none of them, as Wilder says. Lily knew that she was meant for Love, and that the Love she was meant for was a particular kind, for a particular person, not yet met, but somehow known. "I'll know it when I see it...when I feel it...when I see him," she said to herself, confident that she was right. And so she waited for it. For him.

While she waited, though, like all the other young Arcadians of her day, Lily spent her time learning her responsibilities as a citizen. She learned how to hold house, how to work with her fellows, how to add to the gracefulness and reputation of her town, how to respect the towns surrounding her. Most importantly, she learned how to keep balanced in body and mind. This balance was always the aim of Arcadian education, even in the days before Devindra Vale reorganized the university system. It has always been an ideal of Arcadian life, then as now.

All these tasks, and learning them properly, absorbed much of Lily's young time. But in her free hours—which were abundant, back then, in Arcadia—Lily dreamed about Love.

It was Love she dreamed of the day everything changed, for her and for Arcadia. That day brought her to Love. But Love, it seemed, was not always like her dreams.

It started the morning she could hear her parents quarrel. They had never, in her memory, quarreled before.

"Your first duty's your family," she could hear her mother Mae say, even though her voice was muffled, coming up from the floor of her room, through the thick dark blue carpet. "That's always been our way."

"Times are changing, and not for the good," her stepfather Alan said, in a new, worried-sounding voice. Alan was usually as unruffled as he was large. Lily had never once heard anything approaching the sound of fear in his voice, in the three years he and her mother had been so happily married.

She heard it now.

Lily must have told me all this, the start of the events that made her queen. I remember it as a favorite story, clamored for at bedtime. She must have told me, and, later, after she was gone, my nurse Kim must have repeated it. I have it in my head, fresh, as if I'd been there in her attic room up the hill of Harmony Street, in Cockaigne, the house that doesn't exist anymore, not since the Empire overran the town, making that street the scene of an ugly fight that Arcadia lost.

But I can still see it. The house must have been of the early Arcadian type, snug, comfortable, easy to maintain. Flowers growing in the gardens all around, from which came the familiar sounds of the different birds, as well as the sound of one neighbor who whistled every morning. Every morning until the Invasion.

There must have been a change in the air outside. Lily, alerted by a strange new sound, threw off the cool white linen sheets of her bed, and slid her feet into the sheepskin slippers lying there, the same type of sheets and slippers she insisted on all through her life. It was spring, always her favorite season, and the mornings were still cold—though they were clear, too, in a way that my dear nurse Kim always said "would break your heart if you didn't know that the next spring they would be that way, too, and the next and the next."

Only this time there wouldn't be a next.

"They'll leave us alone," Lily heard her mother say dully. "They always have."

"But they won't leave others weaker than us alone," Alan said, and he must have sounded tired, for Mae and Alan had been arguing about this all night, there in their big, wide bed next to the window that opened out onto a flowering cherry tree that was long gone by the time I was born. "And after them, it's us. If we let them have this battle, it's our turn."

There was silence now.

Lily went to her window and threw it wide open. She hadn't yet put another piece of oak on the fire that had smoldered all night in her room's white porcelain stove (you see the details? She must have loved her life there on Harmony Street, to have remembered and told me so much, so many small bits of it, and we had an oak fire in a porcelain stove in our room, on cold days—I have it still). But the cold spring air was welcome. She took a deep breath in and could smell many things: the flowering trees all the way down Harmony Street where she lived, the grass on the playing field at the foot of the street, the clear water in the reservoir at the top of the hill by her house. She could feel a warm current in the midst of all the cold—the coming of spring and then summer.

But she could smell something else, as well. Her small nose twitched.

She stood there, considering. She was worried, too. She had been worried a long time. Her nose sniffed cautiously again at the beautiful mild Arcadian spring air. Yes. She was right. She had smelled it right the first time. From the east—from over the Calandals. She could smell the smells of the Calandals, the high, free, desert smell of creosote and pine. But she could smell something else, on an air current which swept through deep ravines on the Megalopolitan side, and up over the top of Mount MacIlhenny, down into Arcadia. She could smell burning. As she smelled it, she closed her eyes, running her hands down her sides, clenching the soft white flannel of her nightdress. She strained, now, not her ears, but, as it were, her inner ear. With that inner ear she could hear it. A deep, distant, unmistakable BOOM. Another boom. She could hear faint screaming, from far away, from far away over the Calandals.

She knew no one else could hear what she could. It was a moment, she told me much later, where she knew everything had been changed. She knew her old life, which she valued so much, her pleasant life with Alan and Mae and her dog, Rex, where she dreamed in her little attic bedroom of a Love she was sure would come...well. She knew that was over now.

So Lily swayed, standing there, as if she had been hit by an invisible force and was struggling to stand against it. She would have fallen, except for Rex, her dog—a black and gray beast with enormous paws and brown, shrewd eyes. (She loved to tell me, when I was a child, about Rex, and this is something, along with so much else, that I loved about her.) Rex got up now from where he had watched her, on his rug by the side of the stove, and pressed against her legs, trying his best to give her back her balance. Or at least to let her know he was there.

At this, Lily opened her eyes and looked down at him. "You can smell it, too?" she asked. The dog looked gravely back. He could smell it too. "It's here, then," she said nervously, kneading at her nightgown with her hands. The dog wouldn't have answered, she told me he didn't. After a moment, though, he went to the window and raised himself up by his big paws onto the sill. While he looked out in this way, Lily went to the stove and stoked it for a little heat, listening to hear Alan and Mae downstairs. But there was only the sound of bacon sizzling, and the faint smell of the pancakes Alan always made for special occasions. They were going to pretend, then, that everything was fine. Lily knew that if they did this, it would be out of concern for her. She knew this and she appreciated it, but in a way, it made her feel more forlorn and alone. Lily knew a lot of things that a fifteen-year-old in the beautiful, peaceful valley of Arcadia should not have had to know. And there was no help for it. Knowing those things meant she would have to act.

But she would be all alone.

Lily didn't want to be alone. But Fate, as she told me as soon as she thought I might be able to understand, is Fate, and if you don't walk to meet it, it catches you from behind, and who knows what will happen then?

"Maybe it won't come to that," she said to herself reassuringly, as bravely as she could. Lily was brave, no one knows that more than I do. And really, it's only the truly brave who know when they are scared. So she was scared. But she was a little defiant, too. "Anyway, today I've got things to do. There's the Feast. And the marketing to do." (Everyday things, my mother always told me, is what we need to hold on to. Everyday things are what make up everything. And in my life, I have learned the wisdom of that many times.)

Heartened, she began to dress. Thinking about the marketing made her almost sure any worry was no more than a dream. The marketing for the Feast—that was real. The Feasts of Arcadia Before the First Reign are still famous in our history; children learn about them in school. This was the Spring Festival, where all of Arcadia went into the Ceres Mountains, up to the alpine meadows, and made merry, as we used to say, before it became so much harder to do. Lily, like all Arcadians then and now, loved a good Feast. That morning, she thought she'd better hurry if she was to get her breakfast and then get out to the market, which, she could see from her window, was already drawing shoppers from all over Cockaigne.

MAUD HAD ORGANIZED THE RESISTANCE AGAINST THE ENEMY
SO MANY YEARS AGO

Three

"What's your family bringing to the Feast?" Lily's friend Camilla asked when they collided, baskets on their arms, at that morning's market in Cockaigne. I mention Camilla here because much later I came to take a special interest in her grandchildren. I like to think of the generations of Arcadia stitched together like that. I like to think that my mother knew their grandmother as a girl.

Lily showed Camilla her basket, which was filled with wild mushrooms that the Wild Mushroom Man collected in the mountains. It was for her mother and Alan's specialty, the dish they brought every year to the Spring Festival. In those days at the festivals of Arcadia, the tradition was for the households of the village magistrates to compete in a good-humored way, to see who made the most popular dishes. Camilla's father was a magistrate. So was Mae, one of the best, it was said, that Arcadia had ever had. I am proud to say of my own grandmother that she is still remembered. Mae had been elected chair three times already in the last few years, an unheard-of distinction, and it had also been admitted that her wild mushroom casserole was the finest dish a magistrate had ever made. This did quite a lot to enhance her prestige. Skills of that sort were highly thought of in those days. Lily was proud to be doing the marketing for her. The wild mushrooms had to be absolutely fresh for perfection's sake, and the Wild Mushroom Seller knew that, and always saved the best for Mae.

"Look, Lily, he's waving at you! You must have forgotten something." Lily turned and looked through the crowd. Camilla was right. The Mushroom Man, with his dark walnut face and his queer

31

little black hat, was waving her back. She excused herself from her friend, and made her way toward him.

As she neared his table, she saw the mushrooms laid out in front of him. The golden chanterelles, the red and blue boletes, the little chestnut nuggets, and, best of all, the honeycombed morels, all of them so scarce in the mountains now, after our last disastrous experiment with crop starts from the False Moon. In those days, though, wild mushrooms grew in abundance, though in hidden places that only the patient could find. The Mushroom Man was famous for his patience, and usually there was a crowd clamoring at his stand. But at that moment, strangely, the crowd was gone. The shoppers were elsewhere, buying up the mountain fish with the rainbow scales, and the squash flowers, and the long shoots of garlic greens for the Feast—all her neighbors and friends, all laughing, all looking forward to it. (Gone! Gone! Gone are the days of those innocent Feasts. And what have we gained by losing them?) Not one of them had heard anything wrong, Lily thought sadly. She was, as she had always dreaded she would be, all alone.

Not completely alone, though. Rex pressed against her leg to comfort her in the way that only an intelligent animal can.

The Wild Mushroom Man stared hard at her as she and Rex approached his stand. My mother always said, "He looked like a black cloud on a clear day."

"Forgot," he said to her, as he squinted his little black seed eyes. Lily's nose twitched. Rex sat and waited.

"You go see your grandmother," he said. "Quick as you can, and right away."

"My grandmother?" Lily said. "My grandmother's dead." This was true. Mae's mother had died long ago.

"Not her," the Wild Mushroom Man said. "The grand one." And Lily knew by the admiring look on his wrinkled walnut face that he meant Alan's mother Maud, her step-great-grandmother by rights, not her grandmother at all. "Though I loved her more than if she had been my own," my mother would say, and I would take comfort from it, not knowing till much later that the comfort came from knowing you could choose your family at need. "I always felt I had known her somewhere, some time before," she would say.

"We'll be taking her to the Feast," Lily said cautiously, not sure she understood him right. "We always bring Maud." Or she brings us, she thought. My guess is she smiled to herself at the idea of anyone bringing Maud the Freedom Fighter (for that was how she was known even then, in our schoolchildren's history books) anywhere she didn't want to go.

"No," he said. "Go now. Someone with her wants to see you. I met Her in the woods on Her way, and She told me so."

Lily looked at him then. For a moment, it was as if the clamor of the market fell away, and all there was standing there were her and Rex and the Wild Mushroom Man.

Rex whined.

The Wild Mushroom Man thrust out a wrinkled dark-brown hand.

"Take her these," he said. In his palm were a bunch of shriveled black mushrooms. These were Trumpets of Death, and she repeated their other name to herself—trompettes des morts—as she tucked them away in her basket.

"Thank you," she said. The sound from the market came back up, as if it were a normal day after all.

Arcadia in those days was very well organized for marketing. (We seem to have lost the ability to act sensibly about this now, I'm ashamed to say.) On a normal day, Lily would have finished the shopping, and then left it at a designated drop-off point to be delivered to her home. Mae and Alan paid to have things delivered daily, rather than randomly in the regular round of drop-offs. But instead, this time, she hailed one of the boys on the three-wheeled bicycles who spent much of each day ferrying people's purchases from the market to their homes. This was a job boys often had before they turned seventeen and had to think, along with everyone else, about more serious work. And a good job it was, too, because you were out in the fresh air all day, and you knew that what you were doing meant everyone in your village (they were half villages/ half towns then, not the full towns they are today) could walk and gossip and be at their ease because of you, instead of having to lug their groceries in some inconvenient, messy, and more dangerous way.

This boy's name was Colin, and he was a frail boy for Arcadia. (Probably this was because of an illness caught in the days before Hanuman Medical College had got our epidemics under control. We used to have quite a problem with healer-resistant strains brought over the mountains, at least before the more recent discoveries.) He was even smaller than Lily, with blond hair so pale it was almost white, which stood up in a shock on his head. Of course he was in love with Lily. Every boy in Arcadia was.

"Which way are you going, Colin?" Lily said.

I imagine he looked at her just as uneasily as you would expect a teenage boy to look at a beautiful teenage girl. "Dunno," I imagine he said. I don't know for sure. Lily used to rush past this part of the story.

"If you're going up Greensprings, pull me along, would you?" she said briskly. (I know she said it like that. Kim told me later you always knew when Lily didn't want someone getting any closer. "She'd get all sniffy on 'em," she said. "She was always like that with the lads. All except your dad, of course.")

"Don't mind," he probably muttered. And I know—I can see—

she pulled a pair of light silver roller skates from the bag slung across her chest and attached them to her shoes. Because that was how they did things in Arcadia in my mother's youth.

Holding on to the back of the wheeled basket towed by his bicycle, Lily rolled along behind him as he toiled up the hill, up past the edge of the last houses huddled on the Greensprings Road, where the big Museum of Arcadian History now stands, that silly, ugly building Michaeli and Aspern Grayling wasted Royal Funds on in the days of my powerless minority. But in those days, the houses ended there at a wood, the fringes of which covered the lower reaches of the Ceres Range. The road got a little rocky here as it still does, though it levels out a bit after awhile, and Lily, Rex loping at her side, gave a little giggle as she bounced along.

The light here was different from down below. It is to this day. There are times (too few) where I pretend I want to do research at the museum, but I really just go out the back door into the woods, leaving those ridiculous bodyguards Devindra insists I have cooling their heels in the ugly lobby underneath the gigantic picture of Lord High Chancellor Michaeli at his most annoyingly grand. The light there, in those woods, is filtered and green, as if you are at the bottom of the sea. In those days there was only one house, all the way at the end of the track. This was the house of Alan's grandmother, Maud. It was a famous house, The Tiny House in the Wood. (So famous that it was pulled down, of course, since Michaeli intended to build the museum where it stood. Until he found out, too late, that the only suitable site for a huge, impressive building was somewhat downhill.) It was from this house that Maud, Arcadia's most venerable Fighter on behalf of the Great Freedoms, had organized the Resistance against the Enemy so many years ago. Had organized it and had won. Or so our storytellers said.

It was a ramshackle house, when all was said and done. I have heard detailed, affectionate descriptions of it many times, and wish I could have seen it for myself in the days when Maud still lived there. Even then, I'm told, it tilted this way and that. The wood was so old it had turned silver gray. The windows sagged in their sashes, and the floors creaked. But Maud always said, whenever the magistrates of the All Village Council offered to have it set to rights, that she liked it that way. You can see all that in the records. At least the ones that we have.

Colin pulled up in front of the old creaky gate, where Lily took off her skates and stowed them neatly in her bag. (She was always very neat, although never oppressively so.) He gave her Maud's groceries, and took her own basket with a promise to deliver it to Mae. Then Colin, whistling, turned his cycle to sail downhill. In my version of the story, he would be in such a good mood after being allowed to help the beautiful Lily that he would do it with both feet on the handlebars and his hands in the air.

Lily watched him go, Rex at her side, waiting till he had disappeared with a whoop down among the homes below. Then, looking at each other, they pushed open the creaky old gate of the home of Maud Delilah, the greatest Fighter Arcadia had ever known.

Four

Maud was entertaining an old friend, and that friend was Death. Lily recognized her the moment she and Rex walked into the room. She didn't know how she recognized her. She knew they had never been properly introduced. But nevertheless, she knew for certain that this was Death.

This was how she told me the story.

"Was this who the Wild Mushroom Man met today, on his way through the forest?" she thought. Her eyes met Rex's. He had recognized the Guest, too, as she sat in Maud's old red leather-covered wing chair, sipping from a cream-colored china cup. He hesitated for a moment as the two women looked welcomingly at the newcomers.

"Come in, come in. Oh, Lily, how lovely to see you," Maud said, her pale creased face beaming. She didn't stand—that was her right, after all, being old, and having sustained so many wounds in the past—but gestured that the two come closer.

At this, Rex moved forward toward Death, and lay at her feet with a sigh. Death, pleased, reached over to scratch the dog behind the ears. Rex gave another great deep breath, and licked her hand. Lily, when she told the story, was clear that Death liked Rex, and that Rex was not afraid of Death.

"What a nice dog!" Death said, and she looked at Lily and smiled.

Lily went to Maud and kissed her on her cheek. "It felt dry like paper, but cool, too. And Maud smelled, as she always did, of roses," my mother said, not knowing that I breathed in her own scent, which was the same. Lily breathed in deeply then, the way I did while she

37

told the story, and she smiled, too, the same as me. She was very fond of Maud, she said. Maud, in fact, was the most important adult in her life, "more even than my own mother, Snow, and if you should find some other adult more important than me to you, I would always completely understand." But of course I never did.

Maud held Lily's hand and patted it. "Sit there, Lily," she said, pointing to the little hassock at her feet. "Where we can both get a good look at you."

Lily obeyed. And the two women—one old, and the other appearing to be in the full flower of middle age, for Death is not old or young, but always at the height of her powers—looked at her.

"As if," Lily thought, "they've been talking about me. As if they want to see if what they said was true." Lily remembered that she put up her chin a little. She was embarrassed to be looked at like this, by Death and Maud. But she was determined not to show it.

Whatever conclusion it was, though, that Death and Maud came to as they looked Lily over, neither of them said anything about it. Instead they returned to their conversation, as if Lily and Rex had never interrupted them at all.

"I've always liked this situation," Death drawled in her elegant way, looking out of Maud's broad front window onto the woods. "Thank you," she said as Maud urged Lily to pass around the plate of macaroons. "I will." Death bit a cookie reflectively. "Of the place but not quite in it, if you see what I mean."

Maud laughed. "Oh, I do!" she said and her eyes glinted with amusement. Her eyes were a deep black, like buttons, and when she laughed they sent out purple sparks. "That's the story of my life all over, isn't it?" She pulled her plush yellow and black wrap around her arms against the slight spring chill. ("And she always wore black and yellow plush, Snow.")

"And of Lily's, too, unless I mistake myself—which I don't."

MAUD WAS ENTERTAINING AN OLD FRIEND,
AND THAT FRIEND WAS DEATH

Again both the women turned and looked at Lily, at where she sat balanced on a little green velvet pouf. (Somehow miraculously saved from what came after—I have it in my own small tower now.)

"You heard it this morning, didn't you, Lily?" Maud asked. Lily looked quickly at Death, and gave just as quick a nod.

"I don't think anyone else did," she offered, and then, embarrassed, was quiet again.

"No," Death drawled. "No, I don't imagine they did." She looked out the window at the woods, but this time her long, elegant fingers tapped impatiently on her chair's wooden arm. "Arcadia," she murmured. "Beautiful...and blind."

"It's a very good place," Maud said in a voice of faint protest. But Lily could see she was sad. "We fought to make it a good place. And to a certain extent we won, didn't we? We won."

At this she smiled at Lily again, and stretched out her hand, which Lily clasped and then let go. "She's smiling at me as if I'd helped her fight!" Lily thought wistfully. "And I wish I had." Because the stories about Maud were legendary in Arcadia. Village teachers taught them in the schools, their voices still tinged with awe at the idea that one of their own could have been so wise and brave. There were no written records of it, strangely enough, but everyone in Arcadia knew that fifty years before, the Enemy had poured through a mountain pass, opened unexpectedly by a landslide. And it was Maud who led the guerrilla force that had pushed them back, Maud who had been one of the leaders of the great Arcadian Resistance.

So it was said.

But as for Maud herself, she always laughed whenever the subject came up—which was rarely in front of her, so much was the awe in which she was held. But she had hugged Lily to herself once, when Alan was boasting in his good natured way about his mother to one of the magistrates visiting from Mumford, a historian who was interested especially in these old tales, because even then, Mumford was known for its curiosity about fairy stories, legends, and myths.

Then Maud had whispered in Lily's ear, "Never, ever believe everything you hear."

(It was a lesson my mother learned, and that she passed on, almost urgently, to me. "Think for yourself, Snow," she would say, murmuring the words into my hair. "Look for yourself. See for yourself, and don't let anyone tell you what you see isn't there.")

Death stretched in her chair now, in the sun. She yawned. "Too smug," she said finally. "Too self-satisfied. That kind of thing always comes to a bad end."

Maud looked reflective at this. And still sad.

"But the end is never the end," Death said, and now she sat straight up and her black eyes flashed. "Not quite."

"Not even when it's you, then?" Maud said. Lily, straining hard to follow the conversation of the adults, pondered over this.

Death laughed. "Not even when it's me, my dear, dear friend. I am so misunderstood...if I were given to self-pity, good heavens, how you'd hear me moan." She gave Lily a friendly look. "But you see me, don't you, Lily? Do I look so big and bad and terrible and frightening? Do I?"

Lily knew that Death wanted an answer to this question, and so she thought hard about the matter. She thought so hard that she pulled her knees up to her chin and squinted her eyes. Rex watched her, encouraging. She looked at Death, and Death looked young and beautiful and kind.

"No," she said finally, though a little timid, too. "But you do look very strong, and maybe that's what frightens people."

"I am strong," Death agreed. "I am stronger than many, many things. But I am not stronger than Life. And those who say that we are enemies, Life and I, those people are idiots." She sighed again. "But the world is so filled with idiots, I don't know why I bother, honestly I don't, Maud."

Now Death stood up. She was tall, very tall—"even taller than you're going to be, Snow," and I am almost six feet. (I get my height from my father's side of the family; all the women there are that way.) Maud stood up also, and motioned Lily that she was to do so too. They all three stood there for a moment, and Death laughed again.

She bent down toward Lily and looked in her eyes. And Lily saw deep into Death's eyes and saw that she was great and strong and that she was someone you wouldn't want to meet when she was in a rage. But Lily saw more. She saw that Death felt deeply and acted from levels Lily was too young and weak to know anything about. She wondered if Maud knew. "Maybe she doesn't know all of it," she thought. "But she knows more than me."

"That was wise of you," Death said, absently tapping Lily's cheek with one thin finger. It was a beautiful finger, rosy and long, tipped with an oval nail—not a claw, as Lily had imagined belonged to Death. "Always remember how little you know. There are so few of you who can keep that in their heads! I'm a great friend to those who can." At this, Death paused again, lost in her own thoughts. Lily had the feeling that those thoughts were of people that Death had loved.

"It must be a great thing to be loved by Death," Lily thought. Then she saw the great lady turn and kiss Maud on the cheek, and, awe-struck, she realized that Alan's mother was one of Death's loved ones.

"I'll come for you soon," Death murmured, and the two women clasped hands. Maud nodded and smiled and a tear slid down her face. She unclasped one hand and wiped it away. Lily shivered at this. "I knew I shouldn't, but I couldn't help it, Snow." But she knew somehow that she had had the honor of seeing a little, just a little, into a great mystery.

"And as for YOU," Death said turning lightly toward Lily in a whirl, "you I will meet again and again. You're going to need my help. That was why I asked you to come today, to tell you that, and to meet you and be properly introduced, so that when the time comes you will know what's being offered you."

"I heard the BOOM," Lily said, troubled. "What does that mean?"

Death knelt down in front of Lily and tilted her chin up with her long fingers. "It means, dear child," she said gently, "that you must find the Key that has been lost. And when you find it, Lily, you must claim it as your own, to be passed down to your own daughter. You must not give it to anyone else, no matter how they beg, no matter how much you think their claim worth more than yours. Those are your tasks: to find the Key and to keep the Key. Of the two, it is the second that is by far the harder. And the first task is impossible! That is how difficult these tasks will be!"

At this, Death bounded lightly again onto her feet, and her black and gold eyes swept the room. She opened her arms as if to embrace them all, and then, with another laugh full of the enjoyment of life, she was gone.

"Oh!" Lily said. "I forgot to give her these!" And she looked down at the mushrooms that she had carried all this time.

"Never mind," Maud said, soothing her. "We won't worry about that now. We have a lot to talk about, you and I." Maud stood now, and pulled her yellow and black fleece wrap more tightly around her. "Let's go for a walk in the woods," she said. "And then we'll go to meet your mother and father and be in time for the Feast. I think," she said, and her eyes were grave, graver than Lily had ever seen them before, "it will be the last Feast for Arcadia for some time. It's been a long time since I've had a visit from Death, and she's told me many things. And even in Arcadia, Lily," Maud said as she led Lily and Rex out of the weathered front door and closed it behind them, "not as many as should would find such things easy to understand."

With that, Maud sighed and led the way, not through the gate, but up a winding path, along which mushrooms and early spring flowers pushed up through the dirt.

Five

As Maud and Lily and Rex walked up the path behind Maud's house, they could see all of Arcadia laid out in front of them.

It was a clear spring day. A slight breeze pushed everything a little this way and that, and reminded you that this was spring, and everything was still unsettled—that a storm could sweep through in a flutter of an eyelid, black and mean.

But now the air was mild and questioning, as if it were saying, "This is how we all like it, isn't it? Why shouldn't it stay this way forever?" Maud laughed, my mother told me, "as if she could understand the words of the breeze itself." And the great old woman shook her head.

Maud and Lily stood there, looking at the villages blooming like flowers below them on the valley floor. We were a prosperous, hospitable, and fair people, we Arcadians. We still are. But our ancestors were small, as we are small, though we try, I often think with more than a little exasperation, to be bigger than we should. In those days, Arcadians were few in number, and determinedly peaceful; there was no argument about that last, the way there is in our day. At that time, Arcadia had laid it down as law that it would never be anything else but peaceful. This was excellent in theory, but it had this one defect (as Aspern Grayling has so truly pointed out): this made our ancestors proud, too proud, in their moral certainty. They were vulnerable. Their pride was their greatest weakness. But this pride also had this one great value: an Arcadian would never risk her own, and certainly not another's, life without very good cause.

Alan was going to risk his life. That was what the quarrel had

44

been about with Mae.

"Mother and Alan were arguing this morning," Lily said, as Maud stopped to stroke an early-blooming cat's ear blossom, cream and purple against the reddish ground. "And that is something they never do."

Maud looked at her, black button eyes bright. She led the way as they walked on, turning downhill now, toward the top of Harmony Street. "And do you know what they were arguing about?" she said. Lily knew that Maud knew. But she answered just the same.

"They've tried to keep it from us at school, but we all know. Megalopolis. And even though we have the mountains between us, they are so strong." Lily thought about the arguments she had with her own crowd. "The strong," she said, and asked the painful question that was always on her mind, then and later as queen. "Maud. Do they always win?"

"We have to fight them!" one of the boys at her school had said—it was almost always a boy who said this. "We can't wait until they run us over and take all of Arcadia. What would happen then?"

"But they aren't threatening us," a girl had said—it was almost always a girl who said this kind of thing, then as now. "They've sent an ambassador over the Calandals, to Eopolis, asking to buy supplies for their troops. It's a peaceful mission. Everyone says so." This last was said shrilly. Everyone didn't say so. But no one argued just then.

Instead there was a great silence. Eopolis, of course, was the nearest village to Cockaigne, in the northeast. Every girl and boy among them had friends and family in Eopolis.

"It's only a peaceful mission because they're waiting till we'll be easier to pick off. They're fighting among themselves, over there on the other side, I hear. My dad says..."

"It was always a horrible place to live and now it's worse. My

45

mother says..."

"They've left us alone because we were small and not worth the trouble. But my uncle says now they've ruined the entire rest of the planet, they've got nowhere else to go..."

"Why can't they just leave us alone?"

"Why can't they just leave us alone?" Lily repeated, this time to Maud, as the two began descending the last steep stone staircase that Alan had built down the side of the hill. "We have such a lovely life here, minding our own business. Why can't they?"

Maud looked at her, and then rested her hand on Lily's shoulder as if to steady herself as she went down the shaded steps, which were still slippery and moist from a brief overnight rain. But Lily knew Maud didn't need to do this. Even at a hundred and twenty, she was still strong enough to stand on her own. She did this to steady Lily.

Lily thought about Death coming again for Maud, and her heart skipped a beat.

"Let's stop for a moment, shall we, Lily? Let's stop and think of something nice. Let's think of all the Feasts that have gone before, all the Feasts that all the villages have made in Arcadia."

So they did. Lily shut her eyes and breathed in deep. Rex pushed up against her hand, and she could smell his warm doggy smell, and the smell of the still damp ground, and of the sun warming the spots of grass through the trees. She could smell Maud's rose-fresh smell—and she could smell the good smells of all the Feast day dishes being made up and down Harmony Street. Familiar smells. They brought back memories of other Feasts, of playing with her friends in the pale green spring meadows of the Ceres with the late evening sky bowing golden-blue overhead. She could see down to the deep valleys on the other side of the Ceres, and, farther to the south, deep inside Megalopolis, the Klamathas, the mountains that ran parallel to them so far away. She could see her mother and Alan leaning against each other, arms around each other's waist, laughing, as they talked to some neighbors and waited for those who had brought the desserts to set them up prettily the way they liked to on the long trestle tables settled there just for the day.

But then, as she watched this memory play, another memory began to push through it, a strange memory, of another time and place altogether. And that memory was of Arcadia, but it was not of Arcadia. As if Arcadia had been another place altogether. As if the Feasts had not always been. As if there had been a time when Arcadia was mean and nasty and heartless and cold. As if it had been part of Megalopolis, that huge and horrible city that surrounded them on all sides, that miserable place, upon which it was horrible to look, and which was now, thank the Goddess, held back by the Ceres Mountains.

As if she, Lily, had been someone else altogether. And as if Maud had too.

At this, Lily, startled, opened her eyes. Maud looked at her with a sad sympathy. "You remember, then," Maud said quietly. "Good. I wanted to make sure. But don't tell anyone else, Lily. Best to be silent. No one else remembers, nor should they. But for you, you need to know. You need to know that it has happened, many times before, that the strong do not always win."

(And I. Sophia. Her daughter who was to come after her. I needed to know that, too. But I had to find out for myself, which is the only way anyone ever truly knows anything, alas.)

At that, Maud held out her hand and Lily took it, and the two continued down the steep stone steps. Rex followed behind.

Six

The Feast that night was a strange one, my mother said. "Everyone felt it." It was not lighthearted, the way the Feasts before had been, even though the foods were as delicious, the drinks as cool and sweet, the lovers as happy, the children as healthy, the neighbors wishing each other as well as much as ever. But there was something that weighed on them all. Bright colored cloths covered the mountain meadows, but no one sat on them. Everyone moved, milling back and forth, restless. The exclamations over the food were quieter than usual, and even the group of teenagers who drank too much of Amaurote's elderflower wine dropped into sullen silence.

The sky's blue deepened. All of Cockaigne was there, in those days almost seven thousand people, a much smaller population than in our towns now. It must have been strange to see that many of us suddenly go still, all at once, on a mountaintop at twilight.

All turned to look south, down over the rugged valleys below, on to the edges of Megalopolis and to the Klamathas beyond, the imperial mountains that rose up out of the sea and the marshes that formed its far boundary. No one could have said what it was they thought to see. And except for the whistling little mountain breeze, there was no sound.

"Look!" somebody shouted. Lily saw it was Colin, his shock of white hair standing straight, jumping and pointing, his small frame shaking with surprise.

A light exploded over the Klamathas, and, a moment later, a BOOM shook the Ceres, so that the village folk covered their ears with their hands. The light soared upward, straight up, throwing sparks back down behind. Straight up it went and kept going, leaving a thin silver line like a tear in the sky.

Then there was another sound, behind them. This was the sound of a car, coming on very fast, and this sound was so unfamiliar that at first most of the crowd couldn't tell what it was. Cars were only used, in the Arcadia of that time, for the direst emergencies. Otherwise people used silver collapsible skates, like the ones Lily had in her bag, or skateboards, or rode horses, or bicycles, or, as tonight for the Feast, open carriages powered by the sun. But this was a car, and it arrived honking, and when it stopped, everyone could see, from the crest on its side, that it came from their neighbor Eopolis to the northeast. A woman jumped out of the driver's seat, and many recognized her immediately as a sister of one of the magistrates of Cockaigne.

Mae, Lily's mother, as the lead magistrate of the town, hurried to greet her, and listened intently to her rapid talk as several of the other magistrates gathered there as well. The husbands and wives of the magistrates stood in their own group and conferred, for in an emergency, they had their own duties.

As did the daughter of a magistrate. Lily, well trained in these, began immediately to round up the smaller children, putting them into one of the open carriages, and making sure it was safely on its way before turning to the older ones. The magistrates themselves had already left, in the swiftest way each could.

Alan, lingering only long enough to make sure Lily was all right, said, "Stay with Maud," and then was gone. But when Lily went to help Maud into the final carriage, her step-great-grandmother pulled her back into the trees and put one finger to her lips. "Wait," Maud mouthed. And Lily did. Rex, waiting for her in the last carriage, sniffed the air. As the carriage rolled away down the meadow lane, he gave a graceful leap, so silent that he was unnoticed, and loped after them into the wood.

Soon the three were all alone. Dusk was there now, and the sky would soon turn from dark blue to black.

Stars wheeled in the sky.

Maud slowly led Lily and Rex back to the center of the meadow. She stood there and looked into the southern sky. Lily followed her look. There was just the faintest trail now of the blasting light that had shot straight up toward the helpless stars.

"What was it?" Lily whispered, as if she was afraid that it could overhear.

"It was the sign that they have ruined their World, ruined it utterly and completely," Maud said in a weary voice that Lily had never heard her use. "And with their World, they have ruined ours." She took Lily's hand and squeezed it hard. "It was a rocket, Lily," Maud said. "A rocket to the moon."

"To the moon?" Lily said. "But why? Why would anyone want to go to the moon?" To an Arcadian like Lily, that was crazy. (At least, it was then. Alas, that is not true in our Arcadia now.) To go to the moon? That was her thought. A dead gray rock? With the beauties of the Earth everywhere around? Who would do such a thing? What poor defeated people could even conceive of such an incredible waste of time, men and women, and strength?

"They wouldn't go unless they had nowhere left," Maud said softly.

"Nowhere left," Lily repeated.

"Nowhere left unspoiled, nowhere left with water to drink and air to breathe and wholesome food to eat, nowhere..."

"But...but we have these things," Lily interrupted her. "And we...." Lily stopped. So she understood. Maud meant that Megalopolis would come now, to take the Good Life from Arcadia. Once the Empire had the Good Life themselves, and look what they had done

50

to it! They would do that, again, here, in Arcadia. They would strip Arcadia until there was nothing left.

And then they would go to the moon—those of them who could.

Maud didn't answer. She spun about as if she waited for something, something that she expected to come on all sides.

First there was an upward burst of light to the east, over the Calandals, and the same loud BOOM. And a BOOM, more distant now, but still distinct to the west. And then, like a huge gold flower, a light bloomed and the BOOM sounded almost as the same time— and this was over the Donatees.

"As Death told me," Maud said. "She's been there with them. They're using the Donatees as a base. At least, where they can reach."

"The Donatees!" Lily caught her breath in horror. To understand this, you have to understand that the Donatees were sacred to the Arcadians then—holy, almost, untouchable. We have lost that feeling of awe in Arcadia, much to our diminishment. But we had it then.

Something tugged at Lily. A memory. A bad one. She frowned.

"I wanted you to see that," Maud said. "Now we will go back down." And she went over to where her bag and Lily's sat under a tree, and pulled her own skates from her bag. Lily did the same.

In spite of herself, Lily let a surge of joy pass through her. "Are we going to skate all the way down, Maud? All the way down the mountains into Cockaigne?"

And Maud tossed her head. In the light of a saucer-sized rising full moon, she looked young, as young as she had been when she had saved Arcadia once before.

"Why not?" she said. And the two, woman and girl, and the dog running along with them, turned down the mountains, skating fast and free all the way down. Even if it were only for that, Lily never would have forgotten that night. Even if it hadn't been the night when everything changed.

Seven

It was a long way down the Ceres northern slopes to the village edge, and even though Maud and Lily traveled so fast that the sparks flew off the edges of their silver wheels, by the time they arrived at the village hall, the emergency meeting there had been in progress for some time. The representative from Eopolis had the floor. She had obviously been talking heatedly for a while. The magistrates, sitting at their usual long table, had creased faces, as if their very expressions had been thrown out of shape by the news.

"We've sent representatives to every village," the woman said. "We need help. It's never happened that we have not known what to do. But we...we feel a kind of...confusion...." Here she looked around the hall helplessly, as if she felt this confusion now (and indeed she must have, since this is what happens at pivotal times of change, such as the one we face now). "A confusion," she went on, "such as we have never felt, never in the living memory of even the eldest of us. And we don't know what to do." At this she gave a sigh that was half sob, and sat down, waiting for the village's answer.

"What confusion?" Maud said now, her voice carrying across the meeting room floor. She moved forward toward the magistrates' bench. Such behavior would not have been allowed in just anyone, and indeed, with all the procedural court rules now put in place by the Lord High Chancellor, it could hardly happen in our own councils, but in the Arcadia of those days, the wisdom of men and women over the age of eighty was thought to be a resource for all. Anyone over this age was not just allowed, but urged, to speak, in or out of turn. In an emergency, this was a fundamental duty of the elderly.

"Grandmother," Mae said from the magistrates' table, for that was how Mae liked to address her mother-in-law. "You didn't hear."

"Tell me now, then, please," Maud said in her patient way. Just the sound of her calm voice quieted the crowd. "It's a good thing in a crisis to hear a thing said twice. And slowly, slowly...so we can all think it through."

"Not too slowly, Grandmother," Alan murmured from where he stood beside Lily in the back. Alan smiled. Even when he was worried (and Lily knew he was worried now), he was very proud of Maud. (My step-grandfather was, my mother told me, "a very nice man.")

They were all very nice, Lily thought, looking around at the strained but basically pleasant faces of her friends. ("Because they were all my friends, Snow, all of them.") What would happen when they were confronted by someone who wasn't so nice?

The woman from Eopolis stood again, and this time she must have made her statement much more simply and clearly—as Maud said, having to say it twice was not a bad thing. And when she spoke this second time, the frozen look of shock began to melt from the faces of the people around her, replaced by different expressions: indignation, anxiety, furious thought. And anger, of course.

"Megalopolis has sent a delegation to Arcadia," the woman said. "They came over the Calandals at night. I don't know how. It's impossible that they could have bribed some of our people, and none of them have ever understood the mountains, and how would they have started now?

"They say they've come to ask for help. They say they've got plagues and famines and wars..."

"And they say this is new?" Alan murmured to himself. Lily saw him close his eyes as if he was suddenly tired.

"They say," she went on, "that they can buy what supplies we're willing to sell them, whatever kind. That they need skilled labor from our villages to replace those who have died—most especially teachers, doctors, nurses, engineers…"

"Poor bastards probably killed themselves," another man murmured to Alan. This was Colin's father, with hair as white blond and stubborn as his son's. Alan nodded grimly.

"They say they 'come in peace,'" the woman said, and she faltered. Arcadians, even then, were sensitive to language, and therefore to its abuses, and it was a longstanding joke in Arcadia that Megalopolitans so often meant the exact opposite of what their official organizations said.

Maud watched her throughout. Many eyes were on the my step-great-great-grandmother standing straight and tall in the middle of the hall. "And do they?" she said softly.

The Eopolitan woman's doubts were plain to see. "They say that because there are so few of them in the delegation, and because they don't know us, they needed to take precautions. They say that though they 'come in peace,' they have, 'for protection,' taken control of one of the Dawkins families who live on the MacIlhenny ridge, at the topmost edge of the Calandals." She paused. "They don't call them 'hostages.' They call them 'guests.'"

An angry murmur went through the crowd. Now Lily understood the baffled rage on the faces around her.

I have to tell you again about how the Arcadians of my mother's early life felt about their fellow citizens. Each one was as valuable to any villager as herself or her own family. Every death was mourned as sincerely as if it had happened in the household that grieved. "Joy shared," went the Arcadian proverb, "is Joy increased. But Sorrow shared is Sorrow ceased." The Arcadians lived by this motto in those early days. We still have the proverb. But I don't think many would dispute with me that we've left the meaning of it somewhere behind us.

"Those Dawkinses have two small children still at home," another woman said.

"They've said they're caring for them well," the woman from Eopolis said. Her mouth twisted. "And that 'no harm will come to them' as long as the delegation gets back to Megalopolis safe, over the Pass."

There was a moment's silence. Everyone looked at Maud.

"And do you believe them?" she asked in her clear way.

"No," the woman said. "No, none of us believe them." She hung her head. "But what choice do we have but to pretend that we do?"

Lily knew what she meant, and why the Eopolitans had asked for help. The Arcadians of that generation were, we all know, among the most rational of people. They were used to solving their problems by rational means: by discussion, by consensus, by agreement, then by action.

But you can only rationally solve a problem that has a solution. This was a problem without one—at least, without one for which Arcadia was prepared. Arcadia had always counted on its very insignificance, and the protection of its mountains, for its security. Megalopolis was stronger, bigger, more ruthless in every way. Once the Empire turned its eye Arcadia's way, what then?

And that the Megalopolitans had taken hostages was the first sign that they meant to terrorize to get what they wanted. Megalopolis had long since given up any pretense to get it any other way. Colin's father had been right about how the Empire treated its own people. How then, when it had tormented and killed all its own, would it behave to outsiders?

But where could the Arcadians go? Nowhere. And now what could they do? How would the rational method work if there were no known rational answer?

("What choice did they have, Snow?" my mother said when she told me this story. I was too young to understand. I was too young to understand what choice Maud gave them. But I begin to understand it now.)

"What choice do we have?" the woman from Eopolis cried again. And everyone looked at Maud.

She shook her head. I imagine she was in despair at how her words would be taken. As queen, I've felt that despair myself. I know it well.

"There's only one real road," Maud said then. "But I doubt you'll take it. We've all put off what we should have done a long time ago, and now what we have to do to make it up is too hard."

Everyone looked at her, shifting uncomfortably. How many times have I stood in front of a group of Arcadians, all looking at me the very same way!

"Tell us, Grandmother," Alan said. Lily saw him move to hold Mae's hand. She always remembered this, she told me. It was one of the last times she saw them together, she said.

At Alan's words, a murmur of agreement went around the room.

Maud looked at them all, and sighed. Resting on Alan's arm, she walked to the center of the room.

Lily looked apprehensively at Rex. His tail gave a single thump.

"What you have to do," Maud said, "is go on exactly the way you are. Don't stop for anybody or anything. That's all."

At this, everybody looked at their neighbor. They wondered if Maud's mind was finally wandering. Or was she making some kind of sophisticated joke?

"If that's meant to be funny, it's not the right time for it, Maud," one of the men said flatly.

Maud sighed again. "No," she said. "I'm quite serious. Let me say it again: no matter what happens, don't change the way you are. Keep going the way you have."

"And Megalopolis?" someone said in that sarcastic way you talk when you don't understand what's going on around you. The speaker must have been very distressed to be so rude, and in public, too, Lily thought.

"Ignore it," Maud suggested.

"Oh yeah," hooted one of the boys. "Ignore it when they burn our houses."

"Ignore it," Maud said.

"Ignore it when they steal our lands?" a woman laughed shrilly.

"Ignore it," Maud agreed.

"Ignore it when they kill our children," another woman said. She didn't laugh.

Maud looked at her sadly. "Ignore it," she said again, nodding her head. "Ignore it and have more children."

Now there was real silence in the hall.

After a moment, Alan said, in his reasonable voice, "Mother, we can't do that."

Maud looked at him. She looked around again at all her neighbors. "No," she said finally, and she gave the tiniest sigh this time, like an empty teakettle set back on the stove. "No," she agreed. "I didn't think you could." And shaking her head, she took her hand off his arm and hobbled ("Hobbled!" my mother said. "Maud who had never walked anywhere but straight and tall!") toward the double doors at the end of the room. The crowd parted as she went, still silent.

"But what if what they say is true?" a woman cried. "What if Megalopolis comes in peace? What if we can live together, side by side? What if they can just let us be?"

Maud looked at her as if she thought the woman a fool, but politeness kept her from saying so. "They don't," she said briefly.

"They don't and we can't and they won't." She looked around her wearily. And then she said, with all the patience in the world, what she knew to be true. "They can't let us be, for we have proved them wrong. We have proved that the purpose of life can be happiness. We have proved that happiness comes from kindness, from moderation, from compassion...and, most of all, from leaving well enough alone! They can't let us be because we have proved that might doesn't make right. They're afraid to let themselves know these things. So, in their logic, we have to fail. To disappear. To die." She sighed again, looking around the room, and she tried one last time. "What I said already is the only way."

Lily heard the shouting turn then. It sounded ugly and mean, and she wasn't used to this. (She told me she had never before that night heard the sound of ugliness or meanness in Arcadia. Alas, if only we could say that today!)

Rex cowered against her legs. "We should have fought them!" Colin's father called out with an angry growl. "We've talked about it for years, some of us, trying to get the rest of you to see reason. We should have gone over the hills and killed them before they killed us!"

"You don't know what you're talking about!" another woman called back hotly. "Kill them? Kill the millions of starving rabble on the other side of the mountains? And us only a few, and most of those old and children? Talk sense, why don't you? Where would Arcadia be then?"

"Where will we be if they kill us first?" said another voice. "Which they will once they get the scent of it, the bastards. He's right. We should have gone after them a long time ago."

"Gone after them? With what? Your weeding fork and a couple of pairs of skates? Be serious!"

"Be serious yourself! Where do you think you'll be, not defending yourselves and your home, eh? The best defense is a good offense!"

"And where WILL we be?" another voice called out, without waiting, any more than the others had done, for her turn. "Mourning all of our dead, is where. Funerals instead of Feasts!"

"And what Feasts will there be when Megalopolis turns us into its own garbage heap, I ask you?" another voice cried, out of its turn.

One voice shouted out after another. The magistrates called for quiet, but it was no use. They didn't know it, our unhappy ancestors, but that was the last time Arcadia was peaceful and quiet. We've lost the knack of it now, over these last bitter years, and it started that night. The hall erupted with neighbor shouting at neighbor. It's still that way.

That night, the woman from Eopolis looked helplessly on. "It was like this at home, too," she said, though no one seemed to hear. "It's why I came for help." But the hall raged on.

Lily hugged Rex. Even Alan shouted now, at one of his neighbors, the one Lily had seen that morning carrying a net bag of fruit to a sick friend. And the neighbor shouted back. Feeling more than a little sick herself, Lily went to Maud and tugged unhappily at her plush scarf.

"Make them stop!" Lily said. "Maud, can't you make them stop?"

"What?" Maud said, as if Lily had roused her from some dream. "No, Lily, I can't make them stop. No one can. This was Arcadia's fate, you know. To fall down at the last fence."

"What do you mean?" Lily said. The tumult around them increased. Maud, as if still far away, as if she were not in the hall at all, turned and began to walk quickly away. Lily and Rex tried to follow, but there was a confusion of noise outside, a shout from the dark, an explosion, and a whirring noise, and they were caught up in the suddenly alarmed crowd, plunging and hysterical. "Maud!" Lily shouted. But it was no use.

There was screaming from inside the hall and out now, and

voices booming outside, with more explosions suddenly everywhere around. The double doors were flung open, and there was a series of sickening cracks. Lily searched and searched the crowd as it stampeded toward the doors, then, uncannily, the crowd parted, and she saw Maud, standing at the doors—it was she who had thrown them aside. And then she saw Death holding Maud by the arm, whispering in her ear. Maud turned, and, before the crowd surged again, mouthed a good-bye to Lily, who strained to catch one last sight of her. As Lily and Rex struggled forward, they saw Death take Maud by the arm and lead her away.

"Take a few hostages," a good-humored voice said over the screams of the crowd, and Lily saw a group of strangers enter the room, all looking around it with interest and no sign of fear. They were taller than any Arcadians Lily knew, and the three men and one woman were so handsome that it took her breath away.

Especially the youngest among them: a boy? a man? Not much older than Lily, certainly, but already a lord of the universe. Tall, golden, blue-eyed, loose limbed...she had a confused impression of some animal in the forest, and of lying on a bed of grass in the mountains in the spring. It was like seeing her other half, even though until then she had thought she was whole.

At that moment, though, Lily knew she wasn't. Or if she had been once, she never would be again.

And as the boy looked back at her, startled, she saw it was the same with him. She didn't know how, but she knew it was so.

Eight

"Wouldn't you agree," the smiling young man with the hard eyes said, "that it is a good thing for us all to work together?"

"No," thought Lily. But she, like all the other Arcadian children sitting cross-legged around her, was silent.

"And wouldn't you agree," he persisted, holding his hands cupped on his knees from where he sat cross-legged in their midst ("we're all friends here, after all," he had said), "that the Good of All is better than the Good of One?"

"No," thought Lily again. "No, I don't think that at all. And if I don't think it, I certainly can't agree." She tried not to look as sullen as she felt. They had all of them—her friends and her—learned very quickly the bullying that lay behind the pressingly friendly manner of the Empire's occupying force. Not 'troops.' She wasn't supposed to call them 'troops.' They were insistent about that, as about everything else. And none of them wore uniforms, only the most sharply pressed of casual clothes. And they weren't "occupying" Arcadia. They were insistent about that, too. "We are exploring opportunities for mutual assistance. Nothing sinister about that, is there?" A Megalopolitan general had explained this to them all, after they had been herded— all the villagers of Arcadia—onto a communal field outside of Walton. The field was all stubble now, covered in bits of corn and wheat and rye. The Arcadians had harvested it and watched as the Megalopolitans heaved it onto enormous trucks that drove, day and night, through the harsh cut they had made at the lowest point of the Calandals. It was going "to feed needy people," the Megalopolitan social workers informed them loftily. And the assumption was that the Arcadians, being such a warmhearted bunch, would find this some solace. For the fact was that the grains' disappearance meant there were going to be some hungry mouths at home.

Alan, before he disappeared into the mountains with Colin's dad and a half dozen others, had said to her, "Their own people are on the verge of revolt—at least the ones without the money, and that's most of them. If they can make us the enemy, and loot our land, they can buy a little time. But what in the Goddess's name they think they'll do after that, I don't know." But he was going to find out, he said. "Take care of Mae," he said, and then he laughed—they both laughed—at the idea of anyone taking care of Mae. She had already begun a secret line of communication between the magistrates of all of the villages, and she was helped in this by the fact that most of them were, to the Empire, "mere" housewives or small business owners. The Megalopolitans did not understand that in Arcadia the talents needed for these roles were considered supreme, and that such people were for this reason thought to be the only ones worthy of high office.

So through Mae's secret channels traveled much information concerning the less and less full net bags of market day, information traded over the pots and pans that were less and less filled with the food needed for the patient mouths of Arcadia. The Megalopolitans looked on the activities of the women of Arcadia with a derisive eye. More worrying to them was the disappearance of many of the village menfolk into the mountains. But winter was coming. They could deal with them then. They could freeze them out.

Then there were the children of Arcadia. To the Megalopolitan invaders, these were the key to the future. "We have to educate them to Megalopolitan ways, and quickly as we can," urged Field Commander Susan B. Riggs, a rangy ex-commando who stood about seven feet tall. "We have to—as our earlier strategists used to say—win their hearts and minds." There had been something a little scornful in how her colleagues heard her out, especially Conor Barr, the young and handsome military attaché, sent by his phenomenally well connected parents to get some safe (and easily publicizable) real-life battlefield experience. In Megalopolis, it was unusual to find a woman in a position of such authority in the military. But her superiors, recognizing that she would be of unusual value in an environment like Arcadia, had more or less forced her on her commanding officer. Conor looked at the General now to see how he took the suggestions of a woman. Conor's own mother, Livia Barr, was well known for her own 'suggestions,' but she, he thought, was the exception that proved the rule. It was men who knew best. Always, though they kept quiet about it, out of superior wisdom. Conor felt a glow of pride as he reconsidered this truism from his expensive upper class Megalopolitan education. Then he thought again about that girl, the one he saw the night they came into Arcadia. He hadn't dared ask what had happened to her. He hardly dared admit to himself that what happened to her was the only thing that really interested him in this godforsaken land.

The General rubbed his surgery-enhanced jaw and grudgingly admitted the truth of what Field Commander Riggs had to say. If Megalopolis was to hold Arcadia, and mine its resources for the people back home, it needed workers. And those workers had to be willing, too—Megalopolis had found out, to its cost, and almost when it was too late for its own economy to recover from the damage, that it was no good working slaves to death. It was an economic waste the Empire couldn't afford. Happy workers, under the impression that they were working for their own good: that was by far the best. And the Great City couldn't risk importing Megalopolitans into Arcadia to do the work that needed being done there. What if they picked up the subversive values that federation had always held? That was too big a risk. Better, as Susan said, to bring up a generation of villagers who understood that the Megalopolitan way was the best. Better to teach them scorn of their own parents. "God knows, that should be easy enough!" the General exclaimed, thinking of the contempt his own three sons showed for him on every kind of occasion. This had long been a problem for Megalopolitan upper-class parents. There wasn't a one among them who wasn't thoroughly hated by his own children.

Why should it be any different here in Arcadia?

"Don't you agree," the young lieutenant insisted, there in the midst of the Arcadian children who stared at him expressionlessly, "that it is better for a government to decide what is best for the Good of All?"

"No, no, NO!" Lily shrieked inside her own head. No "government" decided what was best for the citizens of Arcadia. The Arcadians decided what was best for Arcadia. Anything else was tyranny. Lily had not just learned this at her mother's knee, and then in school. Lily knew this—she knew it all the way down and all the way through her very self. She knew it, and she knew she had been born knowing it. And she knew it could not be any other way.

"Maud," Lily thought hopelessly, remembering the night last spring—it seemed so long ago now, even though only a few months had passed!—when she had seen Death lead her away for the last time. "Maud, help me now." There had been no time to grieve for Maud. That had been the hardest. All of Arcadia in an uproar, the discovery that settlers on the ridge were killed by the invaders—a 'mistake,' the Megalopolitans said, a miscommunication, and then their feigned anger at the fact that the Arcadians refused to forgive. The accusations that the villagers were using this, "a regrettable error but an honest mistake," as an excuse for aggression. Then the inevitable invasion. It was very simple. Megalopolis was stronger. Arcadia, bewildered, had never even tried to fight. Arcadia had always believed that negotiation and common sense were the way. But it is not the way, as all the worlds know, when one power is so much stronger than the other. There was no negotiation. There was no common sense. There was exploitation and manipulation and planned confusion. Now there was this.

"How can it not be like this?" Lily thought furiously as she tried to keep her expression bland. "What can we DO?" For an Arcadian child was taught from birth to waste as little time as possible in wishing things might be other than the way they are. "If you don't like what's happening, change it." This was what Arcadian teachers taught, time and time again.

And every child in that drab, under-heated room, under the watchful shifting eyes of the falsely pleasant man in their midst, and of Field Commander Susan B. Riggs standing by the door assessing them for her report, every child was thinking the same thing, thinking furiously: "What can be done? What can we DO?"

But as they had no answer yet, they were silent.

"Don't you agree that might is right?" the man went on smoothly and relentlessly, his little eyes glittering with more and more anger as the hour went on. "That all men are ants, but some are meant to rule over the other ants? That Father knows best? That there's no place like home?"

Understand, also, that Arcadian children in those days had been taught, always, the joys of 'Yes.' That 'No' might someday be necessary had not been considered by the educationists of those lovely, lighthearted villages.

"Yes," the man's face pleaded with the children, as his eyes darted nervously to where Field Commander Riggs impatiently waited. "Please say 'yes.'"

That was when Lily knew what she had to do. She knew it suddenly, and very clearly, as if Maud was bending down beside her and whispering into her ear.

"No," she said out loud. And Rex nudged her under her arm.

"What?" the man said, startled.

"No," she said. "No, I don't agree."

There was a pause.

"No," Colin's voice said from the back. "No, I don't agree either. I mean, I agree with Lily. No."

"No," a girl said from the other side of the room. And then some girls from Ventis took up the cry. "No, no, no!" they trilled like a flock of birds. And a family of children from Amana: "NO!" And Paloma spoke. And Wrykyn. And Mumford and Amaurote, too. All the children, of all the villages, in all of Arcadia, shouted out, "NO!"

"DON'T YOU AGREE," the man shouted back, in a panic now, seeing his job disappear into the angry crease on the Field Commander's forehead. "DON'T YOU AGREE THAT TOMORROW IS BETTER THAN TODAY?"

"NO!" Lily said, jumping to her feet and stamping her right one hard. "NO more tomorrows! Today! Today! Today!"

And all the children jumped up, too, and shouted along with her: "NO MORE TOMORROWS! TODAY! TODAY! TODAY!"

A siren rang, and the double doors at the back swung open. A trio of grim-faced men dressed in pressed chinos and polo shirts rushed inside in a wedge. Susan pointed at Lily, and they came and took her away.

"NO!" Colin bawled, and he ran out behind. Rex dodged between the children's feet and followed, managing to get through the double doors just before they slammed shut.

The room was silent. The children were rigid now, and pale with fear. Susan strode to the front of the room, indicating with one gesture that the man in the center was to get out of her way.

"Now, children," she said in her briskest voice. "I know that none of you want to be sent to the Children's Mine, not like that poor little girl we were just forced to take away. I know you are all good children. And the Children's Mine is a very bad place to be. Not a good place for good children AT ALL." At this she gave them a piercing and meaningful look.

The children shook, looked at each other, and slowly, under the penetrating quality of her eye, sat back down.

"Now," she said firmly, "we are going to learn today's lesson: 'Why Tomorrow is Always Better Than Today.'"

"No more Tomorrows." Every child there knew that was what Susan really said. She was telling them there would be no more tomorrows for them, ever again. Every child thought that thought. But every child, now, was still.

As still as Conor Barr was later, standing transfixed at the sight of Lily and Colin and Rex being driven away to the Children's Mine. So still was he, and so still did the scene around him seem, that the General had to speak quite sharply to make him attend. It was time for Conor to go back to Megalopolis and bring the report of the occupying force to the council of the Highest in the Land, and the General wanted to make sure that his own role would be properly represented. It would make a big difference to his pension when he retired if it was.

Nine

I met Susan Riggs much later, during my own time in Megalopolis, and she remembered my mother well. "I knew I'd have trouble with that one, the minute I saw her," Susan told me. She was as rangy and elegant as ever, though her worldview had necessarily undergone a sea change. "Became a queen, did she? And you her daughter. Well. Doesn't surprise me. You've got the look of her. And your grandmother."

By which she meant my grandmother Livia, who was as tall as I am, and as red-haired.

It was my grandmother who had, curiously enough, started the vogue for Children's Mines in Megalopolis. "All these children, just hanging about doing nothing, we should put them to use, shouldn't we?" she said—I've seen it in the Archives. They interviewed her about it, the way they were always interviewing everyone in her family: her husband, the wealthy businessman. Her son, the handsome Conor Barr. Her son's fiancée, the glamorous Rowena Pomfret. They are all over the Megalopolitan history books, and why not, since they paid for most of them?

It was Livia who suggested that since most of the lower classes had nothing to do all day but play games that flashed lights and made loud sounds, that their play should somehow benefit the country at large. So an experimental Children's Mine was organized by a Megalopolitan women's group, the one that also endowed the opera, and equipped the Mine with every modern convenience. The original, set into the Megalopolitan side of the Donatees, was something of a showplace—still in use by the time I arrived. It was painted brightly, and the treadmills the children walked on all day, playing their games and pulling the levers that helped power the night lights of Megalopolis, were coated with a special substance that made you feel like you were walking on grass.

Except of course you weren't walking on grass. The one thing rigorously excluded from even the original Children's Mine was Nature. It was found that Nature, in any form, was just too distracting to the work at hand. Or, at least, even if that hadn't actually been found to be true, that was still the founders' theory. ("And that was good enough," the General told me later, during my own later travels. The conversation I had with him was one I have never forgotten for its sheer smug stupidity and meanness. No wonder his sons loathed him.)

But by the time the Children's Mine Lily and Colin were sent to was built, funding had become scarcer. I think this was because of the impending environmental disasters that only the ruling class was truly aware of, and the vast sums being transferred to the making of a satellite orbiting the planet that could hold them all in case of trouble. Also, there were more and more children who were sent to the mines, as there were fewer and fewer jobs at home for their parents to support them with. Most families were happy to send their kids away to so patriotic a project, especially one that provided three meals a day (even if depressingly healthful and boring ones), along with a safe place to sleep. The end result, of course, was a skimping on funds for the mines that were less in the public eye. So the Children's Mine Lily and Colin and Rex went to was farther up the cold slopes of the Donatees, was left unpainted, was cold, uncomfortable, and dull.

That was the worst of it, my mother always said. The dullness.

It reminded her of her childhood, she said. There was always an exclamation at this; how could an Arcadian childhood have been anything like the Megalopolitan Children's Mine System? Lily was silent when asked this. Of course, I know what she meant now. She didn't mean her childhood in Arcadia. She meant her childhood in Megalopolis, the one that no one but she, and now I, can really face ever happened at all.

No one in Arcadia wants to know where we came from. They're not ready. So my mother's story, for them, the story of Lily and Megalopolis, really starts here.

"Eh, she was that pretty, Soph, your mam. We all loved her, we really did, it was like havin' a princess on the treadmill next to yer, and then she had that dog. She was like you, Soph, that good with animals, like she really talked to 'em and all, do you really talk to 'em, Soph? Always wondered. You've always been like that, too."

My nurse, Kim the Kind. She was a working-class girl from an abandoned neighborhood in the Great City at the edge of the Marsh, shuttered when the plant at its heart suffered an unfortunate explosion, which killed most of the inhabitants and made their homes unlivable for anyone else. "I was away, lucky me, eh, Soph? Away that day trying to get a job in the posh part of town. Me ma wanted me outta there, and yer see how right she was. She went up that day, too—never found her, no, but the social women came and got me and took me up the Children's Mine. That wasn't me first choice, but you know me, Soph, lemons from lemonade. And it was where I met your ma."

Lily used to tell the other children stories, Kim said, "so's when we were on the treadmills, sometimes we wouldn't even look at the screens and the colored lights, it was so int'restin' the stories about where she and that little boy came from." She would tell them about Arcadian summer days, about late afternoons when the sun was still high (there was no real sunlight in the Mine, although the lamps inside were considered of the highest technical grade possible, an almost perfect imitation), about hearing the distant hollow thumping sounds woodpeckers made in the trees, about smelling the strawberry scent of the cedar trees in the sun.

"An' I'll never forget, Soph, she'd tell us about the food they et there": cold tomato soup with little bits of chili and green cucumber floating in it, all of it from the garden. Bread that a neighbor made that day, sour and white and spread with butter from the goats grazing on the Commons at the foot of the hill. Summer food.

Lily missed home very much. Even aside from the worry about her family and friends, even aside from the anxiety about the future, and about Colin, who seemed to grow paler and quieter every day, she missed her home.

"We never got that, the rest of us," Kim told me much later. "Homesick? None of us ever heard of it. Yer had yer place, and yer had yer three a day, and yer had a bit of a laugh, and that was enough, ye know, Soph? That was how we were. It was all right."

Lily missed her home, and she missed something else even more, without even knowing quite what it was or how it had happened. What was it? She wondered to herself as she walked the dreary miles on her treadmill, with Rex at her side, for the overseers had nothing against pets in the Children's Mine. Some early good publicity about the latter in some tabloid or other had made sure of that.

It was the tabloids, in fact, that made her finally understand what it was that made her heart ache in her chest, as if it were trying to move toward something—but what? Not home. Something unnamed. Unnamed but important, the destination, she felt, of her private life.

They had been in the Children's Mine for two months or more, although it was hard to tell time, Kim says, so far away from the sun. "Ye knew when it was by the tabloids," she explained. "They came regular, every week. Those were the ones we got, anyways, not the dailies like the rich kids—have to keep our minds on our work!" Christmas had come and gone, some philanthropists had sent along the usual pudding and oranges, and a photographer had dutifully recorded the children's enjoyment. It was probably that shoot that brought Lily to the publicity department's attention. I know these kinds of departments well, now, and it is with some amusement that I reconstruct what must have happened.

There was probably the usual crisis of funding, not just for the children's needs, but for the salaries of all the administration associated with the Mine. There would have been many such crises at this time, right before the Great Flood. And probably the need for energy supplied by child power was beginning to decrease. The publicity department would have been the first line of defense against any funding cuts. And they would have been absolutely delighted to see Lily and Rex, in comparison to the snotty, rawboned, podgy-faced malnourished lower-class children of Megalopolis (completely unphotogenic, now as then). Lily and Rex must have seemed like a publicist's gift.

"Oh, they'll love that, won't they?" the publicist must have said. She was, I am sure, an energetic blonde woman with the straight hair and teeth of Susan B. Riggs. ("We all looked like that, then," Susan said to me dryly much later. "And the breasts. We all had them done with the same guy. We all wanted to look like Rowena Pomfret.") "People love a dog story! We've got to get a shot of her and the cute pooch for the Press. This could be crucial for our funding."

As Lily was to learn (and Goddess knows, as any queen, anywhere, in any time, knows too), the words 'crucial for your funding' must have acted like a magic formula whenever it was uttered around any Great City functionary. Lily had probably not yet learned to use the phrase to her own advantage, but she would. It was only a matter of time.

Of course, the publicist would have had her way. And Lily's long black tangled hair would have been combed out before she was brought, with Rex, into one of the administrative offices out on the slopes of the Donatees, the ones where the Press was welcomed, the room where the liquor and food were kept.

"Well, if this isn't a pretty lady! And that adorable dog! Where are they from?"

"Arcadia. One of those little towns they've got down there."

"Oh yeah. Our new allies in the Fight Against Want." The journalist would have been properly sardonic: as with all journalists in all times and places, cynicism substituted nicely for any desire to change the current situation.

Lily did describe the scene to me, a little—at least, I think she did. It may have been that she and Devindra later laughed about it ("Because you know, I was like these women at one time in my 'career,' Sophy, and your mother thought that was a very funny idea, me with blond hair!" Devindra would say), and I heard about it that way. But anyway, I know all the Megalopolitans there, the publicist, the consultants, the journalists, were tall, really tall, and slender, really slender, with flat stomachs, and oddly straight teeth. And of course, the women with those enormous breasts the Megalopolitans favor. "Aren't you proud of helping us gather what resources we need to feed the hungry and help the needy of the world?" one of these said to my mother, since that, of course, was the official line of what went on in the Children's Mine.

"No," Lily said. "I'm not."

To her surprise, the women burst out laughing.

"Perfect," one of them murmured, nodding to another who held a misshapen silver camera. The photographer started snapping silently away at pictures of Lily and Rex.

Lily clutched Rex to her. He growled.

THE CONSULTANTS OF MEGALOPOLIS WERE ALL BLONDE AND
BEAUTIFUL, WITH STRAIGHT HAIR AND TEETH

This only made the women laugh again.

"So where are you from, which one of those cute little towns, and what's it like, really?" the journalist coaxed. Lily didn't answer. "Better, better," the woman said cheerfully, as the photographer made a circle with her fingers and started to pack up her gear. "I can make it all up. And trust me," she said as she opened the door to go, "my story will be a hell of a lot better than yours."

So Lily, unknown to her, became the poster child for the Children's Mine. Megalopolitans are a brutal people, I've found, and, like all brutal people, are sentimental as well. The Mine was touted as an 'educational' experience for the children who worked there—'tough love,' the Empire called it—and the general public was a little in love with this view of themselves as Educators of the Young.

Lily, as a particularly attractive version of "the Young," was about to be known far and wide, in the same way that some spokesperson for a candy or a famous athlete selling shoes might be. And that was how it came about that she found what it was her heart was yearning for, when her face had become a famous one, without her even knowing of it, in the Great City outside.

But first the dreary days and months went by. Mind you, the administrators took pains to be kindly. But kindness not truly felt, Lily said long afterward, is nothing more than a burden, worse than a burden, a manipulation, and it simply made the time, which might have passed in nothing worse than a haze, that much more intolerable.

Lily had no experience, in her life as Lily, of manufactured kindness.

Neither had Colin, poor boy. Lily watched helplessly as Colin faded away, day after day. Every morning his hair sank back closer on his skull. Every night his eyes looked a little duller.

"You okay, Colin?" Lily would say, and he would nod. But they both knew it wasn't true. Yet there was nothing to be done about it. Kim saw what was happening. "We all saw it. The lad was that in love with yer ma, and she wasn't in love with 'im. Nothing to be done about it. And there was nowhere for him to go wit' it. And nothing to take 'is mind off it, poor lad."

I think that Kim must have been right. It's been many years now since I've realized that you can, indeed, die for love, and that if you're to survive, you must be very strong. I can believe that his watching Lily drift farther and farther away from him every day, as her heart turned toward something, toward someone else, that must have been a hard burden to bear. For the boy, who was far away from home and from everyone and everything he loved, this must have been the final hardship. And as the tabloids came in with pictures on their covers of the handsome Conor Barr and his glamorous fiancée Rowena Pomfret, and to see Lily's expression, one she probably wasn't even aware had stolen over her face, to know that her heart was with the enemy—that would have been very much, too much, to take.

So one fearfully cold night, as I imagine it, deep in the Mine, Lily would have woken suddenly to a room that was absolutely dark. She could smell Rex, of course, and that was a comfort, and then she could see his eyes glittering as he got up and padded across the floor to the open arch that led out to the dormitory hall. His eyes glittered in the milky approaching light.

Lily sat up. She saw Rex in the doorway, more clearly illuminated now by some light she couldn't identify. She saw his tail thump. Up and down. Up and down. Wrapping a blanket around herself, hardly knowing what she was doing, she got out of the narrow bed and went to his side.

Looking out, she felt a hand reach out from behind and land on her shoulder. She gasped, and turned to see who it was. It was Death.

Death looked beautiful that night, as she always does, to those who have the eyes to see her.

"She's come for Colin," Rex's eyes said. And Lily, understanding, nodded. She swallowed hard. She and Rex followed Death out of the room, to where Colin slept, and watched Death rouse him gently and help him to his feet. Colin looked at Death's face and, Lily said later, he smiled. "It was," she told Devindra later, and Devindra told me, "the first real smile I'd seen from him in weeks."

Then Colin turned and petted Rex one last time. Death said something softly in his ear, and he nodded, turning toward Lily to mouth a last good-bye. Then he put a confiding hand in Death's and followed her to an open door. It was from this door, Lily now saw, from which the strange illumination streamed.

The door shut behind them. The light was gone. And in the morning, the door was no longer there.

Ten

This is where my father truly enters the story.

I met him much later in his life, when he was a different kind of person—the person that his life had made of him.

But at this time, he was a Handsome Prince. How much he was conscious of polishing up his performance in this role I am not sure. My guess would be—not very. My father, even in his last, more introspective, days was not what you would call a deep thinker.

He was an affectionate person, at bottom. I think he must have been born that way. In another world, in another kind of culture, he might have grown up to be a veterinarian, or a grade school teacher, and I think at both of these types of jobs he would have done very well. And been happy.

But he was born in this world, into a pampered class as the rich heir of one of the most highly placed families of a great and powerful empire, one that had effectively (or ineffectively, which was more and more the truth) ruled Megalopolis for unquestioning generations. His choices, therefore, were rather more limited. Great things were expected of him. Megalopolis expected great things of its younger generation just then. The older generation had done its job, and had its day. It had spun straw into gold.

It had spun all the straw of Megalopolis into gold. In fact, it had spun so much straw into gold that there was no more straw left.

As to what should happen when the straw inevitably ran out, that problem it left to its children and their children's children.

Hence the hopes held out for Conor.

At this time, though, few would have considered his position anything but enviable. He was (and I have the testimony of many eyewitnesses for this) the handsomest scion of an almost embarrassingly handsome race. In Megalopolis—and this is still true—if your children aren't handsome, or beautiful, and you have the money and the ambition, they can be made so by science. As a result, the children of the rich were truly gorgeous—my father's wife Rowena was a case of this. I have seen her earlier portraits, and the perfection of her features, combined with an exquisite rose and platinum coloring, was staggering. A bit chilly for my tastes. But beautiful just the same.

He was handsome. His hair was gold wire, amusingly parted with severity on one side, a precious forelock threatening to fall over his forehead. His nose was long and inquiring—even in old age it quivered with a special, attractive sensitivity. His eyes were the cracked blue marble of his mother's, lacking just enough of her intensity to give his face a more approachable look. His lips were thin, and appeared destined to command. His ears and throat were those of a perfected sculpture. And he was very tall, with the rangy, elegant look of some well-made rich child's doll.

He was all of these things. He was young, he was beautiful, he was strong, he was the darling of his people. But he was also very weak. It was that weakness that kept him, young and untrained as he was, from having his own life. His own love. My mother was so much the stronger of the two. But even she couldn't save their love and their life together, not when the tide that pulled at my father was so much stronger than him. And she was in a different current, one that she knew she had to follow, even when it threatened to sweep her out of her depth, out to sea.

It must have felt like being swept away, my father's coming to the Children's Mine.

"He's coming! I heard 'em! He's coming here!" That was the chatter on the day of his arrival, as my dear nurse Kim told me. "It was all in the papers, Soph. Oh, yer dad was coming to see us! Fact-

79

finding mission, they called it. Ooohh. Yer can imagine. Royalty! To us, the poor little peeps in the Kid's Mine!"

Lily hardly heard the gossip going on around her. Her senses had dulled in the aftermath of Colin's death; grief slowed her down. She couldn't see, or hear, or taste, or feel the way she had. "I was different," she told me later. "I had been sharper. Clearer. But it all went away then, as if I were in a fog." Rex watched her and never left her side. The monotonous grind of the Mine, the constant walking always in the same spot, never getting anywhere at all, didn't affect him the same way it affected Lily. A dog can live in the moment. It doesn't much matter to a dog if each moment is absolutely the same. One after another, moments stretch out to Eternity, so what do they matter to a dog?

But for a human, of course, it's different. The only way we know is the forward march of Time. And if every inch of that line is the same, gray and dull and bland, life, before it reaches its goal, stumbles, sickens, and eventually dies.

Rex watched as Lily walked on that gray dull path. But there was nothing he could do except watch her change.

She was thinner now, and more silent. Her black hair hung in stringy coils down her fragile back. Her red-brown eyes got larger and larger in her pinched face. Only her wide mouth kept its generous size, until Rex worried that soon that would be all that was left. That and her eyes.

It's hard to be far away from home. I know this well myself. It's hard to remember what home means, what home is for, what home can help you become. There are lots of ways of being far away from home, and the one Lily experienced was among the hardest. Because Lily was halfway between two homes: the one in her past, which she missed, and the one in her future, which, unknown as it was, she yearned toward without knowing why.

For now, though, there was no going forward. There was no

going back. Everything was as tough and inert and immovable as the sludge and dirt of the one outdoor courtyard of the Children's Mine after a hard rain.

What made it even worse, I imagine, though my guess is that out of courtesy she forced herself to endure it, was the meaningless chatter of the Megalopolitan children around her. Lily was unused to the stupidity and banality of much Megalopolitan conversation. (And in fact, I could hardly comprehend it when Devindra used to shudder and describe it to me later, not until I had experienced it for myself.)

In those days, when Arcadians conversed (and to a certain extent this is still a noticeable trait in our land, thankfully), they bantered, or they informed, or they flirted, or they exchanged views. Sometimes they tried to top each other, for amusement's sake, in a certain kind of lighthearted irony which has rather gone out of fashion now, but which you can still hear, especially in the salons of the better-to-do families of Paloma. But even now, Arcadians speak differently than the mass of Megalopolitans in Lily's day.

The conversations would have been, so Devindra told me firmly, "endless babble about topics of no interest at all." Devindra taught me that this was the direct result of most citizens of the Empire having no share in what became of them, no hope of ever being able to influence events. "So why would their talk be anything but meaningless, Sophy?"

Why, indeed.

It was this kind of meaningless chatter that occupied Megalopolitan children all day long, as a matter of course. They told each other the plots, endlessly, of popular entertainment, all of which seemed to Lily to include scenes of almost incredible degradation and violence. Yet these children, who she liked, and sometimes was even fond of, seemed not to mind these descriptions, or feel pain at them. "Well, why not, Soph?" Kim said to me much later, in her philosophical way.

"Ye live where ye live, unless yer lucky enough to get out, don't ye?"

Lily tried to be friendly, and succeeded, too. But intimacy with such minds was not only impossible, but, in the absence of any other source of solace (other than Rex, of course), actively painful as well.

There was the ceaselessly traded gossip about Megalopolitan celebrities, and about members of the Megalopolitan ruling class. These stories held an endless fascination for the children as they plodded away on their treadmills in the Mine.

Especially the girls.

"Oooooh, she's put on weight, hasn't she, she looks like a fat pig!" they would say, and Lily, to her astonishment, would find that they spoke about some girl somewhere, on some popular show, that none of them had ever met. Or one of them would say, "I don't think much of him, she should dump him right away, he's only after her money, I bet," and the others would offer their opinions. "No, I think he really loves her, you'll see." And Lily would find again that they were talking about some couple high up in the Megalopolitan hierarchy, some couple that they could never hope to meet outside the pages of glossy newspapers.

The people in these magazines, far away from the children in the Children's Mine: they were unseeable, unreachable, unknowable, except by what was printed on the shiny page. And that was mostly lies. But how could the reader tell?

Now, it appeared, one of the stars of those newspapers was coming to the Children's Mine. The whole of the place was buzzing with it. Conor Barr! "Conor Barr is coming here!"

"It's true, I tell you! He is! His mum's sending him on a fact-finding tour! I read it here...and here...and here!" The brassy little girl with the blonde hair and the tight jeans pointed at three of the magazines spread out on the linoleum floor.

The other children crowded around her. All, that is, except Lily, who lay, silent, with her face turned toward the wall. Rex curled watchfully at her back.

Then something happened. Lily's back twitched as if a current passed through it. The others murmured excitedly, "Conor Barr! Conor Barr!" And her forehead furrowed. It was as if the name was a familiar thing, a thing not of home, but somehow an extension of home. Lily, in her dulled, gray state understood nothing, except that the name "Conor Barr" had, for her, some meaning that was yet to be understood. So she sat up slowly and rubbed her eyes. She turned back toward the others. "Who," she asked politely, in a voice that had become fainter and fainter as the weeks dragged on in the Children's Mine, "is Conor Barr?"

The others looked at her. There was no dislike in their looks, but there was no understanding either. The brassy blonde, whose name was Kim, and who was my very own nurse, my Kim, later to be surnamed 'the Kind,' exclaimed, "Conor Barr! Yer don't know who he is? He's just the ooohhhiest of them all, Conor Barr!" She looked at Lily with a hopeful, if slightly confused, expression, and she said, holding out one of the papers, "Here, see for yerself."

"Thank you," Lily said politely and took the paper, as the others looked on with interest. There she saw a picture of a boy—a man, really, still one not much older than herself—who looked like every other Megalopolitan of his class. She had seen them, coming through on field trips for their universities, or acting as assistants to government functionaries on their round. They were all tall and had glossy hair and teeth and eyes, and they uniformly smiled, as if for some camera set right at an angle there, high up in the corner.

If this was Conor Barr, she couldn't tell the difference between him and any other of the boys or men she'd seen down here in the mines. At least, not the rich ones. The poor ones looked different all right—all stunted and hunched and raw-skinned, with their ears sticking out at right angles from their heads. Lily had trouble telling them apart, too. It seemed to her that in Arcadia, each person looked like herself or himself. In Megalopolis, each person looked like his or her class.

"He looks just the same as all the other ones," she said gently, so as not to give offense, and the other girls, even though they laughed out loud at this, seemed not to take any. According to Kim, they saw Lily as a kind of curiosity, and to Lily's relief, they showed no malice toward her.

She was puzzled, though, my mother. What she said was true. And yet...and yet...there was something about this particular boy....

"No, look," Kim said eagerly, and sat cross-legged in front of Lily. The others did the same, looking at Kim as if she were about to tell them a story that was of tremendous interest, even though they had probably heard it a thousand times—maybe because they had heard it a thousand times.

"Conor Barr," Kim said, "is the great-grandson on his father's side of the man who invented the Whaddoyoucallit."

She turned to the girl next to her. "What DO you call it?" she said, but that girl, helpless, just shrugged.

Kim went on. "And on his mother's side, well, I don't know, HER father invented the Whatchamajigger." She looked around at this, and a couple of girls nodded agreement. "Anyway, they're completely loaded, and his father's on the Council, and his mother has all these charities, and they have this humongous villa right smack in the middle of Central New York where the property values are, you know..."

"Humongous," added another girl helpfully.

"Exactly," Kim said. "And he's just about the handsomest thing you've ever seen..." At this there was a collective sigh of agreement. "And every girl in Megalopolis wants to marry him, that's all."

"Or..." another girl said meaningfully, and at this they all went off into gales of laughter. Even Lily smiled, and Rex's tail thumped once or twice in encouragement. The other girls were pleased at this. They vaguely understood that Lily was unhappy, but as for them, they had entertainment enough between the Games Room and the Magazines and the Rumpus Room, all provided by the charitable foundations of Megalopolis. Almost all of them had come from places far grimmer than anything that could be found underground. So by and large, most of them were content. But they understood that Lily wasn't, even if they didn't understand why.

Still, it was better to have harmony than not, so when she smiled, they were all obscurely pleased. Everyone was in a good mood as they settled down to sleep. The boys in the next room huddled over some game of their own. An unusual harmony reigned.

The girls, I guess, all dreamed of Conor Barr. To Lily's surprise, she did, too. But not in the same way as the others.

Lily hadn't connected the pictures in the tabloids to the young man she had been drawn to the night of the invasion of Arcadia. A picture, to Lily, was a dead thing, and the boy she had seen had been alive, a very different thing from a photograph or a film. In Lily's dream, a picture from one of the magazines tore itself up from the bottom to the top, and scattered into a thousand pieces on the floor. Then a voice said, "Here I am." But when she fell to the floor, scrambling to gather up the bits of paper and piece them back together, the voice insisted, "Not there. Here." And then she felt a deep, strong feeling, but whether it was of terror or pleasure, she didn't know, and no matter how hard she tried to pierce the darkness of her dream to see the source of the voice, she couldn't tell who it was, or where. All she knew was that at its sound, a current passed through her, from the top of her head, straight through her middle. And in her sleep, she stirred, deeply moved.

Eleven

On the morning of his twenty-first birthday, in the breakfast room of the Villa in Central New York, Conor, although nervous, announced his plan.

"Mother, I am bringing a woman home," he said (and no one in attendance—servants, courtiers, journalists and assorted hangers-on—knew how nerve-wracking a moment this was for him). "Have the rooms made ready."

I can imagine him saying this. He told me ruefully about it much later, his earlier, lordly, anxious self far behind him. "I was a right prat, Soph," he said. "I was always given to making pronouncements, Goddess help me."

This wasn't entirely his fault. His speeches were doubtless always greeted with awe, manufactured and otherwise.

"Oh, bravo, bravo!" There was applause from the audience. It was probably muted from the servants, since there was obviously going to be more work— even if the woman to be brought there wasn't an official wife, she still would have her demands, they were sure of that. Much more enthusiastic would have been the reaction from the journalists and the hangers-on. Because of recent disasters in Megalopolis, the newspapers had been crying out for more distracting stories. Since Conor was already engaged to be married to one of the Great Tabloid Beauties of Megalopolis, Rowena Pomfret, an heiress herself, there was going to be the triangle story to work. "Any kind of story like that was meat to them," my father remembered. "I don't know what I was thinking, if I thought at all, about how Rowena would feel about this, or what it was going to mean to my future career. I think that must have meant I was already in love with your mother, Soph. Before then, I don't think I ever forgot about my career, not for a second." He sighed and smiled (and in his old age, he had a particularly sweet and engaging smile). "Of course, after... well, it came, and it went. Until it was too late."

As for the hangers-on, they immediately plotted to lure the concubine-to-be to their side. There was constant political war for the scraps from the tables of the rich in Megalopolis, and the war in the Villa in Central New York was no exception.

Everyone approved, it seemed, of this unusual step Conor was taking. Including, to his considerable surprise, his mother. Livia. My grandmother.

"Bring her back, Conor," Livia advised, her voice thoughtful. "And we'll see what we shall see."

Conor froze. He had been packing—it was a habit of his to pack for himself, as he was fastidious in his dress and never trusted a servant to get the creases just so. He had just smoothed down his two favorite shirts when Livia entered the room unannounced. She looked at him. He shuddered, but went on packing. "In a way," my father told me to my own surprise much later, "in a way, we understood each other very well, Livia and I." I know that he had always hated her. She told me so herself, much later, and she appeared to relish, rather than regret, the terror she inspired in her son.

"He did understand me, though," she said, her eyes lighting maliciously at the memory. "A clever boy. Too malleable. But quick to know what you meant."

He understood what she meant now. Even though the marriage with Rowena Pomfret was desirable, even though she had negotiated the contract herself—Conor's father being hopeless at any business matters (he was, as Livia remarked to me much later, "mainly for the Look")—even though so much seemed to pivot on this alliance, and even though Conor had felt a surge of independence and rebellion at his decision to ride into the mountains in search of my mother— despite all these things, Livia wanted Conor to follow his new course of action.

Without waiting for her son's answer, Livia now turned to go out. But before he had a chance to heave a sigh of relief, she turned back once more.

"Oh, and Conor," she said.

"Yes, Mother?" he answered, and he turned, looking nervously in her turquoise-blue eyes.

"Make sure you bring the dog. That will be good for the newspapers. Everybody loves a dog. I can't think why."

And then she went out.

Conor's knees buckled. But he didn't allow himself to falter, not then, anyway. He had made his plan and now he would carry it through.

Twelve

"I've come to take you home," he said. He didn't know why he said it. He didn't know why his voice refused to stay steady. ("Oh, she was beautiful, Soph. But it wasn't that. It wasn't that. It was that she was home to me, and I knew from that moment that there would be no home for me without her.")

"Yes," Lily said, but her voice was sad. She knew that what he meant by 'home' would be utterly foreign to her. This person— this boy—this handsome man—would not be taking her back to Arcadia. She looked down at Rex, who looked up at her and gave a heavy sigh. "No," the dog seemed to say. "It will be a long time until we see our true home again."

And yet, as Lily stood there, a strange happiness grew in her, so strong that she almost (not quite, but almost) didn't care. This happiness was white-hot and strong, and "it almost burned my love of home away," she told me later, thinking I wouldn't understand, thinking I was too young, not knowing that I did understand very well, and that even at seven years old, I knew I was fated, too, to love someone as well as my home. And to have to choose, as she did. To choose to follow my own life. As she did before me, showing me the way.

For Lily, even though this was the only great love she would ever know, there was a still small voice inside of her that insisted on being heard. For Lily, while a great love might, for a time, overwhelm who she was, it would never be permanent. In the end, she would always follow the road laid out for her by Death herself, because anyone who has really met Death sees their own road that much more clearly. Lily's road led back to Arcadia. Lily was Arcadia. There was no getting away from that. Though she would try.

Maybe that was another reason why Conor Barr was, then and ever after, so in love. Maybe he was in love with Arcadia itself. Or with what Arcadia could become.

(I like that idea. But of course I would.)

Conor and Lily rode side by side out of the Children's Mine, down the west side of the Donatee Mountains. Rex trotted along behind. And farther back came Conor's man, with Kim sitting excitedly behind him, arms around his waist. At the last moment, Conor had decided Lily should have her own servant, and his choice was Kim.

(Blessings on my father, for that alone. What would I have done, all these years, without my dear nurse, Kim the Kind?)

The light broke on them as they trotted out onto the steep mountain road, all gray and yellow, as the light over Megalopolis always was. At this, Lily blinked. She pulled up her mare, and in silent obedience to her whim, Conor pulled up his horse, too. The servant behind—who was very well pleased to offer such a pretty girl as Kim a ride back to Central New York—stopped too.

"Why're we stopping, then?" Kim said in his ear, even more cheerful than usual. As she told me: "Oh, it were Adventure, weren't it, Soph? And me not even knowing what Adventures were going to come!"

Conor's servant shrugged. "Who cares?" he said. "Too much trouble to worry yourself about what THEY do." At this his head jerked toward the silent Lily and Conor. "Best advice I can give you, my girl, is look out for yourself now, and let others do what they're going to do."

Now Kim tells me she did not agree with this. "Definitely not! But a'course, I didn't bother to argue." She never did. And this was a very valuable lesson that she later taught me.

THEY RODE OUT OF THE DONATEE MOUNTAINS TO MEGALOPOLIS

As for Lily, she had stopped so that she might look back at the Donatees, the sacred mountains that loomed up so high that their peaks were hidden in clouds. Spring was coming, and she could feel a warm rush of air up from the city below. But the mountains behind were still deep in a winter that lasted nine months of the year. She thought about her friends, hiding there. There would be no way to get to them now, even knowing the secret paths the way every Arcadian child of that day did. And it was so far away.

Better to look forward then. Lily did. She shivered, even though she was wrapped in a white fur-lined velvet cloak, with matching boots on her feet, which had been her first gifts from Conor Barr.

"There it is," Conor said, and his voice shook a little. "Your new home."

There was Megalopolis below. It spread in all directions, its black wires and white towers quivering, as if they were marching forward, up the mountains. From it rose a loud, whining hum and the lights that shone dully everywhere pulsated. The distinctive smell of the Great City rose up even this far into the mountains, battling back the mountain scents of those heights, reaching out backwards onto a marshland and a dead-looking sea.

Many years later, when I came down to Megalopolis along that same winding road, it was a different landscape. The Great Flood had made sure of that. But in spirit, it was all too drearily the same. Megalopolitans had learned nothing from the disaster. They had gone on, stubbornly, the same as before.

Megalopolis was and is a place of considerable grandeur. But to anyone used to a more human scale of life, it was and is a horrible place. A harsh one.

To Lily, who was used to the green and tempered land of Arcadia, it was barbaric, a mistake. It was unimaginable to her how anyone could live here with comfort, let alone pleasure.

This was to be her new home, then. She and Rex exchanged a look. "A bad place," Rex's look said.

Conor, sensing some of this, grabbed Lily's bridle and kicked at his horse, pulling hers along behind him. Lily wrapped her cloak more tightly about her against the wind with one hand, but she kept the other firmly on the reins. She did not know yet what it meant—a bad place. Could a bad place make good people? She looked at Conor, and a surge of tenderness moved through her so strong, she swayed in the saddle. She would always, from now on, be pulled in two directions at once, and there would never be any way to rest. To have one of her heart's desires would mean she couldn't have the other.

All along that tedious gray way, through the endless, crowded boulevards of Megalopolis, where the street noise fought against the howl of the winds that swept through the funneling thoroughfares (Kim described it to me later, long after it had become a great muddy lake), people turned to stare at the woman Conor Barr brought back to the Villa in Central New York.

Lily missed her home very much. She never stopped missing her home. Even after she found her way back to it, after many adventures, it was never the same home she had left. So she was missing something now that was being destroyed even as she rode farther and farther away. That hurt alone made her sag in her saddle.

"Sit up, Lady," Conor's servant said in a friendly way to my mother from where he and Kim jogged beside her on their piebald gelding. "Don't let them say you lack heart."

Sitting straight, Lily gave him a grateful look. That was a kindness. "Maybe these people are not as hard as they look," Lily thought, and she felt some comfort. She wasn't to know yet that both Kim and Conor's servant came from the same small group in the Great City, one that had been beaten and ignored and enslaved for years, and that it was the only one that still retained its old songs and old ways and old heart. How was she to know?

She learned of this later, from her friend Devindra, who was born of the same marsh people. She learned much about the history of that marsh, and the tales that were told there, and how they shaped Devindra, the wisest woman in all of Arcadia.

But for now it was all a great mystery. And the greatest mystery of all was the young man who rode in front of her, his back straight as a lodge pole pine, his golden wire hair kissing the back of his slender neck. "The enemy," her mind said forcefully. But her heart said otherwise. Lily was annoyed at how he never looked back at her, not once, as they rode through the streets filled with rudely staring people. But she found she couldn't listen to her mind. And it was not just her heart who spoke up for him, either. Her body argued for him. And even though her mind screamed out at this in silent protest, Lily knew that what her body and her heart told her was true. She didn't know how or why she knew it, but along with the many feelings snaking through her that bound themselves together and formed a silken, tough rope, she felt a yearning for Another that she had never, in her young life, felt before.

This yearning filled her with sweetness. And it filled her with fear. She exchanged a look with Rex, and she saw that he feared for her, too.

Meanwhile, my grandmother Livia waited for my mother. She stood ceremoniously with Julian, Conor's father and her husband, along with all their household, waiting, calculating how much and what kind of press they were likely to get on this occasion. She made her plans. And she stage-managed her scene with her customary vigor.

"Stand up straight, Julian, for god's sake," Livia hissed.

Julian started, then threw his shoulders back as well as he could.

He looked at his wife. On her face was an expression of the utmost conjugal piety and devotion. Every line on it proclaimed that he, Julian, her husband, was lord and master of all he surveyed. How excellent she was at playing her expected role! He marveled at it anew, as if he had not marveled at it yesterday, and the day before that, and the day before that—and this morning, even, and an hour before now. All their life together he had marveled at her ability to hide her true nature when she needed to, and to always, always get her own way. "I feel sorry for the little girl, indeed I do," Julian mused to himself. He knew that for Conor's woman Livia had the firmest plans. He himself had been the object of some of Livia's plans, and he was inclined to pity anyone else who became their helpless object.

Of course it was hard for Julian (I saw that later, watching him sneak sips from a forbidden bottle in his expensive nursing home every time his nurse's back was turned) to imagine anything but helplessness in any relation with his wife. But he didn't know Lily.

Julian and Livia waited for Conor and Lily now in front of the house, as was the custom when the eldest son brought home his first woman, and all the servants and hangers-on of the house waited behind them. The small children of the house ran shouting down the street toward it, as they traditionally did. And after them came Conor, "followed by a sad-looking skinny little dark thing on the horse behind him!" Julian said later, astonishment at his son's taste still sounding in his voice after all those years. "And next to her, this common, low, mixed breed dog!"

"Good heavens," Julian murmured. "I expected rather more of a beauty queen." Then he gave a start. Livia, in the midst of her broad, respectful, matronly looks, flashed him a glance of pure irritated contempt.

"You would, certainly," she murmured, though anyone overhearing would have thought she was submissively agreeing with his every word. "But Conor is my son as well as yours, and that is as fortunate for us as it will be for Megalopolis at large."

"Yes, darling, I'm sure that you're right," Julian said apologetically— though he didn't at all understand the stupidity of his remark, which apparently was quite clear to her. Julian was used to a different standard of beauty, there in Megalopolis, one more like that of Rowena Pomfret: pale, blonde, sculpted and colored by the finest surgeries money could buy. Lily's beauty was not something he could naturally appreciate. But now it was time to play his part, and Julian was very good at that. He stepped forward majestically, in his role as pater familias and aristocrat, to receive Conor and his first concubine as they dismounted before the Villa.

"You curtsey now," Conor hissed, and Lily looked up at him, startled. His face looked resolutely forward—not at her—and if she hadn't heard him so plainly, she would have sworn he hadn't spoken at all.

"What?" she said.

At this there was a murmuring around her from the crowd, and she knew immediately she had done something wrong. What this could be, she had no idea, but instinct told her to follow Conor's lead. So she turned her face forward and made her expression as lofty and blank as she could manage.

"Don't you know how?" came another hiss from beside her.

"No!" she hissed back. "I don't even know what it is."

"Oh, never mind then," he muttered. "But for god's sake, don't smile."

"Don't worry," she retorted. She learned quickly though, and this time her face (Livia noted with approval) was a perfect and lovely blank. "I've never felt less like smiling in my life," Lily said now through tightly gritted teeth.

There was applause from the crowd as the Lord and Lady of

the Household greeted the young couple. There was much ribald commentary as they disappeared into the house. This too was traditional. About the traditions of Megalopolis, Lily obviously had much to learn.

"And this is your dog, then?" Livia murmured as she took Lily by the hand. "Very good. It should come in handy; everybody loves a dog story." Lily looked up quickly in surprise at the sound of her voice. There was something very familiar about it, though Lily was sure that she and Livia had never—could never have—met.

Livia looked back at her. And Lily saw Livia's sapphire-blue eyes. "I do know you!" she thought. "I do!" But Livia's eyes gave her a warning glance, and Lily held her peace. She felt Rex nudge her hand, and she knew that he had recognized Livia, too.

But recognized her as who?

"Your rooms," Livia said in a loud and formal way, and she held open a tall ebony door. Lily and Rex entered. Conor followed. The door shut behind him, and then they were alone.

The huge four-poster bed hung with green velvet stood in the middle of the room, its white linen sheets turned back on a green satin coverlet. An enormous log burned in an open hearth, and beside it was a table on which was placed a bottle of ruby-colored wine and two crystal glasses.

Lily's eyes flew to Conor's in alarm. To her surprise, he was no longer the haughty stranger who rode ahead of her through the streets of Central New York. Now he sat on the edge of the bed and his look was shy.

"I'll do anything you want, you know," he said.

Lily looked at him more closely. "Why?" she said.

"Because I love you," he said. At this he stood, though he didn't come any nearer. And Lily, still looking at him hard, saw that he told the truth. His look of boyish anxiety went straight to her heart, and without thinking, she walked straight toward him and straight toward her fate. This was the way she had always taken life, and the way she always would. And there was much in it, I think, after all—that way of meeting your life. It would never, in any case, lead Lily astray.

Rex sighed, and laid himself down on the rug beside the hearth. Curling up, he slept.

The hours passed. The log burned to a pile of red embers. Rex, sleeping, breathed steadily in and out. Lily, lying on the bed, propped herself up silently by her elbow and stared at the boy beside her.

He slept, too, deeply and fully, his mouth half open and his brow clear. Lily looked at his face in the dying firelight. It was a half-good face, she thought. "Faces in Arcadia are all good," she thought, "even if no one there is as handsome as this." And she wondered why she had never felt, in looking at any of the boys of Wrykyn, Mumford, Ventis, Amaurote or Cockaigne, the way she felt now, looking down at her lover, a spoiled rich boy of Megalopolis. For this she had no answer. But she tenderly smoothed a hand against his cheek.

It surprised Lily, how very unsurprised she was at all that had happened. For example, she felt no surprise now when the big black teak door opened on silent hinges, and she watched Livia glide in. She felt no surprise when Livia looked over at her, as if to make sure of the depth of Conor's unconsciousness, and no surprise when Livia beckoned.

It was as if it had happened before. Or as if it was meant to happen. Whichever it was, Lily was not surprised. She slid silently out of the bed to the floor, pulled a shift over her head, and wrapped herself in the white velvet and fur cloak that lay where she had let it fall. And she followed Livia.

Rex woke the moment the door opened. And he silently followed the women out, though neither Livia nor Lily heard him behind.

Thirteen

Up and up and up and up a spiral staircase, Lily followed Livia, both women treading noiselessly on the dark red-carpeted stair. Rex, unnoticed, padded behind. Through the slits of the windows they passed, Lily could see the house below. Lights blazed there in every window except one. That one showed only a flicker of candlelight through glass, and Lily knew that was the room she had come from. She thought gravely about what had happened in that room, and pulled her cloak more tightly around her body as she did.

"Why is the house awake?" she said softly. "What is happening?" But Livia only looked back at her and continued up the stairs.

Lily followed. The older woman was like a magnet for her. "It's as if a part of me and a part of her belong together," Lily thought. When she thought this, she also thought, "For now. Not for always."

But why?

She didn't know.

"Look up," Livia said in a clear voice. "Don't look back. Look ahead." When Lily did, she saw the sky.

It was a pale, sickly blue, even in the night, from the force of the lights of Megalopolis. Lily could see only two stars; she couldn't tell which these were. In Arcadia you could place a star by its fellows. That was the way she had learned. "I have no way of understanding this sky," she thought sadly. The sadness mixed with thoughts of the boy sleeping heavily in the room below. "He has no way of understanding me," she thought. "And I have none of understanding him."

And yet her feelings were far from despair. She should feel hate,

99

NOW LILY COULD SEE THERE WERE TWO MOONS IN THE SKY

she thought. She should wish for revenge. "But I don't; no, I don't." And Lily thought again of the sleeping head, gilded by the candlelight, and she smiled.

"Look up again," Livia said, impatient. They were almost at the top of the tower.

Lily looked up and saw the moon. It was large and pallid and watery in the sky, and its face was a curious blank—not the mysteriously smiling face she was used to looking up at when she slipped out of her room to meet a friend on a warm Arcadian spring night. Pondering this, she stepped after Livia onto the roof of the tower—a narrow circle, surrounded by an iron rail. Rex appeared silently at her feet and pressed up against her in the shadows.

She looked again at the moon and she said, "It looks wrong."

"What do you mean?" Livia said sharply.

"It doesn't look like the moon," Lily said.

There was a moment's quiet. "You should be afraid of me," Livia said softly. "But you're not. Why is that?"

"I don't know why," Lily said. It was the honest truth.

"I know why," Livia said, in her same soft way. Her eyes shone, in the fitful moonlight, like a lizard's. Or a snake's. "We have met before, you know."

"Have we?" Lily said uneasily. For a moment, a picture came to her, so vividly that it blotted out the scene before her then. And that picture was of a desert, vast and golden and impassable. A beautiful young man stood before her, his eyes the same color as Livia's. He was smiling at her and holding out his hand. Somehow Lily knew, with a rush of horror, that behind him, all around him, under the sands that stretched out so pure and smooth, were the mangled corpses of the innocent—of her friends. "But I have never been in a place like that before," Lily thought. "I have never had such friends. I have never lived anywhere but Arcadia."

Rex growled low in his throat.

Livia looked down at him. "Oh yes," she said contemptuously. "We've met, too, you and I. Don't think I forget. And if I could have my way, I would call my servants and have you thrown off this tower."

Lily dropped instinctively to her feet and put her arms around Rex. He never moved. He never took his intelligent brown eyes from Livia's face.

"Oh don't worry," Livia said irritably. But she laughed. "I won't hurt your little dog. There's nothing much he can do to me—not this time." She looked at Lily. "Oh, stand up, for goodness' sake, stand up. I have things to tell you. And there isn't very much time."

BOOM. As Lily slowly stood, she heard it. And she saw the rocket trail from the south as the missile exploded into the sky.

BOOM. There went another, to the east. And BOOM. To the west. And then BOOM. BOOM. There were two trails, rising up from the Donatees to the north. From the direction of the Children's Mine. From the direction of Arcadia.

"They are going to the moon," Lily said. The thought filled her with a kind of awe. Not at the thought of man and woman conquering space, not in wonder at the ingenuity of humankind. No. Lily, a child of Arcadia, was filled with astonishment at the idea that anyone who could know Arcadia——Arcadia the beautiful, Arcadia the fragrant, Arcadia the warm—that anyone in a world that held Arcadia, or even the possibility of Arcadia, would want to hurtle themselves toward a gray rock in the empty vastness of space. That idea was a frightening one to Lily.

And yet it was an exciting one, too. She thought again of Conor, who had pretended to conquer her in being conquered himself. She thought of the huge, imperial power of his city, and she felt, for a moment, even more helpless than she actually was—even more small.

Still, inside of the smallness was that flicker of excitement. She frowned as she noticed it. It might not be healthy. It might not be good. But it was there. And she could see that if anything fanned it, it would grow into a monstrous flame.

It made her feel warm all over. She slipped off her cloak and gulped thankfully at the cold night air.

"Yes," Livia hissed softly. "Exactly."

Lily looked at her, startled.

"Look at the moon again, Lily," Livia said. "And tell me what you see."

Lily, obedient, looked at the flat dirty disk that hung there, disconsolate, in the sky. "They're going there, aren't they?" she said. "Those rockets. You're sending people to the moon. That's what they say in Arcadia."

"They're going there, yes," Livia said, pointing to the poor, ugly, yellow thing. "But they're not going to the moon."

Lily, silent, waited for her to explain.

"Look harder, Lily," Livia said. "Look as hard as you can and tell me what you see."

Lily looked. She could feel Livia willing her to look. She could feel Rex willing her to look. She could feel their wills strengthen her sight.

She looked.

"Why, there it is," she said, almost to herself. "Why couldn't I see it before? Why can't everyone see it?"

It was the Moon Itself.

There it was, a shadowed but still beautiful sphere hanging in the sky, to the right and a little above the flat round thing below.

That ugly yellow disk was a False Moon.

Lily could see that clearly now. There were two moons in the sky.

"How?" she said simply. "Why?" And then she said, "And why can no one see it the way we see it now?"

Livia gave a sour smile. "The last question is the easiest. We see what we expect to see and what we're told to see. That is the secret the powerful of all worlds know.

"As to how, that's easy, too. Our technology is great. Well, it should be, considering what we've had to pay for it." She looked around her tower at the gray, wire-riddled, garbage-strewn city below. "It was easy enough for us to build another moon. Haven't you heard, in your little Arcadia?" she said in a haughty voice. "We have become like gods, here in Megalopolis. We do what we will. And we do it because we can."

"Yes," Lily said slowly. "I have heard that. Though we didn't think of you in Arcadia, not as much as all that."

Livia seemed annoyed by this answer, and Lily had a moment's thought that she perhaps should not have been so rude. This thought confused her, and for a moment when she looked into the sky, all she could see was the False Moon.

But if she looked hard and straight, after a moment the confusion cleared.

There was the Moon Itself again, as beautiful and friendly as she remembered it. Only it was shadowed by the Lie.

"As for the 'why,'" Livia went on, "that is a slightly longer answer."

"They say in Arcadia," Lily said, "that when Megalopolis has ruined the world, it will have to go to the moon."

"Ruined the world!" Livia gave a snort. "You can't 'ruin' a resource, you can either use it up or maintain it. If we've chosen to use it up for the greater good of all mankind, I hardly think that can be described as 'ruining' it!" She gave Lily a look of displeasure. "But of course you're only a little provincial, and a girl at that, and you can't have been very well educated. You can't understand that we are at the end

104

of history, that what brought us here was a secret plan to grow and grow and grow until we expanded to fit the universe! We've done that. And now it's time to go into the sky."

"To the False Moon," Lily murmured. She shivered. It was so cold out here on the tower with Livia, suddenly much colder than before. From every direction came noise and the kind of lights that made her head hurt. And all the smells were bad.

"Not at first," Livia said reflectively. "At first, we went to the Moon Itself—but we told no one. Only the Council of Four and a handful of representatives of the Highest Families. And that was when we found them. They had been waiting for us, of course."

"Who?" Lily said.

"Angels," Livia said.

At this Lily laughed out loud. She gave a hearty and sparkling laugh, and she reached down to give Rex a pat.

In her exhilaration, she knew that she laughed not because she didn't believe Livia, but because she did. She laughed not because she thought Livia was joking, but because she knew she wasn't.

It was a laugh of triumph, though Lily would have been hard pressed to explain what the triumph was about. But somehow, she knew it was the triumph of the Moon Itself. "The Moon Itself is still my friend," she thought, and she laughed again to Livia's discomfort. "They haven't destroyed the Moon." And maybe this meant, too, that the Megalopolitans would not be able to destroy the Mountains either. No matter how hard they tried.

"They were there waiting for us, as I've said," Livia went on, trying to hide her annoyance. "They had flown there to wait. They wanted to treat with us—to negotiate. Well, of course, we turned them down. We've had no use for angels on this planet for thousands of years. We weren't about to start treating with them now."

At this, another strange picture floated through Lily's head. She could see the world from above. She was held in a pair of strong arms. The wind whistled past her face as she swooped down over the sea. And she could hear the flapping of wings.

Then it was gone.

Livia looked at her sourly and went on.

"Instead we built another Moon. The situation was increasingly critical down here—something had to be done. Surplus population rioting, water poisoned, air too harsh to breathe—something had to be done. We built another Moon," she said reflectively. "And by and large it has worked rather well."

"But you couldn't ignore the Moon Itself," Lily said, and in her heart she exulted. She could feel Rex happy under her hand. But why? What caused this happiness to rush through her? It was an even greater happiness than she had felt earlier, in Conor Barr's arms, though it was of a simpler kind.

"No," Livia said reluctantly. "Not if we mean to move on. We can't ignore the Moon Itself. It will not let us pass. The angels will not let us pass. We thought, over the years, they'd become bored and move to another place. But they have stayed, waiting."

"Waiting for what?" Lily whispered.

Livia looked away and up at the False Moon. Her mouth pursed into a tight little 'o'.

"Apparently," she finally said, "they are waiting for you."

Lily looked down at where Rex had lain, only to find he had slipped away during this conversation down the spiral stairs.

§ § §

The candle sputtered on the table by the dying fire. Rex paced back and forth on the hearthrug, pausing from time to time to look at the alternately yearning and cruel face of the sleeping boy. What he saw in that boy's face obviously troubled the dog and set him to pacing anew.

In the bed, Conor stirred, holding his arms out to a person who was no longer there. But as his eyes opened, so did the door, and Lily slipped inside. She exchanged a look with Rex. His look warned her against too much excitement, but he could see that she was too far from home and from all she knew to be able to take that kind of advice. Instead, her eyes dancing, she lifted her eyebrows up high on her head. And she grinned.

Rex didn't like that grin. But there was nothing he could do. He lay down with a heavy thud and a sigh.

Lily let her cloak drop, stepped out of her dress, and shivered, hurrying to slide into the warm sheets beside Conor, who, without speaking, gave himself up to her again.

§ § §

"Where were you?" he said sleepily in the dark, after the candle had died and gone out. "Where did you go?"

There was a moment's silence from Lily's side, as if she were carefully choosing the words she would say. "I was with your mother," she said softly.

"My mother," he said cautiously. "That was courteous of her—to greet you like that."

"More than that," Lily murmured in the dark. "As she was showing me the Villa—it's very beautiful, Conor, much grander than anything I have ever seen in Arcadia—she told me about her...your father's...plan."

Conor was silent. It was as if he could hear the false note in her voice. "She was never false," he told me later sadly. "But that night...I think my mother had a spell on her." I know differently, of course. It doesn't take a witch's spell to seduce a young girl with visions of power, after all. Alas, that I should know that.

"A diplomatic mission, Conor," Lily said. And for a moment, he could almost think it was Livia, speaking there in the dark. The thought made him shudder. But Lily pressed her warm body up against his, and the thought went away as quickly as it had come. "They want you to represent the Council of Four. A great honor, as I understand it, among your people. And I'm to be at your side."

"A mission," Conor said.

"To the Moon Itself," Lily said happily. "We leave tomorrow."

"The Moon Itself," Conor repeated slowly to himself. He thought: "Who is this girl I have brought to my home?" And the answer came immediately from the region of his heart. "This girl is your Fate," it said.

"Yes," Lily said. "I've always wanted to go to the Moon."

This was the first and last lie that Lily had ever told in her entire life. Hearing it, Rex gave a low, helpless growl.

"Yes," Conor said, enthusiastic now. He took Lily in his arms again. And the lovers murmured endearments until dawn. While Lily's had a certain truth to them, her voice now had a sweet false edge that made her dog restless where he lay.

Conor and Lily slept. But Rex, instead, spent the hour till dawn staring at the smoldering red ash of the dying fire in a foreign hearth.

108

Fourteen

"I often think about that night up on the tower," Lily said much later to Death. They were walking—trudging, almost—together up a wide, steep path that went first straight ahead, then wound so snakelike that Lily couldn't see what was at the end. "I often wonder what would have happened if I had shouted, or pushed Livia off, or if I had said no to all of her plans. I often wonder that." Lily bit her lip and thought. Rex walked, as ever, by her side.

Death smiled and continued her walk upward. But she didn't say a word. Not just then. And it was obvious to Lily why not.

"But I did none of those things," she said ruefully, "I yearned—that's right, yearned—to know what would happen next. And I said yes. Oh, I said yes. There is no changing that. But what if it was meant to be all along?"

Thinking hard over this question, Lily, too, fell silent. And she and Death continued their companionable walk.

§ § §

How do I know all this? You'll be wondering who told me what they said to each other on that road. Well, of course it was Death. Death herself told me all this, and more, when I met her myself on the Road of the Dead. And then, what I didn't know from her, I know from the Key. These are the important parts of the story, I think. But not, to me, necessarily the most moving, the most touching. Those parts have always come from the loved ones in my life. Curiously enough, even from my grandmother Livia, who saw, quite rightly, a lot of herself in me. "You're tall, like me, hmm. And you have my hair, even if your skin is that dirty brown," she said when we finally met as grandmother and grandchild, many years later. "And you have my energy, which is something I'm not sure I wanted to give you."

This amused me, I remember. "No, Grandmother," I said. "I'm quite sure you didn't."

"Your father never had it—my energy," she said in that grim voice that was such a feature of her last years. "He was, at bottom, a very conventional boy."

About that, I think she was wrong. But she was correct in thinking he wasn't much her son. For my grandmother, though she knew the world with frightening clarity (and it's a clarity I am sometimes frightened to own myself), was unable to love. And my father, who never, even in his seasoned old age, could see exactly what was in front of him—he knew how to love. And he did love my mother. I do know that. Strange to say, it's a great comfort to me, even now, in my sixtieth year.

§ § §

"It's been a dream of mine for a long time: going to the Moon." Conor said this from where he stood behind the crystal window of their temporary quarters, another beautifully decorated room, hung with green silk held up by brocade roses. Outside the window was a view that only the rich could afford, and that only they were allowed—of the Moon Itself. Lily lay behind him, on the bed, in shadows.

"Mmm," she said, noncommittally. "Doesn't he know?" her eyes asked Rex. "Doesn't Conor know that this is the False Moon? He's looking right at the Moon Itself, doesn't he see?" But Rex's eyes told her nothing. They had told her nothing since the night she stood with Livia at the top of the tower. Since that night, when she looked at Rex, all she saw was a dog. He was no longer a guide. He was just a dog.

Lily hadn't bothered being excited when she, Julian, Livia and Conor had filed solemnly onto the shiny, brand new Megalopolitan rocket ship, the one guaranteed to take its occupants to the Moon in under three hours ("Wake up at Home, Eat Lunch on the Moon," as the advertisement went). She had known without being told that they would first go to the False Moon, where all the reporters and laborers, and the holidaymakers who could afford the novelty of a trip to the moon, would see them land and, reassured, go on with life as normal.

"After the ball," Livia had said, "we will go to the Council."

For there was to be a ball. There were many balls given for the rich in Megalopolis, and the rich continued the tradition in the sky. This one was to welcome Conor Barr and his new concubine—and her dog (everybody loved the dog)—to his diplomatic mission on the Moon.

That Conor wasn't aware that his mission was on the False Moon made Lily feel uncomfortable in a way she had never known before. As she observed him covertly from the bed, his elegant shoulders squared, his jaw thrust out, she felt desire and protectiveness mingled. But threaded through these was a single razor-sharp line of contempt. Lily felt contempt that Conor was so easily fooled. And to feel contempt for the one you love is not just painful—it's dangerous as well.

Only vaguely aware of her danger, and the danger to her love, Lily got out of the bed and began to dress for the ball.

§ § §

The Grand Hall of the diplomatic Mission of Megalopolis to the Moon was lit with a thousand candelabra made of thick and twisted gold. The lights darted and flickered in the mirrors lining the walls. Brocade and velvet and fur were everywhere. Everyone wore the heaviest, most lavish outfits they could, for it was cold here on the False Moon.

Conor was noble and handsome in a white velvet suit with a waistcoat of gold brocade. He danced and charmed all the senior women there. They were delighted with him.

But it was Lily who was the great success. And Conor, because of his great, bewildering love for her, was proud of this success—not angry and envious, as would have been normal with a Megalopolitan male, and which just proved the rarity of his ability to love. Livia noted the telltale softening of his expression as he watched Lily dance, in her thin gold silks edged with silver ermine, and her tiny soft red leather shoes. Lily, charming Lily, was observed with obvious approval by all. Even the Ambassador was heard to say, as he bent down to pat an obediently sitting Rex, that Lily was the most graceful child he had ever had the happiness to see. Julian beamed at the praise from someone so high in the Council of Four's esteem. He was pleased, not only for the honor it did his house, but also for Lily and Conor. For Julian also, for all his silliness and vanity, was able to love, much to his wife's contempt, and Lily had already won his heart with her pretty ways—hers and her dog's. Livia watched this with sardonic amusement. How soft were both her husband and her son, she thought with indulgent scorn. "How given to fatal affections of the heart!" And, "how ridiculously obvious that they both like dogs!"

But she didn't have time for these sentimental reflections now. She checked her glittering diamond watch and saw that it was almost the hour. Catching Lily's eye, she nodded. And went out, her green and red velvet train snaking behind.

BUT IT WAS LILY WHO WAS THE GREAT SUCCESS

"Please, Mr. Ambassador," Lily was saying just then as she gracefully looped her frail golden dress's train over one arm. "I think you are the kindest man in...well, if not in the world, then on the moon!"

This made the Ambassador, and, a split second later, all around him, laugh heartily, praising among themselves Lily's delicacy and her wit. Conor waited respectfully at the edge of the group until the great man invited him to his side. "Charming little girl, just charming," the Ambassador congratulated him. And Lily, as was right and proper, modestly backed away, Rex at her side. As she did, the heel of her red shoe caught—it must have been by accident, why else?—in the edge of her train. This was held to be understandable; she must have been overcome with confusion by the greatness of the Ambassador. There was a small ripping sound, and a charming exclamation of annoyance as she examined the tear with a pretty little pout on her rose-colored lips. Bowing to the plume-laden women around her, bowing respectfully as a young girl would be expected to do, she held out the damaged train and mimed that she would find herself a little corner in which to fix it.

No one was at all surprised when she and Rex disappeared after Livia, out the same side door.

§ § §

"It was cold on the False Moon," Lily said, later, in a dreamy nostalgic voice to Death, as they took a turn on the path and entered a green and gold alpine valley. "But it was even colder on the Silver Bridge to the Moon Itself."

"Yes," Death said reflectively. "I remember."

"Were you there, then?" Lily said in a comfortable voice, slipping her hand through Death's crooked arm. Rex, trotting along beside

114

them, grinned.

"Oh, yes," Death sighed. "I was often by you, in those days. Leading you on, you might say."

"And later," Lily said teasingly.

"Oh, yes," Death agreed. "And later, too, of course."

A thousand flowers bloomed in that meadow, that day that Lily and Death walked through it. And the air was heavy with the smell of strawberries.

§ § §

On the Silver Bridge to the Moon Itself, Lily regretted leaving behind her fur-lined velvet cloak. The chill of space penetrated right through the crystal walls of the bridge, and through the fluttering fabric of her ball dress. The Megalopolitan engineers had known how to string a walkway between a false place and a real, but they had not known how to make it as comfortable as their clients would have liked.

"Hurry," Livia hissed, speeding her pace. The bridge beneath them glittered and swayed. Through the crystal slats between the silver, Lily could see all of space spread out at her feet. And in a corner, Megalopolis sprawled across the Earth, gray and brown and flat.

Lily hurried. At the end of the gently swinging bridge was a dark blue door, slightly ajar, from which poured a wedge of brilliant white light.

As they neared it, a shadow crossed the light, and Lily could just make out the figure of someone she assumed was a servant holding a torch to light their way.

"Lady Livia?" a voice said. The voice was neither deep nor sweet, but there was still something oddly compelling about it. Lily revised her first impression. This was no servant.

Livia nodded, and she crossed the door's threshold, followed hard by Lily and Rex. Lily, stood still, momentarily dazzled by the light, which she saw now came from the surface of the Moon. She blinked.

"I've come to take you to the Council. They're waiting eagerly for your arrival," the figure said. Something about it (gentle? forceful? both at the same time?) reminded Lily of someone, of something, of somewhere...but where? She couldn't remember.

She blinked again, and followed the figure's straight, slim back. Looking about, she couldn't help but exclaim. "It's so beautiful!" she said impulsively. Livia turned and gave her a warning look. But the slim figure turned back with approval.

"This is your first time on the Moon Itself?" the figure said politely. And Lily saw, to her delight, that the figure was a girl. A girl very like herself, but with a strength that Lily knew she herself did not yet have. But it was a strength, she realized, that she wanted.

The girl smiled reassurance.

"Yes," Lily answered the girl shyly, and looked down.

Below them, under the crystal of the corridor continuing past the Silver Bridge, the Moon Itself shone, white, silver, transparent.

"It IS beautiful," the girl said, smiling. Her smile glowed, reflecting the light of the Moon. Then she turned back to continue to lead them down the hall. At its end stood another door, also ajar, and from this one poured not light, but the heavy sound of official murmur. The girl stood at this door, indicating that they should go through before her. Livia took a deep breath and swept past. But Lily paused at the girl's side, and looked into her friendly dark brown eyes.

"Please...may I know...your name?" she asked timidly, hoping the question was not discourteous.

But the girl's frank expression did away with any worry. "Phoebe," she said. "My name is Phoebe. And yours is Lily. I know."

Phoebe bent to ruffle Rex behind the ears in a way that Lily knew he liked.

Lily heard a wave of welcoming voices in the next room. Still, she hesitated. She was shy with this girl for some reason, but she felt she had to persist. "And somehow I feel I know you, too." She gave a small laugh at herself, but then her brow narrowed. "Is it possible?" she said abruptly. "Do I know you? From...I don't when. From before?"

"Lily!" Livia's voice came sharply from inside, and Lily, startled, gathered up the folds of her gown and started forward.

As she did, she heard a quiet voice sound firmly in her ear. "Yes," it said. "You do know me. And I know you."

Startled, Lily looked up, again into Phoebe's honest eyes. For another moment, she paused. She almost had it. A memory, some vague snatches of sound, of shouting, of battle, then of a stream tumbling over stones and a quiet voice telling a story beside it. Of lemon-yellow plush and comfort and bravery, too.

Then it was gone.

Livia's voice called out again, more sharply still, and Phoebe's brown eyes urged her to have courage and go on.

Fifteen

"Oh, let's get on with it, for pity's sake. How much longer are we going to wait? Everything depends on how quickly we move, how quickly we find it and use it. Surely we all can see that."

Lily froze as she entered the close, wood-paneled room. There were no windows, and the room itself had a curious quality, as if it were alive, as if the walls themselves heaved in and out with a ragged breath. As if she was in the belly of some large animal.

Rex sniffed the air. He whined.

"Everyone loves a dog, do they?" an amused voice—not the same as the first that spoke—said from the center of the reddish-brown gloom.

Lily blinked. Her eyes began their adjustment to the light. This was difficult after the brilliance of the stars and the Silver Bridge outside, let alone the light of the Moon Itself. But she managed. A person always manages in these circumstances. What is more difficult is to see the stars and the Silver Bridge and the Moon Itself after getting used to the dark.

This was not a difficulty that Lily would escape.

For now, though, she concentrated on the scene in front of her. Four figures, aside from the arrogant one of Livia, sprawled in wide chairs at the room's heart.

Lily blinked again. Rex growled low in his throat. In an instant, Phoebe was beside them, her hand resting warningly on the dog's head. He was suddenly quiet.

"I've never seen him do that before," Lily said to Phoebe, startled. Then, remembering where she was, she turned, with a gasp, back to the men.

It didn't matter though. They hadn't heard what she'd said.

§ § §

"I found out later," she would say to Death on that last long climb of theirs, "that they never heard anything they didn't expect to. Never. And that this was true all over Megalopolis."

"It's true many places in the many worlds," Death would say.

"But not where we're heading?" Lily would say tentatively.

"Not where we're heading," Death would reassure her, and taking her hand, would pull her along in a race up the next little steep bit of the road. When they got to the tree at the top, they would fall, laughing together, onto the grass beneath it, where they would eat a small lunch that Death had brought, give Rex some water, and look out over the deep valley to the opposite side.

That day, Lily would see that valley with so much gladness that her heart would swell in her chest. Somehow she would know that once they had started down, she would begin to forget everything that had gone before.

But except for Conor—always except for Conor—there was no reason any longer to remember.

As she walked down the road past the willow trees, she said, "No, not Conor. Sophia. That's why I want to remember. I have to remember Sophia."

And Death smiled.

So she told me later.

§ § §

"You know where you are, Lily," Livia said, smirking with pride through the red-brown gloom. The walls breathed in. The walls breathed out. It was a labored breath. If this room was alive, it was holding on to that life...just.

Lily stood, waiting.

"This is the Council of Four," Livia said. "The rulers of all there is to be ruled in all the lands. The Ministers of Truth. The Highest. The—"

"All right, Livia, all right," said the second voice that had spoken, still in its amused way. Lily saw now it came from a man seated a little behind the others. He was stocky, with black eyebrows that cut a straight line across his forehead, and he looked like a large garden gnome. "We don't need all our titles here, do we? Among—as it were—friends."

Lily felt Rex tense. But Phoebe's hand was on his head, and he fell still again.

"Can we get on with it, Alastair?" the first voice complained again. Lily could see that it came from the man closest to her, a round, flabby figure, looking older than his fellow, though he was probably younger. He had a peevish face, and Lily disliked him on sight.

"Sorry, Anthony," Alastair said, but so mockingly that you knew it was meant as a joke.

"Well, that's enough of that," said a third man briskly. This one was blond and slim and freckled, with a translucent skin. He wore a blue coat with brass buttons, and his name was Auberon. "The question is, shall we waste time telling her why she's here?"

"Or shall we just show her? I agree," said the fourth man, off to the side in the shadows so that Lily couldn't make out his face. This man now laboriously lifted himself from his chair. Livia rushed to help him, and Phoebe moved quickly to support his other side. Lily could see that he was enormously fat, with a tiny queer-looking head, bald except for three long lank strands of greasy hair that lay across a mottled scalp.

"The Book first?" Anthony said in his whiny voice. Lily caught herself wondering how such a wheedling, nervous specimen could have become one of the rulers of the great empire that was Megalopolis.

"It certainly never could have happened that way in Arcadia," she thought. And this was a sign that Megalopolis had infected her with its poisons. For not only was the spiteful malice of that thought alien there, but if she had been closer in spirit to the land of her birth, she never could have had the thought at all. In Arcadia, it would be impossible to imagine the fates of all people being controlled by just four men.

"Or the prisoner?" Auberon said briskly.

"Oh, the prisoner, I think, don't you?" said the enormously fat man from the depths of his deep yellow-gray wattles as he waddled between Livia and Phoebe toward a door at the rear of the pulsating room.

"Dramatic illustration, of course, why not?" Alastair murmured urbanely, as he indicated with an elegant gesture that Lily and Rex should follow.

Lily hesitated, then stepped forward. The tiny door at the rear of the room opened, as if from the other side. For a moment, the fat man wheezed in its frame, huffing, as Phoebe and Livia pushed at him from behind. He was almost too big to fit through, but by various judicious pushings and proddings the thing was done. He popped out the door with a faint whoosh.

With that, a blue and gold light streamed in from the room beyond, as if in protest at the mean color of the windowless chamber where Lily stood. The light trembled as if it were in pain. There was something awful about it. Awful and strange.

Lily walked toward it. The light grew brighter, and softer, too, at the same time. A rose color lay underneath it, like the early part of dawn. "It's beautiful," Lily thought. Rex silently agreed. "Beautiful and frightening at the same time." But even though she was frightened, she found she yearned to see the source of the light. So she walked on through the door and saw what was on the other side.

It was an angel. A real angel. There was no mistaking it, though Lily—so far as she could remember—had never seen an angel before. It would be many years before angels reappeared in Arcadia. Still, she recognized it immediately.

And it was trapped.

It was hanging upside down from a silver hook, in the middle of a round crystal room through whose walls all of space could be seen, including the False Moon. The Angel stretched, breathing painfully. In...out...in...out...in...out... With labored breath it moved its enormous wings (these wings reached out, silver-white, to touch the crystal enclosure on either side, brushing it, bruising their tips painfully on its hard unyielding surface), and those wings went slowly up and down, up and down, up and down.

"The Angel's breath is what made the room move," Lily thought. "An angel's breath must be powerful, then. Even the breath of an angel as weak and trapped as this one is."

(And how do I know this part of the story? The Angel told me. Much later, when we worked to have her made a counselor of the Arcadian state, a premature move that caused many problems for my reign.)

"Go closer, Lily," Livia's voice said in an unfamiliar, coaxing tone that Lily had up till now never heard her use.

Lily obeyed. She could hear a faint rattle from the Angel's chest as her breath—Lily could see the Angel was a she, now—rose harshly and then fell. She could see the Angel's face, contorted with a kind of suffering Lily had never known. It was serene; there was

IT WAS AN ANGEL. A REAL ANGEL. THERE WAS NO MISTAKING IT.

endurance in it. But with that, almost, not quite, despair.

"Do angels despair, then?" Lily wondered. This was not what she had been taught in Arcadia. In Arcadia, it was thought that angels passed through, from time to time, benevolent and strong, drawn to the villages by the strength of their happiness, joining in their joys, invisibly supporting their revelries, their celebrations, and their feasts. You could never see an angel, Lily had been taught. But you could feel them.

Lily had often felt the angels. She was sure of it. She was sure, in fact, that she had often felt one angel in particular. How this was, she didn't know. Neither had she ever, before now, cared. It was just the way it was, in Arcadia.

It was not, however, the way it was in Megalopolis.

"I didn't know," Lily said carefully, her eyes never leaving the Angel's (and the Angel's eyes were and are dark brown and deep as the deepest canyon in the highest mountain in the sacred range of the Donatees). "I had never heard that Megalopolis believed in angels."

At this, Alastair gave a crack of laughter. Anthony shuffled his feet, annoyed.

"Well, we had to, didn't we?" he said in his peevish way. "When this one forced herself on us."

"Seeing is believing," Auberon said, smiling faintly over Lily's head at Livia. Lily felt approval of her behavior in his smile, and this approval made her feel cravenly pleased. She didn't like this feeling of pleasure. It marred her spirit as if a dirty hand had rubbed against it. And this made her uneasy. It gave her pain.

The Angel breathed another deep, ratchety breath, and Lily knew, somehow, that it had given her pain as well. Lily caught her own breath and tried to control it.

Her head was spinning. "What does it mean? What does it

mean?" an inner voice whispered in her ear.

The Angel twisted on her hook. Her wings flapped slowly and painfully.

"What is she here for?" Lily cried out. She couldn't help herself. "What has she come for?"

"Why have you come?" she asked the Angel silently, trying to keep the pain she was feeling from her face. "Why didn't you stay away from here?"

"What has she come for?" she repeated out loud, looking around at the adults who stood, silent, at the edges of the crystal room. And again, "What has she come for?"

"My dear child," Auberon drawled. "Ask her yourself."

Lily, tears now spilling unheeded down her face, squatted impetuously by the upturned head of the straining Angel. "Do I dare touch her?" she thought. But without a pause, her hand reached out of its own accord, through a long gap in the crystal wall. Lily touched the Angel's streaming black hair.

"What have you come for?" she asked softly.

And a voice rose up from the heart of that room, a voice that belied the tethered feet, the labored breath, the flailing wings. This voice was the sound of the mountains themselves. Lily, who had often heard the mountains' voice, recognized it at once.

"I've come for you," the voice said.

At this, the wings gave one last helpless heave. And the Angel, under Lily's hand, gave one last painful breath and died.

At this, there was an uproar.

"What? What? Impossible!" barked the fat bald man. "She can't be dead."

"Oh, shut up, Peter," Alastair said as he swung open the crystal walls, and bent down to feel the Angel's throat. There was no pulse. He looked at Lily. She could see the Angel's dead eyes roll up in her head.

"Angels don't die, I tell you. They don't die!" The fat man was agitated now. The flaps of flesh around his chin wiggled and heaved with emotion.

"Well," Auberon said dryly from his place by the door, where he leaned with his arms folded, "either she isn't a real angel, then, or she isn't dead. Take your pick."

"Oh, she's definitely dead," Alastair reassured them, getting up now and wiping his hands with a white handkerchief.

"I always said she wasn't a real angel," Anthony said peevishly. "Didn't I? I said..."

"Yes, yes, yes, we know what you said. You said whatever you had to say to be sure you were eventually right. You said she was an angel. You said she wasn't an angel."

"In fact, you said both of those twice," Auberon interrupted Alastair. They exchanged an amused look.

"How can they be talking like this?" Lily wondered to herself. Her spirit was in great pain, as was to be expected from having been in the presence of the suffering and death of a noble creature. "How can they not feel it?"

Looking around the room, she saw they did not feel it. None of them showed the slightest trace of pain or sorrow at all. Livia, in fact, quite the opposite, looked like she was holding some kind of delightful secret to herself. Lily found her expression the most repugnant of all.

Phoebe felt it, though. Phoebe's face, much as she tried to control herself, was cut across by traces of a sharp grief. Lily saw this, and it lightened her own suffering a little.

"I never said she was an angel," Anthony fumed. "I said all along what everyone in Megalopolis knows. Angels don't exist. They're a fairy tale, a fable. A story for children."

"Then what was that?" Auberon said, pointing at the Angel, who twisted in a breeze that seemed to come from nowhere.

They were all silent. The only sound was the breeze that blew from nowhere and to nowhere, around and around the crystal chamber walls.

"The Book, then?" Alastair said to the others, one eyebrow raised.

The fat man, Peter, didn't answer. He gazed at the Angel's corpse with a kind of fascinated horror. Something had upset him deeply about her death, Lily could see. "And yet," she thought, creasing her forehead with the intensity of her attempt to understand, "he isn't sad, and he isn't sorry."

"Oh yes," Auberon said clinically, as he reached up and untied the silken rope that had bound the Angel to the silver hook. Her body slumped lightly to the floor without a sound.

Peter's face took on another look. Lily recognized this: it was a look of fear.

For a moment, she almost grasped what he felt. For a moment, she held it, horrified, in her hand. But then, frightened herself, she let it go. And she couldn't have gotten it back again even if she had wanted.

But it was so horrible, she didn't want to feel it ever again.

"I wish she'd lived," Anthony complained. "Then we could have forced her to tell us who she really was."

Peter shook himself, and his wattles moved ponderously from side to side. Returning to himself, he gave Tony a bleary-eyed look of contempt. "You wouldn't have wanted to know who she was."

"What?" Anthony bleated angrily. "I…"

"You couldn't have stood it. Not for a single moment," Peter said, and, waddling back toward the small door, waited for Livia and Phoebe to help him through.

Behind him, the Angel's body slowly dissolved. It shimmered, shrank, and then completely disappeared. But no one except Lily and Rex saw.

Sixteen

"The Book of the Key," Alastair said with a touch of the irony that Lily had already noted was characteristic of the Council of Four, "is a most impressive technological achievement. All the more impressive since we have no idea, really, how it works."

"Don't be ridiculous, Alastair," Anthony said in his whiny voice. "Of course we know how it works. It belongs to us." But his fellow just looked at him mockingly as he led Lily up to a carved wooden stand on which a large, illuminated book lay open.

The Book of the Key was indeed the most impressive technological achievement that Lily had ever seen. Which was not surprising, seeing as how it was the most impressive technological achievement the Megalopolitan world had ever known...as Megalopolis never tired of telling itself. It was amazing. Death-defying. Unprecedented and godlike.

But it made the skin on the back of her neck creep unpleasantly. And it made her stomach feel a little sick.

This, also, was not surprising. For two reasons.

One reason was that Lily had depths of experience that went past the technological achievements of her race. But of these she had only the faintest of memories. Every child has this wisdom, from the moment she or he is born. But as we are human, we have a genius, too, for forgetting what is most important in our past. And Lily was no exception to this. Still, some of the memory remained, and was enough to make her very uneasy indeed, when confronted by the Book of the Key.

There was another reason, too. And this second reason was

probably the more important.

For Peter had been right. The Angel had not died. Angels cannot die. It had waited, with angelic patience, for Lily to arrive. When she did, when she reached out to touch the Angel, the Angel passed into her. For the Angel had a task: a way to show and wisdom to impart. It is the way of angels to enter into us when these things are so. When their job is finished, they go out again. If we think about it, in silence and solitude, we will see that this is the way things are. We will see that we have felt angels coming and going before...perhaps many times before.

And if we do not see this, it should be cause for grief. For a person—and a country—who has never felt an angel is lost. And to be lost in this world is a dark and dreary thing indeed.

§ § §

But the Book of the Key was remarkable, for all it made Lily feel queasy— and in its own way, it was beautiful, too. The Council of Four stood there, each of them trying to conceal his pride and pleasure in being able to show off the thing to someone who had never seen it before.

"Only initiates are allowed to see the Book," Peter said in a sonorous voice. Then his beady little eyes gave Lily a sharp look, as if to make sure that she understood the magnitude of the honor being done her.

She dropped her eyes demurely. Livia, obviously pleased by the impression her protégée had made, came over and took her hand.

"Look," Livia said. "This book—this precious manuscript—holds the secret of all that was, all that is, and all that is meant to be. You have been brought here because you have been called by the Book itself." Then with a theatrical flair, Livia put her fingers under Lily's chin and pulled it up to look the girl in the eye. "Do you understand what that means?"

"She doesn't mean any of it," Lily thought to herself. "It's just a role she's playing. And she wants me to play one too."

Lily certainly understood what role she was meant to play. And the Angel that was inside her prompted her, so that her actions were everything that they ought to be.

"Indeed I do, Lady Livia," she said in a clear, bell-like tone. "I, the humble girl chosen by Conor Barr, have been called to play a part in the forming of the Great Empire." (If she had been able to see Phoebe's face, she would have seen the girl suppress a laugh at this nonsense.)

Peter let out a heavy, sonorous breath of sheer admiration. "That is well said, well said indeed."

"The Great Empire," Auberon said seriously. "The End Which We All of Us Serve."

"We are the same as our fathers before us," Anthony said in his nasal, unpleasant voice. "We keep the same sacred vows."

Only Alastair looked at Lily skeptically. Maybe he had noticed a slightly false tone in her voice. Or maybe he had noticed she didn't look so surprised when she saw the Book. Whatever it was, something about Lily's performance made him uneasy.

"Look at the book," the Angel's voice whispered inside Lily. "Turn the pages. Look admiring, humble, and afraid. Look all of these things. And I will tell you what to do next."

Lily obeyed.

She stepped up to the glowing pages of the Book. And she turned the first page.

"It's...it's so beautiful," she said. And she meant it, even though, as I've said, something about its beauty made her feel a little bit sick.

This was the truth. The Book was indeed beautiful. Encrusted with gold and gems, each page glowed with pictures so lifelike that one could imagine oneself inside of them. More than that: each picture moved, changed, told its own story.

I know this for I've seen the Book myself. It is indeed beautiful.

And then there were the stories, so many of them. The Book lay open now to the story of how Megalopolis became an Empire.

"Turn to page one thousand, two hundred, and forty-one," Alastair ordered her, still watching her expression closely, as if to reassure himself of something.

Lily, obedient, did so. On that page, there she saw herself.

Herself.

And there was the picture, changing. Everything that had happened to her up until now. Arcadia. The Children's Mine. Conor's and her love (here Lily couldn't help but blush and feel a brief, sharp longing for the lover she had left behind on the False Moon). Livia leading her and Rex across the Silver Bridge.

But there was more. The pictures changed.

"I...I've never seen these things before," Lily said. And the Angel didn't need to warn her to speak shyly. She did this on her own out of her natural awe.

"The future," Peter said softly. And Lily, astonished, knew it was so. She was looking at pictures of the Future. As she did, she saw herself walk to the shore of a great ocean. She was alone. Rex was nowhere to be seen. Without hesitating, the girl in the picture walked into the sea. The green-gray waves closed over her head. She could smell the salt and the wrack and the tar. She could feel the water....

"Somebody catch her before she falls," she heard Alastair say, as if from a great distance.

And then she fainted dead away.

Seventeen

When my mother woke from her faint, she was in great pain, and it was pain that never left her for the rest of her physical life. "Like rolling in a barrel of knives," is how Devindra puts it, and Devindra was Lily's doctor, so she had good reason to know. No one else knew anything about that constant pain, though I think there were some who suspected. But Lily had already, by this time, begun to be silent, about this as about so many things.

One of those subjects she was silent about was me.

Lily and Conor had conceived me that first night together, the night Lily went with my grandmother up into the tower to see the difference between the False Moon and the Moon Itself. Is it really impossible that I remember it? Well. There are so many things that I remember, that I know, that are impossible, and yet I do remember them, I do know them. I try my best to follow Lily's example of silence here. I, Sophia, now so much older now than my mother ever was—I know that she understood more in her silence than I ever have in my restless, constant search for what I imagine to be the heart of things. But one thing I do know, that she taught me, even (impossible as it is) when I was sheltered by her own body at the very start of my story, is that you can never tell anyone anything that they have not first discovered for themselves.

There is, for example, so much that I could tell Devindra, who is so wise, and older than me. But, scientist that she is, she would not, could not believe me yet. Her learning hasn't caught up with what I would say. And her learned disbelief would only postpone, maybe even fatally, her own discovery of all those things she now takes to be impossibility. So, patience, Sophy, I tell myself. The truths that take the greatest hold are the ones that people quarry for themselves. Let them dig! Let them discover! And meanwhile, I'll pray to the One that their discoveries not come too late.

I listen to Devindra more, much more, than I speak of what I know. And this is good for both of us. It has, in the end, made a confidence between us that I treasure. As a queen, I would be hard pressed to do without it.

But I say here that I remember Lily and Conor gravely facing each other, tracing light patterns on each other's skin (the one so golden brown, the other so pale pink and white, the two melding and making me what I am), and then coming together, in more than the way that young lovers have, as if something inside of both told them this twining would lead...to what? To some mysterious and powerful end. To me. To Sophia.

Lily was sure of that. She told me later, even before I was old enough to understand.

I couldn't possibly remember this, Devindra would say. And no one could have told me. My father tried, once, but in the end was defeated by his own embarrassment, as I think was quite right.

I don't know why I've never been embarrassed by these things. Maybe it has to do with my believing that if I can't face my world, and what made my world this way, then I can't change it. And that is my job, the one I'm sure I'll fail at, but nevertheless keep trying to do.

But the question isn't whether or not I'm embarrassed by thoughts of my parents and their physical love, but really how I know about it at all. And how do I know that the Angel entered Lily, and remained as a companion to me—I don't dare say as a teacher, because although she had much to teach me, I'm ashamed of what an indifferent student I proved to be (no matter how willing and hardworking!). But we've had many talks, Star and I, many, many times since. So it may be that I remember what she herself has conveyed, in that wordless way of light that she has, and that I love.

Of course, I don't talk much, if at all, about what Star tells me. Instead I let my dear Devindra instruct me in her own way. She was born to instruct, my favorite teacher! And I've learned many things, hearing her stories in her Tower by the Pond.

It was there I learned first about Rowena Pomfret, the woman— the girl—my father never loved. The girl he married. "She was very beautiful," Devindra told me over a cup of her famous ginger tea, as she watched me carefully with those hawk eyes of hers to make sure none of this hurt (she is always so careful, Devindra, and indeed, I can never make her see that she doesn't have to be, not with me). "She was famous in Megalopolis for how beautiful she was. One of those girls whose likeness is everywhere, and you think, when you're a young girl the way I was, that it's because she is so much more beautiful than you or me."

But of course that wasn't why. The real reason was that the Pomfrets were 'fabulously wealthy' (in the language of the Megalopolitan tabloids), and gave to charity with a widely publicized largesse. They had originally made their money by diverting the rivers that ran off the Donatees and selling the water to the poorer areas of the great city. "That was how the marshes were made," Devindra told me. "They took the water away and then they sold it back." And then they gave to charities that were the most likely to add to their luster.

Rowena was always the Belle of the Charity Ball. Small and fragile, with hair like ironed platinum, and pale blue eyes, she was highly admired. And rich. She was very rich. The rich tend to be admired, I've noted in my travels. Inevitable, maybe, but not on the whole a very good thing. For anyone. Not, certainly, for Rowena.

When I knew her, years later, she was, as she must have been then, vain, trivial, and fearfully strong-willed. You could still see both the beauty and the money of her youth, though the first had become petulant rather than wise, and the second borderline vulgar. She was not a happy woman.

She was not destined to make others happy, either. Which I think must be one of the most awful fates in this world.

She was, however, destined from childhood to marry my father. Destined from childhood by both families, and it was a destiny heartily endorsed by the mass media of the day. My father would be allowed his dalliances along the way (how vulgar that is, too), even encouraged to have them for the tension they would add to the eventual story of triumphant nuptials for the two Great Fortunes of Megalopolis. But the end of that story was never in doubt. For anyone, that is, but my mother.

"She was always in pain, from that day forward," Devindra told me flatly. "Because all she wanted was to love your father and have your father love her back. Oh, she wanted to have you, she wanted to have a happy family. That was what your mother wanted, Sophy. She wanted a happy everyday life. And instead she became a queen."

If it hadn't been for Rowena, she would never have been a queen. She would have lived, instead, in some corner of Megalopolis, content with Conor, and with me. I never would have been a queen. But as a family, we might have been happy, at least until the disaster that was inevitable for the Great Empire actually touched that happiness. We would have ignored it as long as we could. As I see so many families, so touchingly, try to do even now that Arcadia faces its own great disaster.

But none of this was meant to be. If you had seen my mother in the days of her queenship, you would have found it impossible to imagine her as the concubine, even the wife, of some spoiled but handsome rich boy. Of course, she wasn't happy in that role. She was, as I've said, in constant pain, torn between what she'd hoped

ROWENA POMFRET WAS THE MOST BEAUTIFUL WOMAN
IN ALL OF MEGALOPOLIS

for and what was her duty in life. The queenly calm and serenity, I learned much later, were not in spite of that pain. They were because of it. For the cause of the pain (though I'm not sure at all how much of this Devindra actually knows) was that when the Angel entered into Lily, she brought my mother's destiny with her. And the pain came when Lily tried to master it, or at least find a way to accept it with all her soul.

But some destinies are too large for even the greatest soul to master. Or, not master, that's not the word I want. To manage. Some destinies cause permanent suffering in the constant, fruitless attempt to bring them into harmony with an ideal of happiness. And it's the loving, painful quarrel that results that brings its own treasures, unsuspected by the ignorant onlooker.

That I do know.

For aren't I my mother's daughter? I've had my own reason to quarrel, many times, with my own fate (and Rowena Pomfret played a role in that quarrel, too, poor woman). Although mine never had the...well, grandeur is one of the only words I can find to describe it... grandeur and melancholy...of Lily's destiny. She had been fated to be wounded to the heart early on, earlier, even, than the beginnings of the land where she ruled as its first queen. From that wound it proved impossible to recover. But it's from that impossibility that I owe all the warm gifts she heaped on me in my own life, all the material she gave me, that she wove, for me to get and cut and shape and tailor, into the festal garment that suits a happy country best. She was a good queen. She was a good mother. If I could only say the same about myself, how happy I would be!

But this is Lily's story, not mine, not yet (though mine has its cautious beginning here). And Lily would have given it all up to be the simple lover of Conor Barr. If it had been allowed without giving up herself.

Eighteen

When she woke that night, she was back in the green silk-tented room, with the mild, silver light of the Moon Itself shining in over the balcony, with Conor sitting anxiously by her side, holding her hand, and Phoebe standing gravely in the shadow of the carved wooden door. And next to Phoebe, Rex.

"They told me you fainted," Conor said timidly, twining his fingers through hers. "They didn't tell me where. They said..." And then he was abruptly quiet, because Livia, my grandmother, had glided silently in the door.

"Conor," she said, "Rowena is here."

Did Lily know then what was bound to happen next? I think she did. She did truly love my father, which meant that she loved even his weakness and felt tenderly toward it. I know that my mother must have known my father for what he was: "a handsome, charming weakling," as my grandmother later told me dismissively. And I myself have reason to know that the love that goes deepest doesn't necessarily make sense to an outside observer. My father was meant to be a playful, happy lover. That much you could trace on his later, age-ravaged features. You could still see the hopeful, openhearted boy who had never found anything in the world to oppose him, but who had a chance to stay unspoiled through an essential goodness that escaped his mother's eye.

He didn't turn his head now. He didn't answer Livia.

"Conor," she repeated impatiently, "I said, Rowena's here. She's expecting you. Everyone's expecting you."

Did he waver there for a moment? Did some vision of a real

future happiness, one he would have to fight for and that would then be all the more really his, did that come into his mind? What he told me later made me sure it did. That he loved Lily with all his open boy's heart is undeniable. He told me of it much later, and the strength of that feeling resonated still, there between us.

But while Conor had love—affection, and passion, and, at the bottom, a kind heart—he did not have wisdom, or even strength. Well, where would he have gotten them? Wisdom wasn't exactly taught in the prep schools of Megalopolis, and as for strength... strength, I'm afraid, comes in suffering, and he hadn't suffered. Not yet.

I'm sure he told himself he could have it all. He could marry Rowena, the way everyone expected him to, and he could have Lily, too. I'm sure that's what he thought. It's how most young men would (though not all, I'm glad to say). How could he have known what that one misstep would mean for his future? He who never looked past the next spurious accolade, the next trivial prize?

"Conor," Livia said a third time, and I myself have heard a version of the voice she must have used. Even I had difficulty not obeying that voice, and I have a character carefully built by many loving hands to withstand it.

My father did not. His character was to come later. That night, he was just a spoiled, affectionate boy, and he was used to letting tomorrow take care of itself.

He gave Lily, the one and only love of his life, one last pleading look. I can see him do it now. "Save me," that look said. "Make me do what's right. Make me stand up to her, make me stay with you." And Lily, in that moment, loved him with all of her heart, when the Angel's presence had shown her heart to her...at exactly the same moment the Angel showed her what she had to do. What she had to do was opposed to that love, made it impossible in this world, the way this world is presently made, and that was the pain that wracked her from that moment on. To go against your own desire is to swim upstream against an icy current, and that was what my mother did.

She started now. Everything in her yearned to grapple with Livia's will for Conor. But she loved him, and she knew what she had to do. And she had to start by giving him the choice herself, as a gift.

He looked at her again. "Conor," Livia said a fourth time, and he knew there wouldn't be a fifth. "There is bound to be a huge crowd outside with Rowena, and there will be another when we go back down to the Great City. Try to present yourself the way we would like to be seen." At this, Conor pulled himself together, as if slipping on a costume of some kind. He tried a light-hearted shrug, and turned and went out the door.

Livia looked at Lily and gave a wry smile. She lifted her eyebrows and followed her son out.

And Lily, pain shooting through every part of her, her joints, her hands and feet (but mainly through her heart), pulled herself, bewildered, from the green silk-hung bed, and, going to the balcony, yanked painfully at the door.

Phoebe came to help her, but the door was locked. Still, through the crystal glass, the girls could see the crystal-enclosed courtyard below, where Conor greeted a fur-swathed Rowena with a kiss. A million flashes from a million cameras went off, blinding Lily's eyes.

Her hand reached down blindly as she pushed the rising pain back down her throat, to rest there on her heart. Rex was there. She knelt down next to him, and buried her face in his coat. And wept. Because she wanted Conor. She knew she couldn't have him, without using the power of her will. In other words, it was a choice for Lily of using Love or using Power.

It was a fatal choice for her love. It would become a fatal choice for her as queen, too.

Nineteen

Now it's time to talk of Rex. He was just a dog, someone like Aspern Grayling would say. But animals have their choices, and their quests too. Rex had his. And that was no small job—nor was it a safe job, either.

When Rex saw Lily fall on the Moon Itself, he was unworried. He was a dog, and so he could see things that the others in the room could not. He could see, for instance, that Lily had fainted because of the future, and this was something that made him glad. He knew something about Lily's future that she still did not. He knew that I would be born.

He could see the Angel, too, as she really was, not as the others had been able to see her, tortured and bound, in the crystal cell. He could see her standing, grave and watchful, next to Lily. (An angel can be in many places at once, something very few have ever understood. Certainly not Aspern Grayling.) Lily could only feel the Angel inside of her, but Rex could see her. This was the difference between a human and a dog.

"Rex," the Angel said now, coming over to where he sat, unnoticed, at the edge of the room.

"Star," Rex answered. He knew the Angel, knew her well, from other worlds and other times that he knew as well as this one (and this ability to remember, and to see, realities other than the one right in front of our noses, this is another difference between the dog and us). He knew that she had commands to give him; a dog can always feel a command before it comes. "Yes. Tell me and I'll do the best I can."

The others clustered around Lily, lifting her up, chafing her wrists, talking among themselves. While they were busy with this, Star told Rex what he had to do.

"This is what they will do," Star told Rex. "They will take you both back down to the earth, as quickly as they can. For they have discovered the hiding place of the Key. They won't stop until they've found it." A troubled expression passed over Star's golden brown face. "These are a restless people," she said. "Their restlessness keeps them from knowing who they are. From knowing the Key."

Rex knew about the Key. All creatures who keep faith with the Light know about the Key. It is the secret connection of everything that lives—which is the same as everything that is.

"Yes, Star," he said, "I understand." Only Phoebe noticed their talk. No one else would have believed a dog could talk, and so this was yet another thing they, not believing, couldn't see.

"This book has told them that the Key is greater than they," Star said, and she cast a faintly pitying glance at the Great Tome that glowed in the middle of the room. "And they have so little wisdom that they don't understand. They think that to have it in their hand will make them greater still."

At this, Rex and Star exchanged a sad smile. There was not much to be done, they both knew, when men and women were bent on some mindlessly stupid course. There was nothing to do but leave them to it, and hope for better times.

"This book has told them that there is only one who can find the Key."

At this, Rex felt his breath catch painfully against the barrel of his ribs. It stuck as he breathed in and tore as he breathed out. He knew who that one was, of course. It was why he was with her, guarding her, watching her, comforting her. He had always known this day would come. Only...only...only...

Rex looked over to where Lily lay, watching as the men argued over what was to be done, as Alastair picked her up and, carrying her in his arms, followed Phoebe and Livia from the room. He padded along behind, Star at his side.

How could this be? I mean that Star was inside Lily and beside Rex, both at the same time. Well, of course, it's an easy trick, for an Angel.

"I'll make sure she comes to no harm," Rex promised the Angel.

He felt rather than saw her hesitate at this. This hesitation filled him with dread.

"Star?" he said, as he followed the others down the long corridor toward the door to the Silver Bridge that led back to the False Moon. "I'm to go with Lily, of course. She's my person. I'm meant to be at her side." But there was no answer. "Star?" he said again, but this time so gently that only an angel could have heard it. He knew his fate by now. And he would live it, the same as Lily would live hers. This is another difference between a dog and a man. A dog will always do what he is meant to do. Only a man thinks it worthwhile to try to escape his own Fate.

But it wasn't easy for him. Who would it be easy for? He followed them all back to Lily and Conor's room, and he felt very alone.

That was when he caught sight of Phoebe. He had almost forgotten her. But there she was, a girl standing straight as an arrow by the door. She looked at Rex and gave a big, slow, deliberate wink.

And when Lily in her sadness reached down to hug him, he was comforted to know that even when he had left her, gone on his quest, Phoebe would be there to take his place. He knew Phoebe from before, too. And Phoebe had known Lily, though Lily didn't remember. Not yet. Remembering things like that takes such an effort of will, and I think Lily needed all her will to deal with what was in front of her now.

§ § §

Livia had been right about the crowds. The next few days were a nightmare of crowds. First on the False Moon. An engagement party for Conor and Rowena, which Lily was expected to attend with the best grace she could muster. The rooms where she had danced in triumph were now meant to show off Rowena's clothes, Rowena's jewels, the power Rowena had over her fiancé, which included her calling him to her side, in public, whenever Lily was forced by Livia to show herself. Rowena had to be seen to win; that was the story now. And Rowena, without loving Conor, hated Lily. In fact, I have sometimes thought, after my talks with the spoiled aging beauty much later, in the expensive retirement villa she so petulantly ruled, abandoned by her husband and loathed by her son, that her hatred of my mother was the mainspring of her mostly useless life. What did she hate? Her beauty? No, for Rowena, like so many Megalopolitans, only admired one type, a blonde, bland sort, and of that kind Rowena was the most spectacular exemplar. Her brain? No, Rowena would never envy a brain, quite the opposite in fact. The fact that Conor loved Lily and not Rowena? I don't think she cared much about such matters of the heart. For Rowena, what mattered was the public record. And if the media said Conor preferred Rowena to Lily, then that was good enough for her. Better, in fact.

No, the reason Rowena hated Lily was because of Lily's pain. Rowena was not clever, but she was shrewd, and she knew that something large was lacking in her life. Somehow she grasped that what was missing was a Task. And somehow she further grasped that Lily had her own Task, and Lily's pain was a sign of that Task. This filled Rowena with furious envy. In fact, having listened to several extraordinarily irritating and trivial-minded monologues from

Rowena later in life, of the type that passed with her for conversation, I think I can say that Envy was the mainspring of her existence. Envy and the desire to be rid of the Envied. All her life was focused on this one useless goal, and oh, the misery that it caused! Not least to herself. Even the public humiliations she made Lily suffer were not the greatest of the misery she caused, though they were certainly miserable enough. If Lily wore a pretty dress, Rowena demanded it be taken away and given to her. If Conor smiled at Lily, Rowena insisted he come to her side, where she would whisper to him and look maliciously at Lily, making them both laugh, as if at Lily. She would have harmed Rex, too, I think, though only if she had been able to do it without being caught. Megalopolitans are so sentimental about animals; the brutality that their sentimentality inevitably gave rise to was hidden, and this was what they considered civilized behavior. As long as Rex stayed away from Rowena, he was safe, though whether he wanted to be saved was another matter. He knew what he had to do now, and he was both looking for the way to begin, and dreading his task's start.

It wasn't long before they left to go back to the world below. The whole party descended, only to be met by huge crowds jostling and waving on the other side of the massive security gate. There were reporters and cameras, and celebrities and politicians, and many of the common people, bored, looking for the stimulation of any kind of festivity—this one as good as any other.

"HOORAY!" the crowds shouted now. "HOORAY!"

The crowds didn't know what they shouted for, but the reporters said it was to celebrate the union of Rowena and Conor, and the crowds did not disagree.

Lily walked silently behind the happy couple, accompanied by Phoebe and Rex. No one paid them any attention now. The story was somewhere else.

No one, that is, but Livia. Rex was very aware of Livia. She watched them all sharply; she had her plan, and she had no intention of letting Lily get away.

But she didn't care about Rex. Rex was only a dog. And that gave Rex his chance.

The crowd parted, opening a way for Conor Barr, Rowena Pomfret, Lily, Livia, Phoebe, and a beaming Julian to walk to a cavalcade of open cars covered with garlands of scentless carnations. Rex followed behind, forgotten. And as the others stepped toward the bright red and silver machines, he deliberately stopped, as if to suck a thorn out of his paw.

The crowd surged around him, cheering in a bored sort of way. It closed the path in front of him and hid him from sight. This was his chance. He craned his head around for one last look at Lily. But the crowd hid her now.

Rex turned and walked away, at first slowly, in order not to attract attention, then more swiftly, until finally he stretched out into a run. Skirting the massive security gate, he headed for the open fields. On the other side of these fields were the Calandal Mountains, yellow and cold and bare. That was where Rex headed now.

"Rex?" he heard Lily's distressed voice carry over the heads of the crowd on the wind. "Rex! My dog! Where's my dog? Rex! Rex! REX!" Then he heard the faint sound of the car starting up and driving away, though this sound disappeared quickly, washed away by the wind as it shifted its course.

Lily's cries continued in his heart. But he was running at a steady pace now, and he couldn't afford to hear.

§ § §

Rex ran and ran—he ran for many days. He rested in gullies,

or under creosote-soaked bushes on the dry plains leading up to the Calandals. It was cold on the high desert plains, and there were mornings where he woke covered with a layer of frost that crackled on his fur. But he would just give it a shake and, sending it tinkling in all directions, would soon be off again.

The mountains themselves are rugged, even though they are the lowest of the four mountain ranges protecting Arcadia. Rex made his way up their side, zigzagging through the scrub pine and mullein and sage. His paws, by the third day, left a limping track of blood.

On the third day, though, he found the pass he was looking for. Beside it was the burned-out frame of a farmhouse. When he passed this, he came to what had been a spring, but which was now stopped up with rocks and scrub and trash so that no one could drink from it. From here, he could see all the way down to the valley below.

It was changed. Where Arcadia had been green, now it was gray. Where it had been blue, now it was brown. Where it had been gold, now it was black. And a pall of muddy smoke hung over the fields and the towns.

Star had sent Rex on a quest. He was to fetch Death back from Arcadia. And he could see that she was here, all right. He could see, just by looking, that she had been very busy.

Twenty

And now I think I have to talk about Aspern Grayling, even though his story isn't a part of the Legend of Lily the Silent. But it is a large part of the story of Arcadia, and of the problems facing her now. He is a large part of the problems facing me now. The main one: how to avoid the approaching, seemingly inevitable civil war. Or, rather, if that war is inevitable as everyone now, beaten down, seems to feel, how to move us past it with the least amount of harm, and the most amount of hope.

That is my problem as queen, you know. And everything for me, as it was finally for Lily, is about my problem as queen. The happiness of daily life wasn't left to either of us; what was left was the task of restoring the possibility of that happiness for others. Not that I'm complaining. I do rather relish the idea of being a Hero, with the goal of making a polity where no one else has to be one. I inherited this one role from my mother: the Hero who does not, cannot, believe in the ultimate good of Heroism. Very amusing, if only there was someone other than her (and Star) to share the joke.

But to return to Aspern. I have often found it striking that the two most aristocratic figures in Arcadia, Professors Devindra Vale and Aspern Grayling, both come from the poorest and most obscure parts of their own lands. Devindra, of course, came from the Marsh People of Megalopolis, where she never knew her own father, and Aspern (who was born, truth to tell, simple Andy Dawkins, though his mother's father was a Grayling) was the cherished son of a cheerful, feckless, hardscrabble farm family in one of the trailer settlements in the mountains above Eopolis.

It is funny to see the two of them now, though I say that in all fondness. It is a marvel to watch them debate, the two most intensely active, highly tuned minds that I know—Devindra the taller of the two, ramrod straight, with her silvered black hair under her favorite turquoise and ruby turban, her curved brown nose like a hawk's beak, and her poor arthritic fingers clutching her walking stick. How she looks like the descendant of the greatest of foreign queens! Her mother, Tilly, was a washerwoman and who knows what else when the pennies from such scanty work ran out. But Devindra, her daughter, has always looked the part of a noblewoman intent on duty, piety, the care of her family and her goddesses. Her family, in this case, means all of those at Otterbridge University, which she founded at my mother's wish. It's Otterbridge University that is Devindra's real child. Which explains, maybe, why Merope, her actual daughter, hates her and hates what the colleges making up the university have done. And who hates me, the enthusiastic patron of those colleges, who has never done Merope any harm.

But Merope doesn't hate Aspern Grayling. Far from it. Unsurprising, maybe, for he, with his pale, parchment-fine skin, and his blue-veined hands and pale turquoise eyes and his pale fading cornsilk hair, and his long thin nose that twitches at every smell, he has certainly seduced enough people, men and women, in his time. He is remarkable, Aspern, though he calls himself my greatest enemy, and though he is the determined opponent of any wish I might have for what he has always called, not 'the commons' as we do in Arcadia, but the 'common people.' Always with a sneer that reminds me, strangely, of Rowena Pomfret, a woman he never met except in the Megalopolitan tabloids he must have read furiously in his youth.

He hated my mother. I remember that. I remember the cold look of fury on his face whenever he saw her, whenever he watched her patiently untangle old laws and mingle them with new, whenever she gave audience to Arcadians he considered well beneath him, let alone her, whenever she settled disputes peacefully, according to rules of fairness rather than power. I was only seven years old, but I knew he hated her. And I clung to Devindra, who loved her, and I even clung to Merope (oh, mistake!) because she was my own age and belonged, I thought, as much to her mother as I did myself.

It was only when I was older, when I was first princess, and then queen, that I saw the truth about that. Watching Grayling and Devindra debate the future of Arcadia before an increasingly anxious audience over the years, I began to see the widening fissure between the two sides, the two visions.

Both were an aristocratic vision, at bottom, if we define aristocratic as caring little for possessions, even for life, beyond the service they can give to the values of honor, courtesy, dignity. But Devindra's aristocracy is always of the mind, always inclusive, always striving to bring in more and more, whether people, or experiences, or ideas. Aspern Grayling's aristocracy is one based on power, on a bedrock belief that some are more worthy than others, more meant to rule, that anything else is chaos, base anarchy, dissolution...death. By death, he never means the Death that Lily knew, and that I met later, but a death formed by his distorted image of his own life, an imaginary adversary to defeat, something...someone...to triumph over, as in his world view everything must triumph or be defeated, with no middle ground. There is no living in harmony with Death, no partnership or even truce possible to Aspern. It is always kill Death or be killed. It is either triumph or be left humiliated, worthless, in defeat.

It is a ruthless worldview. It is a view I can't accept, and Grayling counts this refusal as my great weakness, proving my feminine unfitness to rule. To Grayling, it is the harshness of the view that proves its truth.

This is sentimentality to me, of the worst kind. And there we have our disagreement, Grayling's and mine.

But I've run even farther ahead of myself than I had meant. I need now to go back to my mother's story.

Twenty-One

"Don't cry, Lily," Conor whispered as they walked toward the car. "I'll get you another dog. I'll get you anything you want. I'll make all this..." he gestured around them at the crowd, at Rowena, but with a gesture that made it look as if he was waving in a lordly way to the cheering Megalopolitans that surrounded them. "Make all this up to you," he muttered, knowing very well that none of it could be made up to Lily, none of it could be made up to anyone. He knew very well, my father, that the world he lived in was bad, crumbling at the bottom, and rotting at the top; he knew that the only true thing he had ever had in his luxurious and pampered life was his love for Lily. And he knew that he was going to betray that love now. He was ashamed of it. But he knew he would do it anyway.

Livia looked at him ironically, and he looked away, not meeting her eyes or Lily's gaze. What else could he do? He was Conor Barr, the idol of millions. There wasn't enough left to him from that Conor Barr to strengthen just plain Conor. There certainly wasn't enough to strengthen him to stand up for Conor and Lily. That would only come later. Too late, my father said. But about that I'm not sure. It may be that it's never too late to be true to Love.

But now was not the time for Conor Barr to stand up for himself, let alone for Love.

"Get in the car with Rowena. Now," Livia hissed. And Conor, obedient, gave Lily one last look, and hurried ahead with his father to join his fragile, fairy princess fiancée, leaving his true love behind. Behind with Livia.

And with Phoebe. Who was she, and what was she doing there?

No one had said anything to Lily, but in that dark moment, she felt a hand squeeze hers. Surprised, she looked down and saw it was Phoebe's. "Rex knows what he's doing," Phoebe murmured. "It will be all right in the end." Lily listened to this carefully, puzzling over it. There was much for her to puzzle over just then, my poor, dear mother. But it was painfully working out the possible answers to the puzzle that made her emerge, finally, as queen.

Conor was wrong. Lily had not been crying. She knew that Phoebe must be right, that Rex was not lost. (And who was Phoebe? And why did Livia seem not to see her? Seem to pretend, or not know at all, that she wasn't even there?) Lily knew that Rex would never have let himself be separated from her without a good reason. She trusted him to know a good reason from a bad. Only it had frightened her badly, his leaving so suddenly like that, leaving her to fend for herself among these dangerous strangers. Still, there was Phoebe, whose dark brown eyes saw so much, and who held onto Lily's hand. And up ahead, in the car, next to Conor's servant in the driver's seat, was Kim, who bounced with excitement when she saw Lily, her sharp little nose bobbing in the air. Just the sight of Kim comforted Lily. There was always something about Kim, even much later in her life, that made those around her cling to a little bit of hope, no matter how dark the surrounding world became. She was that for me, oh, many times when I was growing up. Some people are like that, I thankfully observe. And it was lucky for Lily that Kim was one of them, now.

"Friends," Lily thought to herself, looking at Phoebe and Kim— or was it the Angel inside of her speaking? She couldn't tell. But the voice went on. "Friends. Allies." And Lily heard.

She let herself be led to the car, settled in it between Phoebe and a watchful Livia, covered with fur rugs, and driven away. She was quiet when they turned off from the main road, leaving the cavalcade of red and silver cars, and headed down a narrow, badly kept road.

§ § §

They drove quickly and were soon past the crowds, speeding through open countryside. This was not the kind of landscape Lily was used to. It was blasted and stunted and brownish red, and every so often a murky pond oozed up from its clay. It was the Marsh Land, where the Marsh People lived. The Marsh had once been a clear river, and the land around it a prosperous one. But since the damming of the river, things had changed.

"Isn't this lovely!" Kim exclaimed from the front seat, craning her neck around. "I do like a bit of Nature." And she gave a contented sigh.

Lily saw Phoebe laugh soundlessly to herself. But Kim was oblivious to any absurdity. Livia gave a sour smile.

"Yes," she said in an acid-tinged voice. "The Council of Four has worked long and hard to preserve our natural heritage. This is a park that will be here for generations to come."

"Isn't it beautiful, Lily?" Kim said with her usual ebullience. But Lily, who this time pressed Phoebe's hand under their shared fur rug, didn't answer. Instead she schooled her face as well as she could into a look of blank admiration. Phoebe looked disapproving at this, which also comforted Lily. Lily was already missing Rex very much.

Barbed wire fences flashed by them, and bleached bones lying half stuck in the clay. And then there was the smell of something fetid, something brackish and sour.

"What is it?" Lily cried in spite of herself. "Where are we going?" At this, Phoebe looked more approving, and gave her hand, under the fur rugs, another comforting press.

"To the sea," Livia said, and she inhaled deeply as if the horrid smell was something fine.

Kim clapped her hands and bounced up and down in her seat. "The sea!" she said. "I was born near the sea!"

"But," Lily thought, "I'm sure the real sea doesn't smell like this." Looking at Phoebe's blank expression beside her, she was sure of it.

§ § §

The sea did not look the way Lily had always imagined. For one thing, the strand in front of the murky, lapping water was covered with soldiers, all silent, holding guns and wooden staffs. There seemed to be hundreds of them, stretching out in both directions, on either side of a straight path down to the sea. There were so many that Lily couldn't see the end of them.

The car pulled up before a smartly dressed officer, who saluted them crisply.

"Lady Livia?" he inquired, and then, seeing it was, he waved them down the path through the troops, the path that crossed the strand toward the flat black sea.

"Hey!" the driver protested, putting on the brakes of the car. "I can't drive there. We'll sink into the sand!"

"Go on!" Livia hissed. "Idiot! Just do what I say! Drive on!" And Conor's servant, shaking his head and muttering, did what she said.

"Horrible old bitch," he thought to himself. But he did what she said. Everyone in Megalopolis always did. A redoubtable woman, my grandmother!

Now even Kim shivered. As they drove slowly through the silent ranks of soldiers, whose eyes glittered from behind their black wool masks, the Angel spoke inside of Lily.

Lily listened carefully. At first she hesitated. But then Phoebe pressed her hand again, and Lily knew it meant Phoebe could hear

156

the Angel's voice as well. It was a comfort, she told me when I was very small (for this part of the story was my favorite, I made her retell it over and over), to know that the voice she heard so plainly was not only her imagination.

"Though to say 'only my imagination,' Snow, is to put it the wrong way. Try to remember that. It's only in your imagination where the answers to the really hard questions can be found."

She had reason to know that was true. So she listened. And she obeyed.

"Stop the car," she said. It surprised even her, the clear sound of her voice. The driver, startled, craned his head around.

"Yes," Livia said nodding. "Do what she says."

It was quiet there, on the strand, even with the hundreds of men and women standing there. The car juddered to a halt, and all you could hear was the halfhearted movement of the sea.

Lily scrambled over Phoebe to get out of the car. "Lily!" Kim hissed. "Lily, where are you going?" But one look from Livia, and she was still.

Lily got out of the car, and walked the now short distance down to the sea. When she got there, she just stood, looking out over its dark expanse.

"What's she doing then?" Kim asked fretfully, but the driver, now scared as well by the look in Livia's eye, shushed her.

Then Phoebe got out of the car.

"No," Livia said vigorously, and made a move to stop her. But the girl was too quick for Livia, and before she could be stopped she was striding to Lily's side.

"Well, then," Kim said, and before anyone could stop her, either, she was out and off. "I'm going, too." She ran lightly on her long, coltish legs until she was almost upon the other two girls, at which point she stopped, shy. But they turned and seemed to welcome her, and then the three of them stood there, between the soldiers, looking out to the sea. As the rest of them watched, Lily turned first to Phoebe, then Kim, and said a few words. The other two girls paused, then nodded, first one, then the other. And at this, Lily turned and came back alone.

"I know what you want me to do," she said, looking at Livia. "I can see it all. You want me to go into the sea." And when Livia was silent, she said, in a scornful voice, "That's what THEY are for..." her arm swept around the soldiers standing, watchful, there. "They're to drive me into the sea."

Livia still did not answer.

"You don't need them, you know," Lily said gently. "I saw what it was in the Book, what I have to do. And I'll do it all right. But on one condition."

At this, Livia's eyebrow raised inquiringly.

"If I can find what you want and bring it to you, you'll give me safe passage back over the mountains to my home. To Arcadia."

Lily missed Rex badly, but she knew where he had gone. It was where she longed to go, too.

Livia nodded, seemingly amused. I would have been warned, if I were Lily, by that look of amusement in my grandmother's eye. But I think I know her better than Lily ever did. I am so much like her, you see.

And then, Lily was bracing herself to give voice to the other part of her condition. She held up her hand. "Wait. Safe passage for Conor, too. For Conor and me to go across the mountains to Arcadia."

At this, I know, my grandmother's face became grave. This happens to her expression, sometimes, when she feels a particular triumph, some particular glee at a turn in events. It's her way of hiding the fact that she has won. She knew she had won now. So she said, sounding aggrieved, "You would take my son from me?" Her face, I am willing to swear, was that of an old defeated woman, who was losing everything she loved.

This would have amused my grandmother no end. She would have been doubly amused to see Lily's struggle go across her face. Lily, who felt the justice of a claim Livia did not really feel, was incapable of feeling. It would have cost Lily much to hold out in silence.

"And if I'd known you were in the offing, granddaughter," Livia said to me much later with a nasty look in her eye, "I would have denied safe passage to you." In fact, she tried then to claim my mother had tricked her, all those years ago, and that by right, she could keep me with her as long as she liked. But I am not Livia's grandchild for nothing, and like, in that case, won out over like.

My mother, while just as strong a spirit as either of us, was a more loving one. She hated to interfere with love of any kind, even power that masquerades as love, only meaning to win more for itself. So it must have cost her much to hold her ground. But hold her ground she did. Until Livia, histrionically, pathetically, gave one broken sob and nodded her head, hiding the gleam in her eye.

Lily turned back and returned to her friends. Livia and her soldiers watched as the girls conferred. Phoebe stood with her arms folded, serene. Kim bounced up and down on the balls of her feet, nodding furiously. Then the three girls linked arms—there was just enough space on the path for the three of them, standing abreast, to pass—and walked toward the sea.

Livia jumped up, alarmed. "No!" she shouted, scrambling from her seat onto the strand. "Stop them! That's not the way it's written! It's written that she goes alone! Stop them! Stop those girls!"

But the soldiers had no orders to stop Lily, only to force her into the sea. So they watched in silence as she walked, arms linked with those of her friends, into the dank cold water. Of the three girls, Lily was the smallest, and after her disappeared Kim's yellow-brown ponytail, and Phoebe's white-gold hair.

"NO!" Livia yelled, and she stomped her foot on the strand. But she was too late. All three girls had gone into the sea.

Twenty-Two

Under the sea, everything was changed. To their surprise, none of the girls felt frightened, my mother told me, but rather "felt just exactly the way things were meant to be, Snow."

(For this was my favorite story as a child, one I had from my mother, and from Kim, and even from Star.)

There is a lot you see under the sea, my mother told me. Kim, too, told me "there's ever so much more than you see on land, Soph," as she tucked me into the huge bed I'd inherited from Lily. "I think it musta been cuz of how dead quiet it is there." There under the sea, she said, noise is not constantly pushing and pulling at you. You can just move in one direction and see, quite clearly and plainly, where you're headed.

I've never been there myself. But I have imagined.

And then, they weren't alone. (How I loved this part of the Story of Going Under the Sea!) Almost immediately, as the three followed the slope of a hill down under the clear blue water, they attracted a crowd. Now there were three dolphins swimming alongside, their bottlenoses and their silver bellies showing as they twisted and rolled along. There was a wedge-shaped formation of rays complete with teeth and whipping tails. There was a line of green eels. And, overhead, as the girls looked up, there were hundreds, "maybe thousands, Soph, just imagine it! You never saw such a thing," of tiny, eager fish. They were all the colors of the rainbow, Kim said: "red and white and yellow and purple."

The girls laughed but they made no sound. They smiled at each other and held hands. And they walked on.

The farther they went, the more company they had, underwater creatures of all kinds: shrimps, and squids, and swimming sponges; sharks and soles, and red and orange snappers; rainbow-colored mackerel, and marlin...

And then...there was a Manatee. Big and bulky and with a strangely ill formed back tail. They only caught a glimpse of him at first. They were so overwhelmed by all the show around them, by the welcome they were getting from the Sea, it was hard to take it all in. Hard to take in any detail past the larger feeling of joy that came on them now.

The more company the girls had, the happier the girls felt. This was a particular feeling that all three recognized as the same that had swept them, together, into the sea. They had not been driven to it, as Livia wanted (which must have frustrated her utterly, if I know my grandmother). They had gone together. None of them could say why they had done so, but I can tell you that they had gone together for love.

And so the company that joined them now joined them for love. They didn't know it, any more than a fish knows it swims in water. They accepted it as natural, and they just walked on.

The three girls held hands now and walked straight forward, catching sight, from time to time, of the Manatee as it swam shyly along, first behind a dolphin, then beside an anemone. It was as if the huge, clumsy creature wanted them to see him, to notice him in some particular way, but was too bashful to call attention to himself.

Lily gave him a closer look. He had flipper-like hands, which he used in a precise, almost dainty way. His tailfin was almost round, and flat, and propelled him more gracefully through the water than you could imagine, if you looked first at his enormous brown and wrinkled bulk. All the more surprisingly since the tail was lopsided, as if he'd been injured somewhere. If he had been able to walk, he

162

would have limped.

This reminded Lily of something. But she couldn't quite remember what.

Then there was his face. Lily could see that it was long and silly, but with a kind of noble nose topping the whole. The Manatee was very silly-looking indeed, and wistful, too. Lily pondered this. It seemed to her that she had seen this expression before, that somewhere she had once known someone very like the Manatee. But the moment she thought this, that thought washed away in the water around her and was gone.

As she looked over at the Manatee, trying to puzzle some sort of sense out of him, she saw him duck his head, putting one flipper over his eye and peering out back at her from under it. Then the huge unwieldy creature drew himself up to his full length—he was, indeed, very long; I used to laugh and clap my hands at this point in the story when Kim would describe how long—and swam ponderously forward. He swam beside the girls and then, with a churning of the water, gave a bow that was courteous in the extreme. Lily, observing him close up now, gave a start. The Manatee looked at her intently from his tiny gray-brown eyes. There was something about those eyes that was very familiar indeed. They were silly, and, tiny as they were, they bugged out a little. Lily knew that she had looked into those eyes many times before, and in many places, too.

But how could that be? She puzzled to herself. How could that be so?

The Manatee turned with the girls now, and swam along beside them, his tail flapping comfortably as they went. Lily watched him, but for now he kept his silly muzzle pointing straight ahead. Just for now he didn't meet her eye.

Down and down they walked, deeper into the sea. Or rather, they didn't walk down—they walked, no matter how far, as if on even land. It was a long, flat plain the girls walked along with the fish swimming beside, one that stretched out farther than you could see.

It was the sea above them that got deeper and deeper as they walked. Deeper and deeper and deeper, until, when they looked up, they could see nothing but water overhead for miles. And to their further surprise, the farther they went, the lighter the seawater became around them. First it was a shiny blue-green, then turquoise, and then, as they neared their destination ("though how we knew we had a destination, much less that we were near it, none of us could have said," my mother told me later), a pale gold-blue shimmered all around them, turning any other color it surrounded into a deeper, realer version of itself.

All of this Lily saw. "I could see quite clearly, Snow, there under the Sea."

The Manatee, as he swam, courteously holding Lily's arm on one of his oval-shaped, velvety fins, looked more and more to Lily, as they went on, like the most comfortable armchair by the warmest fire you could imagine. His dark gray pelt took on a burnished look, as if reflecting the cheerful flames there. And his eyes, though tiny, shone deeper and brighter, too.

And then there was Kim. She changed too. "Ooooh, I did and all, Soph. I were never the same again, no never." Her blonde hair turned golden as they went on in that blue-gold light. Here and there it escaped the black plastic clasp she used to hold it back, and floated in tendrils around her face. The fish, swimming with them, teased her by nipping at the floating ends. "Oooh, they made me smile, them fish!" But she never said a word.

As for quiet Phoebe, her face changed, too—it became whiter and whiter as they went on, until it glowed like the Moon Itself, and the more her skin glowed, the quieter she became. The quieter she became, the more her smile shone like a sharp silver crescent on her face. And Lily, seeing this, realized that, since they'd come together under the sea, her silver-haired friend hadn't said a single word.

It was only then, when Lily marveled to herself at this, that she realized that she, too, was silent. She opened her mouth, experimentally, just to say one word, and she found, not that she couldn't, but that she wouldn't. Although why she wouldn't she could not have said. And Lily, as she walked along the golden sand that showed their footprints for only an instant before the sea washed them away, pondered this.

Without knowing it, Lily and the others had passed through the Sea Change that happens along the long walk to the Mermaids' Deep—for it was to that very place, known to all the girls from the stories of their earliest childhoods (known to all of us from all of ours, as well), that they walked now. After this, none of them would be the same. Each changed in her own way, which, of course, is the way it is with change.

THE MERMAIDS' DEEP

Twenty-Three

What can I tell about the Mermaids and the Mermaids' Deep? Everyone knows the nursery tales. Or should. On the other hand, it occurs to me that so many true and useful things have been forgotten here in Arcadia, that it's worth repeating the old, established facts about the Mermaids and their Deep. There are so many things that need to be known and remembered and so many things that are, instead, unknown and forgotten. We believe in preserving memory, Wilder and I. And of all the memories worth preserving, there are few worth more than those of Mermaids and the Mermaids' Deep.

There are a lot of stories about Mermaids, in Arcadia and Megalopolis, and a lot of fakery, especially on the False Moon. A mermaid to most people these days is nothing more than a pretty device. And the reason for this is not because Mermaids themselves are frivolous or vain, but because they are not. They keep themselves to themselves and don't much care about the outside world. They have enough work to do where they are, in the Mermaids' Deep, tending the Mermaids' Well. Too much to do without worrying about publicity, too.

Mermaids existed before just about everything that we know in our world. They lived under the sea even in the days before the world had risen out of it. From the beginning, they have been a happy people, and a conservative one, and—though you might not think it—highly mobile, travelling here and there, powered by their great curiosity. The pictures that show Mermaids with a mere fish's tail are ill-informed, for each Mermaid has two strong legs, of varying colors depending on her age and her ancestry (some iron blue, some fish-scale green, some iridescent rose or violet, some turquoise and silver, some gold or bronze). A Mermaid is born knowing how to put those legs together to form a single propelling rudder that moves her through the water with incredible speed.

But she can walk on the bottom of the ocean when she has to. And on the surfaces of the world, too. Many has been the time in human history when a curious Mermaid has ventured out onto land. But in all those many times, she was never seen for what she was. She was never recognized. Most of the Mermaids who tried this hopeful experiment were driven by this lack of recognition, grieving, back into the Sea.

I've always thought this was a terrible shame. And all because no one could see the Mermaids for what they are.

The only way for a human to recognize a Mermaid is to meet her under the Sea. It's easy, Lily told me, to see clearly there.

"But wait!" I can hear my dear subjects cry. "If we can recognize a Mermaid under the Sea, and there are as many of them there as you say, and if they have been there for so long, how is it that we have never heard of anyone who has seen them? How is it that they are unknown to Science? How is it that no scientist in Megalopolis has ever caught them on camera or in nets, and how is it that no people have ever ventured underwater to capture and enslave them, as you would think would be natural?"

In fact, I can hear Aspern Grayling say something like this. He is always saying things like this, whenever such topics arise.

Here are the facts. The Mermaids are a peaceful people—but they are warlike in their peacefulness, and in this, they are unlike any other species ever seen by Man. By this I mean that they aggressively pursue their right to be passive, to be ornamental, to be helpful and nurturing and kind. There is nothing a Mermaid likes more than to sit

on a rock, gazing into a mirror and combing her long hair (again of
a color depending on her age and ancestry—roan, or metallic green,
or bronze, or pure and dazzling white). She likes to sit like this for
hours, combing and contemplating herself and her thoughts. There
must be something in it, too, because a Mermaid will, in a flash, turn
into the fiercest of beings if disturbed at this occupation. She will
never strike the first blow, but woe to the Man who does—for that
Man will never return to his home above the Sea. A Mermaid will
not allow herself to be interrupted at what she does. And the reason
we have not heard much of Mermaids (and the little we have untrue)
is because there are few men (women, it seems, are differently made
in this respect) who can look at a Mermaid without an overwhelming
urge to capture her, chain her up, and drag her to where she doesn't
want to go. A Mermaid will never allow this. And what's more, she
has the strength to back it up.

After many tries at capturing a Mermaid, Man has simply given
up. Because of the many defeats he has suffered, to protect himself
from the knowledge of his own violence and foolishness, he now
pretends that Mermaids never existed at all.

It's simpler that way, for some people—Aspern Grayling and all
his followers—are of this kind. But just because you say something
to feel better about yourself doesn't mean that the thing is so. Just
because you say you are just and wise and good doesn't mean you
are. I recommend that even when you keep silent about this kind of
foolishness out of loyalty (and loyalty is a good thing, never doubt
that), you never allow yourself to be fooled. In the silence of your own
heart, always remember that Mermaids exist, in huge congregations,
and if no one else around believes this is so, well, too bad for them.

If you understand this truly, and hold onto it hard, it might even
be that, one day, when a Mermaid comes out of the Sea, you will
know her for what she is.

§ § §

Lily and Kim and Phoebe met with a tremendous welcome in the Mermaids' Deep. Lily had never felt so warmly received in any place, not even in Arcadia where there was always a warm welcome for anyone, friend or stranger. The Mermaids crowded around the girls, each one more beautiful than the next, each one with a round, jewel-colored face, like the fish that had acted as their escort—faces that shone with delicate scales of ruby, or sapphire, or topaz, or amethyst, or emerald, or diamond. Their legs, of course, were covered with scales, and because this was early in the Mermaids' Spring, with the planting just begun, the colors of these scales were just turning brighter from those of the Mermaids' Winter. So they were quieter in color than they would be later in the year, now pale gray-green, or purplish black, or the color of a newly budding plant. And their many-colored hair waved in tendrils about their round moon faces.

Kim put her hand up to her own escaped locks and gave a silent laugh. "I looked like 'em, didn't I, Soph?" she said to me later, merrily. Lily told me the same. Kim did indeed look, as they walked on, more and more like a Mermaid. And Phoebe had turned so much like this new company now that Lily had a hard time in picking her out from the crowd.

On each Mermaid's face was a crescent smile as sharp and distinct as Phoebe's had become, though each differed from its fellows in color. Some smiles were silver, like Phoebe's own, and some were copper; some were brass, and some were gold. But the smiles, welcoming as they were, stayed fixed, never moving into words.

There are no words with Mermaids, except in their songs, because words are for use in talking about the past or dreaming about the future. And in the Mermaids' Deep, it is only ever Now.

Now was time for the Mermaids' Feast. The guests gladly sat at the enormous round table where the Feast was held. Lily sat next to the Manatee who, his shyness conquered, stared at her with a strangely expectant look. On her other side was a Mermaid— an emerald-faced Mermaid with golden hair and purple-black legs colored like winter seaweed—who courteously poured from a pale pink jug made of a single seashell a pale green wine that tasted of the spring breezes in the mountains of Arcadia. Then when the wine was finished, the Mermaid would give a nod and, putting her legs together, would stand, give them a flick like a tail, and disappear, only to return moments later bearing some new delicacy.

All through the meal—which was course after course of the finest, best chosen, most well-portioned of foods—Lily noticed that the Mermaids would frequently get up from the table and disappear, returning, after a moment or two, with another course of food, or with golden instruments on which they would play a wordless song, or with a carafe of an even finer wine than had gone before, or with a new set of plates with pictures painted on them. And what pictures! Kim tried to describe them to me. "Phoenixes and unicorns and lions and salamanders, Soph!" Lily traced a unicorn horn on her plate with one finger, simultaneously scooping up the final bits of a briny sauce and putting this in her mouth. She had seen it was a habit of the Mermaids to wipe their plates in this fashion, a pure expression of pleasure. So Lily courteously did the same. As she ate and drank, she found she could understand all that was going on around her, even though no words were spoken. So Lily understood that after the Feast, they were to go to the Mermaids' Well.

When Lily looked around to see if her friends had understood this, too, she saw that the Manatee and Phoebe had gotten up, unseen, from the Feast. They stood a little ways away from the others, their heads together, as if in conference—though even at that distance, Lily could clearly see that they were both silent. Then, to her surprise, they swam away. It wasn't the swimming that surprised her. It was the way that Phoebe swam. Lily's friend swam with her legs together, as naturally as if she were a Mermaid herself, and her legs shone, now, with a covering—it looked like—of pale blue-gray scales. And her hair streamed out in tendrils behind her.

Twenty-Four

The Mermaids' Well was in an oasis of stone and sand, surrounded by waving sea palms. As Lily and Kim neared it, led by the emerald-faced Mermaid, they could see the Well was round and squat, and made of the same yellow stone that surrounded it. Kim squeezed Lily's hand in excitement—"though at what, Soph, I'd swear I couldn't tell ya." An ebony-faced Mermaid with chocolate-colored hair and dimly burnished bronze legs swam to the Well, holding a reddish bowl out in front of her. Through its rim, two holes were pierced on opposite sides.

The purpose of the holes become clear at the Well's edge, as the Mermaid tied the bowl to the long brown tendrils of her hair.

Kim's breath came out in a long hiss of bubbles. "Ooooh. Me eyes were wide at that!"

The Mermaid let the bowl down bit by bit, her hair lengthening as it went, until Kim and Lily heard a quiet little bump, of the sort you might hear in a little boat on a lake on a summer afternoon while you're lying on the boat's bottom in the sun, just as it reaches the shore.

The ebony-faced Mermaid now pulled gently at her hair, and as she did, Kim put a hand over her face, holding her breath.

"I couldn'ta said why, but it made me that happy to see her doin' it, Soph. That happy."

Kim leaned forward as if to get as close as possible to what was being pulled up from the Mermaids' Well. And when the bowl rose to the top, and the Mermaid pulled it up and over onto the sand with a well-practiced yank, Kim gave a silent shriek, and fell back.

Out of the bowl fell what looked like an enormous ugly insect. Kim ran from it, hiding behind Lily's back. Lily, laughing soundlessly, pulled her around and made her look again. It was true, the contents of the bowl looked at first sight like some hideous bug: a cockroach, or a cricket, or a giant slug. "As we watched the 'orrible little thing, it started to change, like." Kim, sheltered under Lily's arm, watched, fascinated, as the bug waddled out from the bowl, shook itself off, rooted itself and began to grow.

As it grew, it turned into itself. It turned into a Tree.

Kim, delighted now, clapped her hands. "Oh, it were a beautiful Tree, Soph, just beautiful!" More beautiful, even, than the sea palms that waved gently around the Well.

And as the Tree spread its branches, they saw it was not just any, but a particular kind of Tree.

It was, in fact, a Family Tree.

And more than a Family Tree. It was Kim's Family Tree.

This seemed incredible to Kim, but so it was. Pulling Lily by the hand, she went up to it, mouth open, and looked up. On every branch of the Tree there was a name written in dark green script, and above each name was an ornament of some kind: a stone gargoyle here, a clutch of flowers there. At the bottom of the Tree, on one of the lushest of the lower branches, there it was in script, the words: "KIM THWAITES." And above her name was a shining gold cradle that hung by a single broken chain.

Kim looked with amazement at this Tree. For Kim had never known where she came from, having been born after the days of the Great Accident III, when all records, except those of the very richest families, had been lost. Kim went shyly to the Tree and touched the little cradle hanging there. And there were tears in her eyes. "You could see that even in the water of the Mermaids' Deep," my mother would always say softly at this point in the story. So Kim cried. As she told me, "it's a sorrowful thing not to know where you come from, Soph. Planning where you go is always hard, but how much harder if you don't know where you've been!" And Kim had always longed to plan where she would go, but had almost given up hope that she could. "If you're just a piece of trash floating along," she would say to me later, many, many times, "you don't think you have much of a say, then, do you?"

But now, as Kim looked at the cradle hanging so precariously above her name, there rose in her the beginnings of an Idea. It wasn't the first Idea that had ever come to Kim—if you looked inside her, in fact, you would have seen, I'm positive, the merriest jumble of multi-colored intentions and resolves—but it was the strongest by far. And for a moment, she stood there patiently and let it form itself and grow.

Lily saw all this happen to her friend, doubtless again because of the clarity of the water in the Mermaids' Deep. And she silently asked the Well, "And me? What do you have for me in the Well?"

At this, the ebony-faced Mermaid swam toward her and, taking her by the hand, led her to the Well. Lily moved easily over the gold sand, and the water washed away her footprints as soon as they had formed at her feet. She stood there at the edge of the golden circle, and then, holding her breath, looked in.

She could see a lot of things, she told me, way down deep in the Mermaids' Well. She saw music and dancing and the carving of stone statues. She saw heraldry and viniculture and the breeding of horses. She told me about those things, explaining carefully what they were when I asked. She saw vases carved with pictures from the stories told down below among the sea's inhabitants. And she saw fields of flowers and white sheets drying on them in the sun.

But that wasn't what was important. What was important was that Lily saw, lying on a muddy ledge halfway up the deep immensity of the Mermaids' Well, a Rose-Gold Key.

The Rose-Gold Key.

There was no mistaking it. Half covered in green-black murk that it was, it shone up through the clear water. And Lily knew it had been waiting for her. It shone now with its recognition of her, and she knew she was meant to fetch it and take it back to land. She knew that was what she was there for.

But it was so far down the Well. How was she to get at it?

She looked around for help. "Always remember to do that, Snow, when you need it." She saw Phoebe smile at her, with that sharp silver crescent smile, from across the Well. Kim, too, had joined them, and the long yellow-brown tendrils of her hair waved in the water.

As Lily looked at her friends standing with her at the Well, she said, silently: "Who will help me get the Key?" At this, Phoebe reached up to her silver smile and plucked it—ping!—away from her face. "Like it were ripe or sumpthin', Soph," Kim said, laughing at the memory. Phoebe's own mouth appeared behind it, pink and raw, but the silver smile shone in her fingers like a fisherman's hook.

Lily took the smile with a nod of thanks, and tied it to the waving ends of Kim's long hair. And then Kim bent over the Well. With Lily guiding the strands of her tendrils, the waving hair plunged lower and lower, pulled down by the silver crescent hook. Until it reached the ledge. And Lily, closing her eyes, fished for it and felt it catch, and felt it lift, almost as if it was lifting itself, reaching up itself toward its true fate. It whooshed up the water of the Well, and danced out with a tiny 'plop,' bouncing once against the sandstone sides, and up to where Lily caught the Rose-Gold Key with both hands.

As she caught it, the Mermaids' Deep fell away. And she was in Arcadia again. All around her was her home. But her home, now, was burnt and mangled and gray and reddish brown.

Shuddering, Lily tried to cry out, but there was a wind that blew ash and bits of burnt paper and cloth so hard that nothing could be heard above its wail. She knew where she was. She could see the mountains: the Calandals, the Donatees, the Samanthans, and her beloved Ceres. She reckoned, given the distances, that she was somewhere between the towns of Amaurote and Paloma. She had been there once with Alan, her stepfather, for reasons he had never told her. She had never asked.

"But this can't be the same place!" Lily thought. "Where is my lovely Amaurote, with its flowering trees? And over there, that heap of ash—that should be green Paloma."

Then she heard, over the screeching of the wind, the voices wailing with pain: the pain of loss, the pain of torture, the pain of wrongful death.

"Rex!" she called out, because suddenly Lily knew that this was where Rex had gone. And she knew that, holding the Key, she could feel everything and everyone everywhere. "Rex! Where are you?"

Then she was suddenly elsewhere. In the mountains. She was there in time to see two stone-faced troopers from Megalopolis herd two small children into a shed, the kind the people in the Calandals used to store their winter wood. "So it's the Calandals, then," she thought. "Over Eopolis." She looked more closely at the hut, and at the remains of a farmhouse, burned, behind it. "It's the Dawkins place. I've been there with Alan." He had taken her there before, she had never asked why.

The troopers were young, and both very handsome, pale and blue-veined, with cornsilk hair. They were serious about their work, and you could see in their expression that they didn't particularly relish it, but they knew their duty. Efficiently and quickly, they pushed the children inside, and then set fire to a pile of wood left haphazardly against the shed. They did this, Lily saw, to teach a lesson to any

Resistance fighters hiding in the woods.

"This is what happens to traitors and those friendly to the rebels," one of the troopers said loudly, apparently addressing the trees around her. And Lily saw what the troopers couldn't. She saw Alan and Colin's father, and a young boy, maybe fifteen years old, hiding in the trees, the boy in a lightning-struck hollowed-out oak, a hank of pale brown hair across his forehead. He was clutching Rex.

As Lily watched, helpless, Rex looked up at the boy, and licked his face. When Alan and the other man burst from the trees, the dog pulled itself from the boy's grip, even though the poor child clutched after him soundlessly, and hurled himself after the men as they ran through the gathering smoke toward the burning hut. None of them made it that far.

That was how Rex found Death, and gave her Star's message.

And Lily turned back to the boy, knowing there was nothing to be done for the others, the pain not yet having found its mark. Her first instinct was to comfort the Living, before she could miss the Dead.

But she couldn't reach him. As she watched, she saw his face go wild, and all she could do was pray silently that he would keep still and only come out when everything was clear.

Someone must have heard her prayer, because that is what he did. Young Andy Dawkins, who had come home from school at the first sign of trouble, to find his parents murdered and his home destroyed, and then watched his brother and sister burn. That was the fire where Andy became Aspern Grayling.

How do I know? I know because he told me. And when he told me, it was without expression, except for his habitual one of urbane sophistication. And it was not in a conversation about his family. It was in a conversation we had once, late at night, about how he hated dogs.

Lily screamed, then, not in terror, or in anguish, but like the release of steam from a pot that boils over on the fire. It was a sheer need to let out the pressure of the feeling building up in her, to let it out so that she could go on and do what she needed to do. The scream was silent, but it was powerful, and it shook her frame so that she dropped the Key.

At this, the vision shimmered and disappeared, and Lily stood once more beside the Mermaids' Well. The Mermaids and the Manatee and her friends all stared at her in silence.

"I have to go back," she said. And these were the only words that Lily the Silent ever spoke in the Mermaids' Deep.

Yes. The Manatee nodded his velvet-gray brown head. He swam toward her. And waited for her to stoop, hesitant but firm, to retrieve the Key, after which he offered his back. Lily pocketed the Key, and, grasping the sea creature by the soft scruff of his neck, clung to him as he shot through the water back the way they came.

"Wait!" Kim cried out behind them, and these were the only words Kim spoke under the sea. "Wait, oh wait for me!" She jumped up and down crying. "No, I got to go with you!" She turned to the Mermaids around her. "She needs me! I know she does! I saw it in the Tree!"

Then, as if that was what she had waited for, Phoebe, legs forming a tail like a fish, swam quickly to Kim's side. The other girl thankfully hugged her around the neck. And they shot off, following the Manatee and Lily, back the way they had come, to the surface and to what was now the Road of the Dead.

For there had been other dead, back in Arcadia, that Lily had not yet seen.

Twenty-Five

When they came out of the sea, the Dead were there waiting. There were thousands of them, stretched out along the road—a sea of the Dead.

Rex was there. It was his mission to bring Death back to Megalopolis from Arcadia, and, like good dogs everywhere, he had done his job. Death was with him, grand and free, her black hair blowing in the dank wind, her green-brown eyes crackling with fire. She stood there at the front of the Dead. Rex sat patiently beside her.

When he saw Lily come out of the sea, he leapt up. Death put her hand on his head and said, "Not yet."

Rex sat down again and waited for Lily to make her way out of the sea. This was hard for him. He didn't mind Death—as we know, it hadn't been difficult to find her, and while it had been hard to go to her and bring her back, it was hard for one moment only. But after that moment, when Rex woke up, he remembered many things he had forgotten, and he knew they had been many. That was how it was when you passed from Death to Life and back again. But the one thing he could never forget, no matter which land he roamed, was Lily, and what it had been like to be alive and be with her as her dog. That would stay with him now through Eternity. It had happened and could never be changed.

So even though Rex now had the infinite patience of the Dead, when he saw Lily, the memory of his heart leapt up.

Lily saw Rex before she saw Death, and so of course she ran toward him out of the sea, up the sloping sand beneath. She was so

WHEN THEY CAME OUT OF THE SEA, THE DEAD
WERE THERE WAITING

eager to reach the shore that she forgot the Manatee, who couldn't follow as her feet touched bottom in the shallows. He watched her go and he thought, "These partings—they are the same in every life. Always painful, always sad." He lifted a flipper to one eye and gave a quick blink twice. But he, like Lily, had duties that couldn't be put off or ignored, and with one last pang, he silently saluted her as she ran up the strand toward the Dead, and then turned, with Phoebe who had set a bewildered Kim on her feet on shore before turning back. Both of them, with a wave of flipper and feet, disappeared back toward the Mermaids' Deep.

You wonder how I know this? The Key changes everything. You see a lot of things that you would have missed before. Sometimes you would rather have missed them. But once you've held the Key, you really have no choice but to see these things. And then to act.

That was Lily's situation now, as she came out of the sea from the Mermaids' Deep. And even now, when I'm so much older than my mother ever was, my heart aches for her.

"Rex! Rex! Oh, Rex! I had the most awful dream!" Lily, laughing and crying at once, ran up to where the dog sat patiently and threw her arms around his neck, burying her face into his fur.

Only when her arms clasped together they clasped nothing. There was no doggy smell. There was no warm fur under her cheek. And no wet nose nuzzled at her throat.

There was nothing there.

At this, Lily fell back, silent. She looked at Rex, and he looked back at her sadly, his tail thumping soundlessly on the ground. Lily looked from Rex to Death, who stood beside him. She looked one question, and Death gave her one nod. At this Lily's silence deepened and increased. And she said nothing again all that day, as she and Kim walked through the Marshlands into Megalopolis at the front of the Dead.

"Who are they all?" Kim whispered to her as they walked to the front of the silent crowd. Death and Rex led them, and their feet made no sound on the gray mud. The only sound was a thin wind, the wind, so Devindra has told me, that always sounded above the Marsh.

It was a comfort to Lily that Kim held her hand. It felt good to have that warm, living skin next to hers. So instead of answering, Lily stopped for a moment, ducked her head onto Kim's shoulder, hugged her, and continued on, still holding her by the hand.

And this, I have found in my life as well, is generally the best answer to questions of this kind.

By then, the Great Silence of the Dead had silenced even Kim. This was different from the silence of the Mermaids' Deep. Though both mean wisdom, they are wisdom of different kinds. For human beings, no cold wind blows through the silence of the Mermaids' Deep. That silence means every good: protection, kindness, and the civilizing possibilities of life.

But the Silence of the Dead: what human being still alive can say what that means? It may well mean every good beyond what the living can understand. But there is no way of knowing this without becoming one of the Dead yourself. And for this, no human is ever really ready. No matter how much we might long to be, even in longing to follow our deepest loves.

Lily, her hand in her pocket clutching the Key, knew she was not ready. Although at that moment, in the midst of the Dead, her heart yearned toward Death, who walked so fearless and strong ahead of them all.

Still, Lily's deepest love was not among the Dead. He was ahead of her, with the Living. So her heart moved in two different ways, and that, I have reason myself to know, is a very painful kind of movement indeed.

You might put it this way: her future was with Life, but her past was with Death. And this left her present, a riddle that is very hard for anyone to solve, even a woman who is learning, already, what it takes to be a queen.

One of the most important lessons is how Death appears in this life. And how she is like that. And how she isn't.

Lily then thought she had never seen anyone as beautiful as Death, no one as vibrant and good, no one so filled with purpose and holy rage. Death was angry. Lily who held the Key knew this. She could feel it. And she could feel why.

Death strode ahead, in a fury with those who had misused her powers for their own stupid ends. Death was enraged with Megalopolis. She was outraged that the Empire had presumed it knew when and how to call on her, and for what uses. Star had known it would be this way when she sent Rex on his quest to Arcadia, where Death had been lured by Megalopolis, under the falsest of pretexts. "To do nothing more," Death thought to herself in her rage (so Lily could feel through the Key), "than further the pygmy projects of a pygmy world, a world that has never given me my due—no, nor my sister her due, either!"

By her sister, Death meant Life.

"She's angry, isn't she?" Kim whispered, and Lily nodded in reply. "Oh, she's beautiful, though." And Kim, walking two steps behind Lily, still clutching at her hand, wasn't scared. (She was hesitant, she was unsure, but "I weren't scared, Soph, that was the weird thing. I weren't scared at all.")

"They all dead, then?" she whispered. And then she repeated her first question.

"Who are they all, Lily? Do you know them then?"

Lily nodded. Her heart was too full for her mouth to make a sound. For she did, indeed, know them.

184

It was the Dead of Arcadia—all of the Dead—who marched on either side of them, parting as Death and Rex led the two living girls to the front of the line. And Lily recognized them. There was Colin, with his shock of white hair, his face cheerful now, like a breeze—not shocked and worn the way it had been when Lily watched Death lead him away. Colin gave her a wave and set himself again to marching.

There was Camilla, who waved and laughed, too, as Lily and Kim passed.

And there was Alan. He walked along, whistling silently, surrounded by a tumbling pack of Dead Boys, who obviously admired him as much in Death as they had in Life. As Lily hurried to keep up with Death, Alan gave her a big, broad wink.

It must have been hard to keep from running back and throwing her arms around him. But Lily knew, from holding the Key, where her duty lay. It was ahead of her, with her love, in Life. Not behind. And she knew from her first mistake when she came out of the sea that to throw your arms around the Dead and hug them to you was a useless act: useless, meaningless, and sad. So instead she gave him a tremulous smile, but when Kim looked at her inquiringly, she didn't say a word.

And there, marching along beside them, was the Mushroom Man and his dog! He ignored Lily as she passed, "the same," she thought, "as he would have ignored me if he came upon me while he was hunting in the woods." Why should it be any different now that he was Dead?

They had almost reached their goal now, which was the front of the silently moving throng of the Dead, and at their head was Maud. Seeing her, Lily did almost cry out, but the old woman smiled and put a finger to her lips.

Death was a discipline, even for the Living, Maud's look said. And Lily was learning this discipline fast.

Still, when you learn anything new—anything worth learning—
you don't master it all at once. You have surges of new strength,
followed by a falling back into weaknesses you often never suspected
you had. It was that way with Lily now. When she and Kim came up
beside Death and Rex, and fell into step beside a silent Maud (how
much more grateful Lily was now for Kim! how she wished Kim
would chatter more now! but even Kim was silenced by the Silence
of the Dead), she wanted to cry out: "But where are you going? Do
we go to defeat Megalopolis? But where will you go when we're done,
oh where? Where will I find you again? Will we ever meet again? Oh
where?"

She didn't cry out. The discipline of the Dead had begun its
work, and what was started in the Mermaids' Deep in Lily was here
complete. She was now, in the outer woman, no longer a girl. She
became, even more than before in the Mermaids' Deep, Lily the
Silent.

That is also how it is. You don't become something completely
new all at once. You get a taste of it, and then you swallow it down,
and then, after awhile, it becomes a part of you. I've had that
experience, too. And this was the way that Lily became the person
Arcadia made its queen.

But even Lily the Silent couldn't quiet her own heart. She never
could, not even later, after the journey over the mountains, after
she became queen. Her heart went on calling out, "All of you I've
ever loved. What happens to the Dead? Is there happiness among
the Dead? Is there love among the Dead? Is there peace? Is there
joy?" Her heart cried out so loudly that Lily thought she could hear
it trilling like a bird in distress, one that watches, helpless, while a
fox stalks the nestlings in its nest. It was a song, but it was a song
of grief.

Like all true songs—if you listen truly—the song of Lily's heart demanded an answer. And behind her, the answer came. Behind the march of the Dead was the sea, and the Mermaids rose up, now, above the surface of the sea, and sang one of the songs that are the purpose of their being—that is, the Lament for the Dead. Mermaids are silent except in singing one of their three songs: the Praise of the Gods, the Joy of the Born, and the Lament of the Dead. All of these songs are versions of the One Great Song, whose name is secret, but which is called—when it needs a name—the Delight of All.

The Lament of the Dead is, of course, the saddest of these songs, and yet, as it is only a movement of the One Great Song, there is the kind of joy woven all the way through its harmonies that can reconcile those souls that are ready to hear it to their fate.

Lily must have been ready, because she heard the song and was comforted. All around her, and through the Key, she could feel the Dead give a silent murmur of content, at the Mermaids' singing, and she could feel them march forward faster, determined to win the battle to come and then pass on.

"Pass on to what?" Lily's heart said. The Mermaids' Song, though, was confined to the Lament for the Dead, and Lily was forced to go forward now without an answer.

She went forward, on the Sad Road Back, to her destiny and theirs, the Destiny of the Arcadian Dead. Every step was a hard one to take, but every one she took wakened something—or someone—inside her. And that something—or someone—was alive, and it urged Lily on, filling her with new strength as they went.

"That was you, Snow, though you don't remember," my mother would say to me drowsily before we both went to sleep, me in her arms in her big, queenly bed. And she would fall asleep with a long lock of her black hair across my forehead. But I would lie awake, remembering.

Twenty-Six

As Lily went forward on the road, she could see a parade up ahead, barring their way.

"Look at that, would you?" Kim said, wide-eyed. She squeezed her friend's hand. "What's all that about, then? Who's all that for?" And then, with a low whistle. "Is it for us?"

Lily looked at Kim and squeezed her hand back. She shook her head. No, the parade was not for Lily and Kim. She knew that. Hand on the Key, there was much she knew.

The parade was for Conor Barr. And his brand new wife Rowena. It was their marriage march. The happy young couple sat in a horse-drawn carriage covered with scentless white peonies, pulled by four snow-white horses waving white plumes. Rowena sat with her small hand firmly clasping Conor's wrist, her other waving benevolently to the crowd of Megalopolitan living who now mingled unknowingly with the Arcadian Dead.

"Oooh!" Kim gasped. "Isn't she beautiful!"

And she was beautiful. All brides are, but Rowena had improved on this general rule of nature with a first-rate stylist: hair, makeup, dress, all the best and most gorgeous money could buy. This was the start of the fashion for all things False in Megalopolis, which was to go to such absurd lengths and reach such ridiculous heights in later years, even among the masses left after the Great Disaster. But now, at the fashion's start, as usually happens, it began with a kind of dazzle that couldn't help but fascinate the eye. Rowena, as a fashion leader, had experimented with the new artificiality, and her strange, glittering beauty that day was a tribute to her success. Her deep violet eyes lined with green glittered under her long, curling eyelashes. Her perfect nose twitched. Her bow-shaped lips formed a flowerbud moue. Sapphires flashed from her ears.

She dazzled, did Rowena. At that moment, no one had eyes for anyone but her. And it was this dazzle that protected Lily. No one noticed her in the shade left by Rowena's light.

Rowena told me about that day much later, in that thin, querulous, overbred voice of hers, in the expensive Retirement Villa she lived in on the False Moon at the end of her life. That was the day she returned to, over and over, as if it had been the most important of her life. I think maybe it was. She was never meant to be a Mother ("so painful, Sophia! Children ruin your life!"), or really even a Wife ("I hated hated hated growing old, Sophia. You'll see. You'll hate it just as much as I did"). She disliked being a Lover ("So...so messy").

What Rowena was meant for was to be a Bride.

"My hair was gold, Sophia, not just any gold, but a gold a dozen artists had worked three weeks without sleep to perfect, the kind of gold you dream about, or read about in stories, but never see in life. Except that day! Look, here, I kept a lock of it..." But the bit of hair she eagerly pulled out from a fraying velvet-covered box was faded, and the old Rowena looked at it sadly for a moment before her desire to see differently triumphed over what was in front of her, and she looked at me, complacent again. "My make-up was done by the foremost painter of the day. How we laughed as he dabbed at my face, and—I remember!—said the tint was more beautiful than the rosiest summer dawn. And the dress, Sophia! The creation! A thousand silkworms couldn't have spun a more translucent silk than our Megalopolitan scientists made, a white never seen before except on the finest, pink-tinged pearl, a dress made of dozens of yards of the fabric, but a dress so fine you could pull it through a gold ring without strain. That was the most beautiful dress that had ever been seen in Megalopolis...in all the world! And my shoes...studded with tiny diamond chips that flashed every which way when I walked...." At her description of the shoes, the old Rowena's monologue slowed and almost stopped. Then, a final dreamy word, "I always loved shoes the best. Always." And then she was gone from me, in a dream, I hoped, of her marriage day, when she was the center of all eyes, and still happy. I left her, without having got the answer that I looked for that day, but still, with that bit of memory passed on to me by the poor, faded, rich, and unloved creature shrinking visibly by the moment in the expensively covered bed before me, in the expensive retirement villa over which she petulantly ruled. As I went out, the nurses went in. "Her husband and her son never come to see her. Never," one of them muttered to me as she let me out the front door. I didn't tell her that I already knew that; instead, I promised to come again. And I did, one more time, but by then she was lost in her dream of triumphant girlhood, and I don't think she remembered who I was. If she had ever known. "I was the most beautiful bride," was all she would say, that final visit. "The most beautiful beautiful bride."

My grandmother told me a bit, also, about that day. "Megalopolis needed a beautiful bride," she said with that grim humor that I appreciated—maybe I was the only one in the family who had ever appreciated it. In any case, Grandmother always responded to the smile I could never hold back from her, no matter how horrifying the details of her conversation, no matter how clear she made it that she had never had the good of any of my dear loved ones in mind. But how she burned to have power, my grandmother! How much energy was there! "We needed a big party, the biggest the world had ever seen, something to distract the population from noticing the Great Disaster looming, the one we still hoped against hope to avert." She smiled sourly, I remember, as if she looked back at

Rowena's glowing, demanding beauty, and found it as thin and silly as she and I both knew it really was. "That backfired. No one had eyes for anyone but Rowena."

What she meant was, "I was too busy stage-managing Conor's wedding to notice Lily had returned with the Key." And knowing my grandmother, I can well believe this irked her till her dying day. Which was not a happy one. I know. I was there. I have been there at the deaths of many loved ones and family, and of all of them, Livia most hated Death. And when you hate Death, she does not treat you kindly.

Lily and Kim stood there, watching the cheering crowds of bored Megalopolitans shouting with pleasure as Conor gave Rowena the obligatory kiss.

Death nudged my mother in the ribs with her elbow.

I can see this. Star and Kim have both described it to me, and, having met Death myself, I can well believe this was done in a certain mordant spirit.

"Look down," the Great Lady whispered. And Lily, looking at the mud on the road in front of her, saw a large Brass Key lying there. It glinted in the light reflecting off the passing cavalcade of cars. It was bigger, bolder, more noticeable in every way than the Rose-Gold Key, which Lily had safe in the pocket of her coat.

"Pick it up," Death suggested, and Kim swears there was the hint of a laugh in her voice. Lily did what she was told, and just as she straightened up, holding the Brass Key wonderingly in her hand, there was the sound of screeching brakes, the headlights from a car swept over her and she froze.

"Ah," a voice said dryly. "I see you're back."

It was Livia, following the wedding couple's carriage, in an open car with Peter and Alastair, both looking bored. Conor's servant was driving. He hopped out and opened the back door for Lily to get in beside Conor's mother, and then he helped Kim into the front seat beside him.

When Alastair saw who it was who'd gotten in beside him, his face lost that look of ennui. He leaned forward. "You've found it?" he asked eagerly. "The Key?" And when she nodded, he held out his hand. His expression was greedy. Peter's eyes gleamed over his head.

Lily gave him, as she knew she was meant to do, the Great Brass Key. His hand closed over it with a sigh. Peter exhaled a long breath. Both men turned their heads forward and resumed the look of boredom that protected them from the crowd.

In her pocket, Lily's hand clutched the Rose-Gold Key, which seemed to grow heavier as she held it there.

"Hurrah!" the crowd shouted, throwing flowers—provided, for the occasion, by the State—into the air. "Hurrah for Conor Barr and his bride!"

The driver started up the car again, and leaned over to give Kim's knee an exuberant pat. "See that? Hear that roar? It's a great honor to be the maid of Conor Barr's woman, lass, even if she's never the legal wife!" he shouted up over the general noise. But Kim, when she looked back at him, gave an uncertain smile. "Is that what I am, then?" she murmured. For she knew she had become something else. Something much more. She was not the same Kim who had gone into the Sea ("and I never was again, Soph"). She looked over at the Dead, stopped now, standing blocked by the parade, watching it silently go past. And the car drove away from Death.

"Listen!" Kim shouted over the fireworks and the singing and the chanting and the laughs, "don't you see them, then?"

"See who, lass?" the driver shouted back, cheerful as ever.

"Them! Them over there! The Dead, you silly fool! The DEAD!" Kim waved her arm toward Death, where she stood at the head of the thousands of shadows, with Rex at her side.

"Get over your joking!" the driver laughed.

They couldn't see them, then. Kim's eyes looked for Lily's in the back of the car. Lily, her hand being absently patted by a glitter-eyed Livia, shook her head.

"No," Lily thought. "None of them can see the Dead." Except possibly, she thought, for Livia, who had turned, craning her neck, chewing on her thumbnail, and looking reflectively in Death's direction. But Lily couldn't be sure.

The parade marched on. Conor led it, Rowena sitting straight up and gleaming at his side. The crowd roared its endless approval. No one noticed how frightened Kim's face was, or the tear that fell down Lily's cheek.

Lily craned her neck until the last minute she could, to catch a last glimpse of Rex, as he sat patiently by Death, his tail thumping without a sound. But no one in the crowd saw her look. Not even Conor knew that she was there, and this filled her with sadness. Lily's heart thumped sluggishly in her chest as the parade—noisy, glittering, alive—ignored the Dead, and, ignoring Lily's yearning for Conor, ignored the Living, too. The parade ignored both these facts and marched on by. Only Kim could see them that night. But my dear nurse was always so modest, I doubt it occurred to her that she alone, aside from Lily, was able to see plain facts that were invisible to the rest of the world.

And Lily, of course, could see and hear all the things she couldn't see and hear before. She could see many things that were there, that no one else could see. It wasn't until much later, when I found and held the Key myself, that I knew what this must have meant to her. Tremendous isolation and responsibility—what should be told? And what should be left unspoken? At that moment, though, she didn't need to worry about that. No one in the rest of the world wanted to know what she could see. Not just then. The rest of the world was distracted. It could not, just then, see past the promised Grand Party.

Twenty-Seven

The Feast at the Villa in Central New York, celebrating the marriage of Conor Barr to Rowena Pomfret, was a far grander affair than the Feast in the Mermaids' Deep. And so it should have been, given the amount of treasure Julian and Livia lavished on it. "This is the proudest day for a proud family!" Julian announced to representatives of the media, before passing around innumerable bottles of champagne. And Livia dazzled the nobility and the lesser ministers under the Council of Four with the lavishness of her hospitality.

There were roast peacocks with their plumage, and roasts gilded with real gold on the edges of their marrowbones. There were ice sculptures of swans filled with eggs of fishes now so rare that it took three explorers and their bearers five days of marching into the desert surrounding eastern Megalopolis to find even one in the last deep-water lakes hidden there. There were pyramids of cunning apples, brilliant red, which had been crossed by Megalopolitan scientists with a kind of oyster that was nasty to eat but which formed the most flawless of pearls. And each of these apples, too, hid, in their hearts, a pearl. You had to be careful not to bite on it too hard, or you'd crack your teeth. This had already happened to Conor's servant, to the great merriment of the rest of the servants' table that ran down the side of the great room.

"You're not laughing, lass!" he said reproachfully to Kim as she sat, shivering in spite of herself, in the place of honor at the head. And he grinned to show off his jagged broken tooth and make her laugh. She smiled and patted him on the cheek, and he wondered at her. "You're not the girl I remember," he growled with affectionate puzzlement. "What's happened then?" But Kim only smiled and shook her head.

"Shhhh," she said. "It's speeches, now."

And indeed it was. At the grand table filled with Megalopolitan dignitaries of all descriptions, each resplendent in his sashes and his orders and his official evening dress, side by side with the Megalopolitan wives, each vying with the others in the splendor and richness of her attire, an array of the rarest wines made their appearance, and greatly contributed to the wittiness and exhilaration of these toasts.

"To my noble friend Conor Barr, whose progress I have watched with pride and pleasure—may he not forget his old friends!"

"Hear, hear!" cried the other dignitaries wittily, as the wine sloshed out of their platinum goblets onto the tablecloth below—and one or more shirt fronts, as well, much to the annoyance of the dignitaries' wives. "Stout fellow! Tell it like it is!"

"May he remember always that the business of Megalopolis is business, and let him make it HIS business to keep that faith alive!"

"Hear, hear!" the others shouted with even greater enthusiasm. And some among them even wiped away a tear, because a Megalopolitan nobleman is always a little sentimental when it comes to his own religion, which he regards as sacred above all else—even above his own wife and daughters (though not, of course, above his sons). And they are still like that to this day, though you would have thought by now some more modern ideas would have penetrated. I attended a similar feast in my days in Megalopolis, and I can promise that nothing has changed.

Conor, flushed with unaccustomed amounts of wine and praise— though he was certainly used enough to both, so the amounts that night must have approached the spectacular—rose unsteadily at the head of the table to answer these toasts.

Lily sat, unnoticed by all, slightly behind Livia. The pain that had come on her when she'd awakened from her faint on the False Moon, and which had faded away in the Mermaids' Deep, returned with full force. She felt ill, and ugly, and unsteady on her feet. She didn't even try to catch Conor's eye.

"Something was happening to me, Snow," my mother said, snuggling up against me in her big bed, one cold winter's morning before she died. "I didn't know what it was. And I was scared." She kissed the top of my head, and then she said, "But of course what was happening was you. And that was the best thing of all."

I know now this was not the total truth. I know now the best thing that could have happened would have been for my mother and my father to have quietly moved to a farm somewhere up on the Megalopolitan side of the Ceres Mountains, high above the flood plain, to live there a modest, quiet life with their family, far away from the Greater World. The kind of life I would want for my own children and grandchildren. The kind of life we are struggling here in Arcadia—Devindra, I and the others—to remake for our world....

Our world. And all the worlds that move with her.

But back then I did appreciate that my mother didn't give that version of the truth to me. The story a seven-year-old wants to receive is that she is the center of her mother's world, and that truth my dear mother, Lily the Silent, First Queen of Arcadia, never hesitated to give.

She knew, she told me, that she would never again be as beautiful as she had been in her younger days in Arcadia, and in her first days with Conor in the Great City. "It isn't true, none of it!" Kim contradicted indignantly. But Devindra, who had seen the early pictures of Lily when they screamed out of every tabloid in Megalopolis, told me later that it was a fact: Lily looked different after she came back from the Mermaids' Deep. "Although to my mind, Sophy, my dear, she was more beautiful than before." Lily looked now at the glittering Rowena, dressed in the finest bridal clothes ever seen in any of the worlds, and she was ashamed. Or so she said.

But I think it was something different. I think what she felt was the humbling knowledge of who she really was, which is something entirely different from ashamed. I think it was that she knew what had to be done, and didn't want it, felt she wasn't capable of it. But still, it was pulling her forward. Her desires moved her toward Conor, who stood flushed and overly excited, responding to the toasts of his admirers, moved her toward him, toward battling Rowena for him, and toward what she thought of as fulfillment. Happiness. But her...I hesitate to call it her soul, I can hear Aspern Grayling's contemptuous laugh as I do, and certainly we have had some fine battles over Arcadia's soul, and none to compare with the battles to come. But as I say that, I gain confidence, I know Arcadia's soul, and I know my own. And even, this many years later, I know the soul of my mother. She knew it too. She looked inside herself after the Mermaids' Deep, and she knew her soul, knew that inside her that night it was protecting mine that was just being born.

How do I know all this? I know this because I have held the Key.

Lily pondered this fact, hugging it to herself, as she hugged the new life inside her. And these facts she quietly pondered joined with that new life, and made it grow in unexpected ways. Which was lucky for me, her daughter.

For now, she tilted her head up gravely, and prepared to listen, with the admiration expected of her for his brilliance, leadership qualities, and wit, to the speech of Conor Barr.

"Friends..." Conor began. But then, outside, there came an uproar. A loud wave of shouting from the mob.

A faint expression of annoyance passed over Livia's face. "Ah," she said urbanely, making the quick recovery that was usual with her. "A Fortune Teller. How auspicious! Hurry!" she said to the servants who leapt up to open the huge bronze doors. "Food and drink for the Fortune Teller, and let us all hear what the Fortune Teller has to say!"

The massive doors swung open, and in a moment, as if appearing from nowhere, the Fortune Teller stood there.

"It's very lucky," Conor whispered to Rowena as she sat, upright and glittering, beside him, her white and pink hand holding a crystal goblet of pale gold wine. He had, of course, sat immediately back down when the Fortune Teller appeared, as was the tradition in Megalopolis at times of triumph, transition, or crisis. All this Conor explained to his new wife. "Auspicious. He's come to the Feast to pass judgment on the design for which we gather."

"And what is that design?" Rowena asked coldly. She had no interest in any design other than the celebration of her Glorious Achievement in marrying the man—the boy—that every other woman in Megalopolis longed for. ("Politics," she spat later, when I visited her in that cold villa of hers, hoping for an answer to a question I never dared ask. "Conor was, like all men, only interested in politics." She looked at me tragically, and said in that whiny overbred voice of hers, "Never Love." Poor Rowena. Love was her religion, but she knew it not.)

"That we rebuild our whole society on the basis of new technologies that will save us all!" Conor said proudly. "My family has always been at the forefront of such initiatives. You know that, Rowena! The False Moon is only one of our projects. Now there will be dozens of others!" His eyes gleamed as he watched the Fortune Teller eat and drink the small amounts of ritual food necessary on these occasions.

The Fortune Teller, unsmiling but calm, looked back, and then

THE ARRIVAL OF THE FORTUNE TELLER WAS MOST AUSPICIOUS

looked aside at Lily. But Conor, still feverish with excitement, did not
follow that look. Not yet.

"And I will be the one leading the projects, Rowena!" Conor
boasted, lolling in his seat, blinded by a momentary vision of his own
greatness. "I— with you by my side!" Then he hushed her, kissing
her on the top of her head, though it had been he, and not she, who
had spoken.

("I am so ashamed when I think of that night, Sophia," my father
said to me much later. I forgave him, of course. What else could I
do?)

Now the Fortune Teller stood and walked to the head of the
room.

"Thank you for the food and drink, Lady," he said in his calm,
almost placid, voice, which nevertheless carried into every nook and
cranny of that enormous hall. Everyone buzzed. How they love, in
Megalopolis, a Fortune Teller! It's still as true today on the False
Moon as it was then on the mainland.

He nodded at Livia, who stood reluctantly and curtsied in
return—a stiff, formal bob, as if she would do what was required of
her by custom and not a bit more.

I laugh when I think about it. I can see my dear grandmother in
this scene so clearly.

The Fortune Teller noted this, and his eyes laughed. He held
up his hand, and the room was so silent that Lily could hear the
skittering of a rat as it disappeared into a hole in the wainscoting,
holding a bit of smoked eel in its teeth.

"In return, Lady," he continued. "I will give you two pieces of news
you would like to have—though one more than the other, maybe."

"Thank you, Sir," Livia answered him formally, in what was the
ritual exchange. She hesitated for a moment, and then she said, "I
choose to hear first the one that will bring me the most joy."

"The most joy now or the most joy hereafter?" the Fortune Teller asked, and Conor, whispering, told Rowena that this question was what he must always ask, by the laws of their people.

("As if I didn't know," she said scornfully to me later. "I was as well born as he was. Better. But the Pomfrets never pushed themselves forward the way you saw the Barrs do. Of course, we were a much older family, by twenty years or more.")

"But it means nothing, really," Conor explained further to his annoyed bride. And Livia said, with only a hint of impatience, "The most joy now, Fortune Teller, for now is the only time we have."

The Fortune Teller nodded. And when he spoke again, his voice was entirely different: no longer placid and gentle. And that voice boomed: "Conor Barr's child will rule over all. Of that there is no doubt."

Livia stood there, blazing in her triumph. She had a moment of doubt—a moment that my mother alone noticed. She had been unsure of what the Fortune Teller would say. The Fortune Teller had not been bought. Ever a risk-taker, Livia had left that one small matter unfixed. And see, here was her reward!

"Conor's son!" she called out, triumphant. "Conor's son will rule over all!" Dramatically, she held out her arms. "Come to me, my child!" she called out, her eyes, I am sure, only darting for a moment right and left to be sure that the representatives of the media were given the best possible of photo opportunities. "Let your mother be the first to embrace you upon hearing this news!"

Another uproar. Conor hurried to his mother, who clasped him to her bosom (somewhat stiffly), while everyone else in the hall fought to be the first to congratulate them. Corks popped by the dozens, champagne poured into tumbler after tumbler. The noise was incredible. Lily shrank from it, pulling herself away through the crowd, trying not to double over from the pain she felt all over her skin.

That was when Conor saw her.

Over his mother's shoulder. He saw Lily move slowly away, cradling her stomach with one forearm, and then, in that moment, she looked back at him.

He stopped. Everything stopped. He told me that.

"It was as if Time had slowed and then stopped, and as if only she and I were allowed to move in that space. As if we could go to each other and no one else would see."

I didn't tell my father, but that is probably what did happen. That was one of the theories that the scholars of Otterbridge University proved, in the first decade of the research led by Devindra Vale in the Tower by the Lily Pond. The theory that feeling, not thought, produces the flow of Time. That stronger feeling can stop it.

My father told me he hurried to Lily's side. He was sure no one else could see. While the rest of the room froze, he reached out and touched her timidly. "I was afraid that she hated me for what I'd done. The way I'd betrayed her. I couldn't put it into words myself, not then. Too young, too stupid, too concerned with my own vision of myself as a Great Man, Sophy. But that was it."

My mother didn't hate him. She flew to him. Imagine. Everyone and everything frozen around them, like all the trees around my mother's room that cold winter's night when she told me this story. And two living breathing warm young human beings finding each other.

Clinging to each other for dear life. And then parting. "Later," Conor mouthed. "I'll come to you later." It was then Lily remembered Livia's expression at the side of the sea. And her heart sank.

He was back in his chair next to Rowena, nodding and smiling to the crowd, all in a flash. As if the moment had never happened. And the room unfroze. Time started up again.

Livia continued the ritual exchange with the Fortune Teller.

"Well?" she said. "I liked your first prophecy well enough. What's the one that doesn't bring me joy?"

The Fortune Teller looked back at her, startled, as if he had been looking at something far away. "More of a warning than a prophecy, Lady," he said now slowly. "A silly saying, a cliché practically, I'm ashamed of it, to tell you the truth." At this, he gave an embarrassed cough. "It's only this," he said apologetically. "Beware of the Sea."

"And what's the meaning of that?" Livia asked, attempting without much success to suppress her irritation.

"Maybe nothing," the Fortune Teller said, shrugging his shoulders, picking up a champagne bottle for himself off the endless heap, and making ready to go. "It's not me as makes 'em up, you know—I just tells 'em as I hears 'em." He gave a grin, went up suddenly to Livia, murmured something under his breath, and then he was gone.

Kim told me that. But I was never able to get Livia to tell me what it was he said to her before he disappeared. "I've forgotten completely," she said to me tartly. But Kim always said, "Whatever 'e told 'er, it made 'er gather 'erself up right then and there."

Now Livia's color had returned, and her steadiness. "I knew," she said, "or I thought I did, that we had the Key. And that was the only thing that mattered," she said to me, remembering that night.

I remember her looking at me when she said this, and her eyes had that twisted look that scared so many of her underlings, but which I always, for some reason, found oddly attractive...and this may have been why she confided all this to me. Although my grandmother had so many undiscovered depths, I never did know for sure.

"Of course, I was wrong," my grandmother said dryly. And even all those years later, her capable hands closed involuntarily into two dead fists. "We didn't have the Key at all. That little girl had carried it off...."

For the feast was over. Lily, knowing Conor would come, went back to what she thought of now as her old room. And in her pocket, Lily's hand closed around the Key.

Twenty-Eight

As she lay on the broad tall bed in the arms of the sleeping Conor Barr, her face was pale, despite her golden brown skin and the reflection from the dying fire. And she was cold all over, even under the gold satin coverlet. She didn't bother pulling the covers up around her chin. She knew it was no use. The cold came from inside, not out.

"Anything can happen, Lily!" she had heard Conor exult, whispering in her ear before he slept. "Anything!" He was too excited. Pushed and pulled to and fro by forces he didn't understand, inside of him and out, he no longer could see what was real.

"In my mind," my father told me later, in that faintly wry tone he took when talking about his younger self, "it was all triumph. It was all 'Conor, Conor, Conor.' Whatever Conor wanted, Conor was going to get." My father laughed again, that sad laugh of his. "Young men are such idiots," he said, smiling. "We think it's us against the world, and we never think the world is likely to win."

I know he loved her truly, though. Even though he had waited till his new bride slept before slipping through the corridors to her room. Even though he slept soundly now, as if she were a trophy, or a prize, anything but a human being, and never worried now about what would happen to her or me, the child she still hadn't told him was going to be born, even though he smiled in his sleep at dreams of having everything he wanted and his own way, and having everyone admire him while he did, supporting him in his triumph, and never doubting for a moment that he deserved it. Still, I know he loved her truly. Didn't he prove it, much, much later, when he was a much, much older man?

And she? She had that great capacity for Love, Love of all kinds, as I should know. He was her first great Love, and the last she would ever have of that kind. But she knew Reality, because she was a girl who knew she was a woman, not a boy thinking he was a man. Reality told her she could not stay.

"Come with me, Conor," she'd pleaded before he had fallen, in her arms, asleep. But he, just as Livia had known he would, only laughed. "Go with her?" my father said to me later. "Leave all that advantage? Go to some provincial place where I'd be unknown and poor, when all we had to do was stay put to have everything our hearts desired? I didn't think she was serious. I told her, 'You're the one I love. What does it matter what everyone else thinks? We can arrange it to suit ourselves.' But she wouldn't listen, of course. Well, of course she wouldn't. Wasn't she a person in her own right? Not that I knew that then."

That was something she realized, I think. That she wasn't a person to Conor, no matter how much he loved her. She was an object, a thing. And this was not how she loved him. She saw that to him her child would be an object, a thing. And she had the Key. She knew this had to change. She knew that because she had walked on the Road of the Dead.

As she lay there staring at the dying fire, it was as if a pearl dropped from her heart down and down and down. She listened carefully. But though it dropped for a very long time, it never reached the bottom. That night, she failed to hear it land.

Then there was another sound she missed tonight: the sound of Rex breathing evenly, on the rug beside the hearth. Lily listened and listened, and scrunched her eyes up with the effort of listening, but you can't hear what's not there, no matter how hard you try.

Shuddering, she buried her head in Conor's chest. He murmured in his sleep, and pulled her to him. There was warmth in his arms, but even as she held them to her, and clasped her own around his chest, she could feel the warmth dying. There was soon to be no more warmth for her there, no matter how much she desired it. Because Lily knew that her desires were not the most important thing in the world. She had drawn this knowledge up with the Key from the Mermaids' Well. This is an important knowledge, maybe the most important knowledge for a queen. My father had not achieved it yet. It would be a long time before he did.

Pulling gently on Conor's arms, she prized them apart. She sat up in the bed, paler, even, than before, watching silently as Conor Barr slept. He had one hand lying palm up on his forehead, and that forehead wrinkled as if, even in his sleep, he planned the grandest of plans. ("And I did," my father said, smiling. "It's true. Especially in my sleep, I was a Conqueror of Worlds.") He muttered something, as if momentarily distressed, and she moved without thought to comfort him. But a sound behind startled her and checked her hand.

Lily saw it was Death, standing inside the huge carved door, wrapped in a heavy cloak against the cold, though Death can't feel cold, no, or warmth either.

Quicker than her thoughts, Lily covered Conor with one arm, guarding him against Death. She was quick, my mother, when it came to protecting those she loved. I have reason to remember that.

This time, though, Death just laughed at her, indulgently. "No," she said, throwing back the hood of her cloak, and heading toward the fire. "I haven't come for Conor Barr, Lily. I have bigger fish to fry."

But Lily warily kept her arm across my father's sleeping chest. She watched Death as she sat at a loom that appeared there, where Rex had once slept. Death worked the loom, watching it critically as she did, its shuttle clattering with a comfortable familiarity.

It was a strange thing. But with Death's arrival, warmth returned

LILY COVERED CONOR WITH ONE ARM,
GUARDING HIM AGAINST DEATH

to Lily's arms. She puzzled over this, and I'm not sure she ever understood it. I'm not sure I understand it, even now.

"If you go now, Lily," Death said quietly, over her work. "I'll leave him be for many, many years. As you know, I always keep my promises."

Then Lily knew what she had to do—the way an animal does, without thinking. Lily gave Conor's lips one quick kiss ("I felt it in my sleep, Sophy, I'm sure of it," he said), then slid down to the floor, and began to dress. This was still her room, and all the clothes he had given her were there. She dressed in the warm clothes he had meant for her to wear when they went into the mountains for the winter sports—sheepskin-lined wide wool pants, a linen shirt that buttoned up high on the neck over a winter vest, and a pair of stout green leather boots. She looked at her velvet and fur cloak fit for a queen, and hesitated. Instead, driven by an instinct she did not yet wholly understand, she shrugged herself into a fur-lined leather hunting jacket of his, left carelessly over a chair. She felt carefully in the pockets for the scarf and gloves and hat that she knew he would keep there. And then, to her surprise, she felt the Key.

She hadn't put it there. But the Key would not be left behind.

Death nodded her head and the shuttle flew across the warp. Lily came closer and saw the cloth stretched out on the loom. It was covered with pictures, top to bottom. People running up a dark street, an enormous wave following them. Two roads, the one to the left with a knight valiantly fighting a helmeted foe, the other solitary, weaving past streams and ponds, heading down to a green world.

As Death wove, Lily saw a picture emerge: a knight battling with his foe—only now the foe's helmet was off, and you could see...the knight was battling himself.

"They've invited me here," Death said, smiling wryly. "By the grandeur of their conceptions." She stopped her work and sighed.

"Oh, if they only knew how tired I am of man's grand conceptions!"

And Lily's hand tightened over the Key.

All at once, she could hear shouting, and the sound of thousands of feet tramping, and the loud roar of the sea. She could feel terror all around her, and the deep desire to get to higher ground.

"That's right," Death murmured approvingly. "That's a good girl." And this was the last time Lily was called a girl, when she was called one by Death. And there was no going back.

Now there was a little scratch at the door, as if from an animal, and when Lily opened it, Kim, wrapped in a blanket coat that was way too big for her, looked back at her with an expression of timid resolve.

"Ohhh," Kim breathed, taking in Lily's dress, as Lily quickly and silently shut the door behind them, so the two women were alone in the hall. "I knew it. I knew you were going." Lily turned to go down the hall, putting her finger to her lips. "Well," Kim whispered fiercely, "you're not going without me, then, you know that, don't you." Lily, grinning, gave her a quick hug, and the two disappeared down the back staircase, and let themselves silently out onto the street. Neither of them looked back.

Twenty-Nine

On winter nights in Arcadia now, we hold Storytelling Around the Great Hearth, in the Central Round Hall of the Palace. It's meant to knit us together, to strengthen those bonds between us that are shown by the Key to so clearly exist. It's our new tradition, invented by myself and Wilder the Bard. Traditions have to start some place, after all.

That first night, I remember, I knew we had chosen right. Wilder held forth in the way that only Wilder can, when he is both the teller and the tale. It wasn't just his talent that kept the audience enthralled, I told him when we were alone again in his room in the Tower: it was his experience, his wisdom, all that he'd learned on his own long hard road. When he wove the tale that first night, I could see him weave the tapestry of Arcadia anew. This part of Lily's story made our fellows hold their breath. No one made a sound. No one went out of the room, to the bathroom, or to get a snack. They had wandered in and out at other parts, all of which they knew well, but when he came to this part in the story, and the kindly wind sang outside, and the puffy snowflakes swirled in little tornados you could see through the long windows of the Round Hall, and it was warm inside, and dark but for the fires and the candles in the sconces set onto the slim wood walls—all that came together, I remember. We could smell the hot cider in the mugs we held. And Wilder held us, too.

He was modest about this later, and sad. "For Goddess' sake, Snow, it wasn't me, it was the story." Then, troubled, "All the story I could bear to tell." But in this, I understand more than Wilder himself. My understanding was dearly won, as no one knows better

211

than he. I know that the magic that held us was that he was in the story, too. And yet, because of his own part, he can never speak the end. That is always left to me. It was that night. Wilder could sing up to a certain point, and then, like a bird when you throw a cloth over its cage, he was, like my mother, silent.

But until that point...this is the way he told his portion of the tale that winter night when we first gathered around the Great Hearth:

"In Arcadia, there is much history, and legend too, about the hard and dangerous travels of Lily the Silent and her companion, Kim the Kind. Many strange and terrible things are told of the days before the birth of Sophia, later known as Sophia the Wise. But the most terrible is of the final night they fled, out of the Villa in Central New York, back to the mountains. Back to higher ground. For this was the time of the Great Earthquake, and after the Great Earthquake—as every schoolchild knows—there came a Great Silence more ominous than any sound. After the Whole World held its breath in fear, the World once more let out that breath...and with its breath came the Great Wave. All who had stayed on lower ground were destroyed, utterly destroyed. There was nothing left."

At this, the audience held its breath. And Wilder, sad but determined, carried on, taking courage as he wove the tale.

§ § §

"Kim and Lily hurried toward the main road that night. Kim turned toward the stables, where they would find horses, but, 'No,' Lily said firmly. 'It's better we stay on solid ground.' Why she said this, Lily didn't know, but about this she was sure. Kim didn't argue. She followed.

"When they came to the road, they were no longer alone. There were hundreds of people—Devindra Vale, who was there that night, walking out of the Marsh, says it may have been thousands, though only a small part of that survived the final winter's journey over the mountains into Arcadia. The endless, restless crowd moved slowly and silently up toward the mountains. Without wondering at this, Lily and Kim joined them. They blended in right away. Most of these refugees were women and children. Here and there was a man, although not many, and of these, maybe only one or two finished the trip.

"On every face was a look of dread. 'We saw Death,' the wanderers murmured among themselves as they fled. 'Death with the Dead.'

"A woman holding the hand of a little blonde girl who had her brown skin and black eyes said to Lily, 'Only some of us could see her. The others just laughed.'

"And Lily and Kim saw what she meant by 'the others'—heard them, too. As the silent procession continued toward the mountains, pressed behind by its own fear, jeering folk lined the road on either side. They held glasses and bottles, for the celebrations of the wedding of Conor Barr and Rowena Pomfret were meant to go on for two more days, and the bystanders had been at the freely distributed wedding cheer for most of that night. This group was mostly men, though there was a scattering of women among them. 'What do you think you're running away from then?' they laughed. 'Bunch of ninnies. Scared of the dark. Seeing things that aren't even there. Fools!' But the folk heading for the mountains ignored them in silence and pressed on.

"This was when Kim realized the wisdom of making their way on foot. The drunken, angry men yelling out insults as they passed by were in a dangerous mood, the way men, and crowds, fueled by aimless celebrations become. To ride above a crowd like that would have invited...unwelcome attentions. 'You were right then, Lily,' Kim whispered. Lily nodded grimly—she held the hand of the little blonde girl while her mother stopped to redo the straps of her knapsack—and they continued on.

" 'She's quite taken to you,' the mother whispered to Lily, with a fond, sad look at the daughter who clung to Lily's hand. Lily smiled faintly and nodded again. This girl was Clare, afterwards Clare the Rider, who was never seen in Arcadia far from one of the marvelous horses she trained, the horses for which she was famous far and wide. Everyone in Arcadia wanted a horse from Clare the Rider, but she sold them only to a certain few, and how she chose those few will be told later, in the tale about her dearest friend, Sophia the Wise.

"It was Clare who helped Kim the Kind the night that Sophia was born. It was Clare who kept the fire lit at the mouth of the cave and who kept watch there against any enemies until dawn. Her own mother was dead by then—fallen, in the dark rush up the mountain, down a sheer and rocky drop.

"After this, Clare clung to Lily all the more."

§ § §

"But all of this happened later," Wilder continued, after taking a draught of mulled wine. "For now, the refugees surged forward, silent and with one will. Our scientists say it was because of this unity of purpose that the time they made was remarkable. Seven days and seven nights they moved, as if making up a single animal, resting all at once, eating quickly and sharing what provisions they had among them, and then continuing on. How they knew to do this would be a mystery to the scientists of Megalopolis, who say it is impossible for so many individuals to act together, without a leader, without force. But in Arcadia the facts are known. The answer is the Key.

The Key was among them, and the Key knit them together, and it was because of the Key they knew when to stop. It was because of the Key that they knew when to start. And Lily, pale with the effort of carrying the Key, knew this even that very first night, but as she had now become Lily the Silent, how it worked was something she would never tell."

§ § §

"It was the Key that opened the door to the new world," Wilder continued in his most solemn voice, and even the children who knew this story by heart stared at him open-mouthed and wide-eyed. "You all know how our Arcadian scientists discovered this later, after much debate about the meaning of the facts. It was the Key that opened the door to the Great Wave, that catastrophe that killed everyone left on the plains of Megalopolis, everyone who had not climbed the Ceres Mountains, and everyone who had not been rich enough, or well enough connected, to catch the last rocket to the False Moon. Our scientists, you know, have labored long and hard to understand the physics of what occurred. There's been debate; there have been factions. Professor Devindra Vale, the leader of the scholars who eventually uncovered the truth, was the first to hold out her hand to the other side, saying: 'We wanted to know this as little as you. But now that we do know it, let us hold it together, and see what it means for us in the future—to what direction it points, to what duties it calls us.' It was hard, you all know, for us to accept these truths. For some of us, impossible. But in the end, we hope Truth prevails. Even if we also know that prevailing might take, as it has in Megalopolis, a very long time."

§ § §

215

When Wilder came to that part of the story, I remember, Devindra put her knitting down on her lap for a moment, wiped her eyes, and hid a sad smile behind her hand.

§ § §

"It took another three days," Wilder continued, "once they had reached the foothills, for them to get up into the mountains, and many, despite the efforts of their fellows, fell along the way. There was never an abundance of food, but there was enough. Barely enough. The Ceres, on their south side, keep green in a normal year for ten months out of twelve. And though this was no normal year, still there was food to be found, much of it left from the oldest days, the days no one can remember, when both women and men had settled there, leaving behind patches of now wild greens, trees with bright orange fruit, edible roots and berries. And of course there were the mushrooms Arcadian mountains are famous for providing.

"There were wise women in the group, women from the marshlands of Megalopolis who had lived, secretive and unheard, afraid of the periodic purges of the Different and the Odd that happened in that great city. These women knew much about wild foods: which mushrooms healed, which ones hurt, which were good to eat, which gave an agonizing death. These women quickly passed their knowledge to others—to the young girls traveling with them, in particular. These showed themselves deeply interested in the lore of the older women, and our queen has told us that this gave her the idea for the foundation of the colleges of Otterbridge University. She began by watching the younger women quizzing the old, comparing what she heard to the truths the Key had taught her. All this by the fires made at night from the brush of the Ceres, where, Queen Lily told us, the new Arcadia was born in these meetings between young and old.

"One of these young women was our own Devindra Vale, the great physicist of Arcadia you all know, and the founder of the University herself. You have heard her say that the Flight from Megalopolis was the Foundation Stone of the New Arcadian Science. And she never, ever lost her taste for woodland mushrooms."

At this, I remember, Devindra smiled again. This time at Wilder, who wouldn't look at her that night. She had long forgiven him for his part in the story, but he—he found it impossible to forgive himself.

Bravely, though, he went on.

§ § §

"On the tenth night, they camped in silence on a sheltered ridge, a fierce wind blowing around them down the mountains to the plains below. They gathered there, huddled around brushfires, all silent. The view of Megalopolis stretched out beneath them. The city glittered on its plain like a string of jewels.

"Lily, silent, looked down at the city and remembered a string of colored gems—flashing white and orange and pink and sea-blue and red—that Conor Barr had given her as a gift. She had worn that strand the night of her triumph at the ball on the False Moon. She had left it and everything else behind. And it was that necklace that our own queen, Sophia, brought home from her adventures in foreign lands. You've seen her wear it at occasions of State.

"Lily had left it behind. Along with everything else she owned.

"Except the Key. And except the child who would be born too soon."

§ § §

That was me, of course, that baby. It was no surprise that when Will came to this part of the story, a deep emotion rose in me, through my chest, up my throat, and into the back of my eyes. But my own birth is such a small part of the story. It doesn't count for much against the greater tale. That is the story of the birth of a new Arcadia, the one Lily tended so anxiously, the one that I inherited, along with a duty of care toward it. The one that Aspern Grayling so despises, and aches to dismantle in favor of...what? "In favor of Power," he would say. It's difficult for me, who feels gently toward him, while sternly toward his works. Didn't he and I come out of the same disasters? How can I help looking at him with love, even while he demands the destruction of everything I've pledged to protect and foster?

He says that's why he does plot against me. He says that it's my weakness that makes me unfit to lead.

But is it truly a weakness, I wonder? And was it Lily's? Sixty years later, past the events in those winter mountains, I feel the ground firm under my feet. It's not weakness, Aspern, I tell him those rare times we meet in secret to see if our differences can be resolved. It's strength. And it's the only way forward.

"Is it?" he says to me scornfully. "You who let the murderer of your own mother live?"

§ § §

Wilder stumbled when he came to this part of the story. It was too much for him. I saw that, and helped him. I picked up the thread of his tale.

It's understandable that he would fail. But I tell him he can't let himself fail forever. Too much depends on his finally being strong

218

enough to own his experience. All his experience. And his experience, of course, is mine.

If anything has made me fit to be queen, it is that I own these experiences, everything from this moment on until the Death I can see ahead of me. My own Death will be a peaceful one, I know that. Unlike the Death of my mother. Of Lily.

When I say this to Wilder, his head droops, and I fear, sometimes, that I'll lose him to despair. But I needn't fear. At the last minute, I know Wilder will remember he is a bard, and remember his job, and, hard as it is to face what he has done, he'll tell the tale whole.

But that first night, around the Winter Hearth, it was too soon, too hard for Wilder, no matter how strong his professional pride. So I had pity on him, my partner in making the stories of Arcadia anew, and I took up the story myself.

§ § §

Lily smelled disaster in the cold air. She told me, Kim told me, Devindra told me. They all knew. They would have to get over the mountains, somehow, before...before...before....

I know Lily shivered, thinking about it. Kim looked up at her sharply, then looked away with a thoughtful expression. Clare slept with her head in Lily's lap, and Lily methodically smoothed the child's hair as she did.

Then it happened. "Look!" someone called out. And look they did. They saw a rocket go up from Megalopolis. Then two. Then three.

"They're leaving," one of the women said dully. "Them with all their science," another one said—the one who had found the abundant mushrooms that fed hundreds that night.

"They know," a third woman said.

"And they woulda left us lot behind," Kim said, her eyes sparkling indignantly. A murmur of agreement went around the fires.

Lily stayed sunk deep in thought. She remembered that other night she had seen the rockets take off from Megalopolis for the False Moon. Soon—two, three nights at the most—she hoped they would be in that meadow, on the Arcadian side of the Ceres. And then...home. She would be able to see home from there.

The thought filled her with a sadness she couldn't name. As if she knew it wouldn't be so—not the way it seemed to her that night.

Reaching gently into her pocket, so as not to disturb Clare, Lily grasped the Key.

The wind blew.

Then the silence of the throng was cut by a gasp, a sharp intake of breath from a thousand throats.

"Look!" they cried, as if with one voice. As my dearest Devindra, the scientist and Distinguished Professor, has often said, this was the moment when she realized, to the depths of her being, that everything she had learned in the laboratories of Megalopolis had been wrong. "And if not wrong, then limited," she says now thoughtfully to her students as they sit around her cross-legged on the wide green of the college lawn. "The wrong picture. More than the wrong picture. The wrong frame."

Because then, what stood before them all, at the edge of the ridge, overlooking the great city, were two doors, one open and one shut. Two doors that just stood there, as if it were perfectly normal for two doors to appear at the edge of a ridge in the mountains, framing the view below.

At least, that was what the one on the left did. Open wide on its cold stone frame, it showed a view all the way down to the sea.

All was silent. "No one went near the doors. You can imagine it was like witchcraft seeing them hang there!" So said the scientist

Devindra much later, she who had spent her early life scorning the idea of sorcery and magic, and who now stared at...what? Was it proof? Proof of what?

A few of the women crossed themselves. They didn't know why. They only remembered that their grandmothers and their great-grandmothers had done the same when they were in distress. These women were now in distress themselves. And they did not know how to meet that distress. There was nothing to meet it in what they'd been taught.

"What's it mean?" Kim whispered. Clare was awake now, and clinging frightened to Lily, who murmured soothing words to her, and gently put her aside. Lily knew what she had to do. She had the Key, and the Key told her. Dusting herself off, she stood. Taking a deep breath, she thrust her hand back in her pocket, once again grasping the Key.

Another deep breath. And then she walked, slowly, toward the closed door.

No one stirred. Lily kept up her walk. Then she was in front of both doors, staring at them in silence.

I think she knew then. I think she knew all her fate. It was uncanny. It was...Aspern Grayling would deny it ever happened. He wasn't there, but he would deny it ever happened, and blind people would believe him, because it's easier to believe him than to make room in their tiny worlds for what truly Is.

Lily stood there. "Oh, it was as if she were having a conversation with them doors, Soph!" Kim told me later. The door on the left, made of some light silver metal, swung even more widely open in the wind, as if inviting Lily to step through. Through it, Megalopolis shone like the strand of jewels she had left behind.

The door on the right was a thick wooden one, carved all over with curious animals of a type never before seen: half human/half bird, half human/half lion, half human/half ape. There were angels carved across the lintel, and devils and demi-devils down the sides of the frame. And the carving was so cunning that all these figures seemed to stir into life as Lily stood there.

On the left-hand side of that door was a burnished wooden handle. And beneath that handle was a lock. Lily paused only for a moment, taking the deepest breath she could, and though she never told anyone what went through her mind at that moment, Kim, back at the fire, could see her thinking to herself, "Breathe in. Breathe out. Breathe in. Breathe out..." With each breath she walked closer to the door. She took out the Key. She fit it to the lock. It joined the lock as if it had never been apart.

"Breathe in. Breathe out. Breathe in...."

Lily turned the Key.

There was a cry from Clare. A trio of shaggy ponies appeared at the edge of the ridge, drawn by the force of the event. They were wild ponies, left from the ancient stock that the old women and men of the mountains had bred long ago.

The ponies stood shaking their manes in the wind. One of them, a black pony with a thick, ragged gray mane, let out a loud trumpet of a neigh.

Lily swallowed. She put her fingers up against the door gently, against the figure of a woman with a horse's body—a centaur. As she did, the carved woman neighed in answer to the pony. Startled, Lily would have drawn back, but the carving's front arms seemed to reach out and grab her thumb. Then, as Lily moved forward, the right door swung open. It swung open wide...wider...wider still... expanding across the ridge until it covered the other door, obliterating it from sight, and stretched out and out and out until it was a carved wooden frame, with wooden angels and devils chasing each other around and around, stretching out to reframe the view. Lily followed it until it stopped. And the carving of the woman centaur let her go.

Lily took one step back and gazed through the open door.

That was the moment of the Great Earthquake. As everyone on the mountain watched, Megalopolis began to shake and groan and split down to its roots. So deep and terrible was the Great Earthquake that even there, on the ridge in the Ceres Mountains, the terrified people could hear the earth's cries...and the screams of the people as they ran to and fro, with nowhere to cling safely, nowhere to hide.

"It went on for hours," Kim said later. "Or anyways, that were the way it seemed." In fact, it lasted no more than ten minutes. And when it was over, the lights of Megalopolis were out, to be succeeded, quite shortly, by red and orange flames. Here and there at first. Then everywhere.

This was the moment of the Great Silence, which Arcadian physicists still find such a fruitful, and often frustrating, part of the landscape of natural fact. Everywhere was silence. Had anyone wanted to, they could not have uttered a sound.

"I tried it meself," Kim has said to me many times. "Couldn'ta said a word if I'd a-wanted to. No."

Not a bird sang, not a frog croaked, not a wolf howled. Not even the flames crackled, now consuming what had been Megalopolis. They did their job in silence.

Burning, the flames raced across the picture in the frame. From three sides, they raced toward where the missiles had taken off. And then the Great Silence was rent, as if from top to bottom, by a Great Noise so loud that it seemed like Silence itself.

"It was no noise like you and I know, no, nothin' like that. It was so loud it was quiet. Dead quiet. It rushed past us like a hurricane, even far away as we were. And it left some of us deaf, as if it exploded our eardrums, from the inside."

Then there was a Howling, as if the whole of the Landscape in the Frame, as if the Whole of the World were crying out in pain and regret for what had led to this, the acts that had ended in this...and then there was a loud rushing sound—"Like if you could hear under water in your bath when you pull out the plug..." said Kim—and the blazing flames below went out, in patches, one by one, bowled over by a greater force. "And we didn't know what it was till things cleared up and we could see again—oh, that was a lot later, Sophy, you were almost born then—and we saw it was a huge wave, a tidal wave from the sea, and it just mowed everything down."

But no one on the ridge, that night, knew about the Great Wave. Arcadian physicists later hypothesized that the Megalopolitans had prepared some vast power source, which these natural disasters had twisted and turned to their own end. And their end was the End of Megalopolis. For that was what it was.

"For awhile, then, we thought it was the end of us, Sophy, dear," Kim said to me later. "But it wasn't. Not by a long shot. We were tougher than that, all right. Some of us."

But not all. Because that was when Winter, called too soon to every nook and cranny of the World by this loud cry of Force, strode across the land. And he came first to the mountains, where he is more at home than anywhere else. He came quickly, in thick white sheets of snow and freezing wind, and by the morning, there were many dead of the cold and of the sheer terror of it all.

Then came the great scramble for shelter among those who were left. There was a moment where the fear was so great that it killed more people than the mountain, more people than Winter himself. This sobered those left, which was lucky for them. They remembered they needed each other, and it was that understanding that let them survive. That and the Key.

Winter lasted months. A mountain that, in fairer weather, could have been crossed in two days now became impassable. Lily, who had known the mountain as a child, was able to lead her now small group to a clutch of caves. It seemed so long ago since she and Colin had played robbers inside of them.

The three little ponies were with them. No one knew why they followed Clare, but they did, as did every horse she ever came near from then on. And this was a piece of luck. The ponies knew, after many generations wintering on that mountain, where to dig to find the tender shoots still hidden, where to look for acorns and pine nuts, where to find streams with fish hiding sluggishly in icy inlets. One of the ponies proved to be a mare about to foal, and so there was milk.

"Three long months of this," Kim said, shuddering at the painful memory of it. She has never had her health back again, after those months.

"Then, you were born," she said.

I never tired of hearing that part of the tale when I was young. And so, that first night around the Hearth in the Round Hall, I made Kim take up the last bit of the tale.

§ § §

She hesitated, of course, because she was worried (she told me later) that she was no storyteller such as Wilder, but then, "A' course it's me as should tell it, I was there, warn't I? I've as much right to the story as he does. It's my story, too, innit? The story of thems I love." So my nurse, Kim took up the tale that night. And I think it was best told in her more homelike way.

"Born in a cave, you were, with just me and Clare and the ponies

225

SOPHIA THE WISE WAS BORN IN THE CERES MOUNTAINS

looking on, all anxious. Your mother did it all, and never said a word—hours it took, and she never said a word. And you only cried once when you came out, like you were surprised. When it was over, we wrapped you up and gave you to her and we cut the cord, and after that you were still. I was worried it meant there was something wrong, but Lily, she knew it was all right. And then, oh, I don't know, but it was spring, somehow, things got better bit by bit, until one morning it was warm again! Warm! And the birds singing! And sunshine everywhere! We could see down the mountain now. Where Megalopolis had been, now was just one big bright blue-green sea.

"Your mother was still weak, but she was always stronger than the rest of us even when she was that way—you know what I mean, you're a little like that yourself—and she made us all get up and led us to a place, all green and covered with new buds, which seemed to make her sad. She'd been there last, she said, at a Feast. We don't have them now. I dunno why. But there we were, where one had been. And then we walked down the other side of the Mountain into Arcadia."

Of course I knew the rest. We all knew the rest. But I begged Kim to go on. And the rest of her audience sat rapt.

"Oh, then, sad times, you know. You all know all this from the history books, don't you?"

"Go on, Kim." I said, urging her. "Do go on."

Kim sighed, but she went on, lacing her fingers together on her lap there by the fire. "Well then. It was all a mess, all of it. From what I heard, the place, our place, this 'ere Arcadia, never got over being occupied like that by the Great Empire—we Megalopolitans could be dead cruel, and a place never gets over a thing like that. Lily's ma had been a big...I'm not sure what...some kind of leader, like they had in the old days. So when we got down there, there was nobody in charge, like. And your ma, she was like magic, Soph. (I mean, yer majesty, sorry, I keep forgettin'.) All yer 'ad to do was look at 'er to know it. They all knew it. So they asked your mother to be their queen and lead them."

"And she said no," I said, keeping my voice expressionless.

"She said no," Kim nodded. "Three times they asked. Three times she said no. Finally, they just wore her out—that's what I think. And she spent all her time trying to get everything steady. Which wasn't easy. If you ask me, a bigger group of fruitcakes I'd never seen than that court of Arcadia. But your mother told me to be patient. She said it would be all right in the end."

"But it wasn't."

"No. It wasn't. Three times when you were small (I mean, when Queen Sophia was a royal tyke), she tried to step down, and three times the cities begged her to stay on. Then was the fourth. She was firm this time. She said she would keep the Key, but step down she must, and step down she would. She had never wanted, she said, to be a queen."

"No," I said thoughtfully. And then added, "Tell me what happened then."

"Aw, Soph...I mean...aw, never mind. You know what happened then. You know I don't like to..."

"Tell me," I said. And the room around the Central Hearth went absolutely still. "And tell them, too," I added softly. Kim looked at me through her eyes swimming wet with tears. For what? For her old friend. For me, her nursling. For Arcadia itself, Arcadia that surrounded her, listening to her tale.

"Ah, well, then," Kim said, resigned, wiping her eyes with determination, "she told them she was going. Told 'em they were going to have to stand on their own, sink or swim. She and I were laughing together in the throne room—she was so relieved to think all that would be over soon. I don't remember where Clare was..."

"She was with the horses, in the meadows near Wrykyn, getting ready for the Fair."

"Yeah, of course. That's where she was. And you were with Devindra somewhere, you were that interested in 'er experiments, even then, a little tyke like that, we all wondered at it. But of course you were Lily's daughter. A queen, ye know."

We were both quiet then. We both knew I hadn't wanted to be a queen.

"Go on," I said. That was when Wilder pulled his bard's cloak over his head, in sorrow at what he knew she would say. His fellows nearby looked at him, doubtful, and pulled away, leaving him seated there alone.

And I? I stood and went to him, putting my hand on his shoulder in reassurance. In comradeship. But that night, he didn't move, or look up at me, or say a word.

"Then," Kim continued, same as the many times she told the story to me as a child, she told it to all of us, later, in the Great Round Hall, "a messenger came in and said there was a man outside, a stranger, who wanted to talk to Lily the Silent. I remember she turned all pale and she said, 'Let him come in.'"

"She thought it was my father."

"She thought it was your father. One of the mushroom women had come to the palace, and said she'd seen in her fire that your father was alive and would come to find you again. And Lily the Silent knew enough to believe the mushroom women when they saw something in the flames." Kim sighed again. "But, heigh ho. It wasn't your father after all."

"No. It was Will."

"Will the Murderer. That's right." Kim carefully looked down at her interlaced hands. "Him," she said. "The young idiot, wound up by people who knew better, him with his knife and him with his stupid yell, 'Death to Tyrants!'—and when had your mother ever been a tyrant, I ask you? And everyone else asks it, too." Kim stopped here, shading her eyes with her hand, though she wasn't sitting in the light.

"He killed my mother," I said, as gently as I could say such a thing. "He killed Lily the Silent."

Kim, her eyes still shadowed by her hand, nodded. I went on.

"He killed her and you, Kim, ran to her, and she was dead. And when you looked up, there I was, standing in the doorway, a little girl staring at Will."

"Yes," Kim said, very quiet. But the hall was quieter still, and heard every word. "And you remember it, though you were that small."

"I remember it," I said gravely. "I remember it well."

It's understandable that Wilder hates this part of the story, and can't bring himself to speak it out loud, can't bring himself to look up during the telling of it, can't bring himself to look at Kim, who in turn can't bring herself to look at him. Though of course he has written it down. He has written the whole story down. And he has whispered it to me. Even though it was this part of the tale that led to his bardhood, and to the great service he has done for Arcadia. He doesn't like to be reminded ("as if I don't remember it, and every night, Snow, in my dreams!") that before he was Wilder the Bard, he was Will the Murderer, and that he—my trusted companion, my friend—is he who killed my mother, Queen Lily the Silent, the First Queen of Arcadia, while I, too small and helpless to do otherwise, looked on.

But there is more to the story than what I told that night, more than what all of us told, or tell, around the Great Hearth. What I have never told anyone, not Wilder, not Devindra, not Kim, not Clare, is that at the moment when my mother died, I saw the Angel fly out of her and into Wilder—Will the Murderer then. I saw that, and I ran to Will (this was never told before now in the story, because how

230

would it fit? How would my listeners understand it?). I clung to him, and refused to let him go. And afterward he, who had murdered all I held most dear, was my greatest teacher, and my greatest strength.

This is a great mystery. I am just beginning myself to understand it. Is it anything that you, who come after me, can hear? Anything that you can begin to understand?

'DEATH, WHERE DOES THIS ROAD LEAD?'

Thirty

"Death," Lily said reflectively as she walked along the mountain road through the wildflowers and the berry bushes, with Rex close by her side. "Death, where does this road lead?"

Death smiled her beautiful smile, but said nothing. On the Road of the Dead, it was a warm, soft day, with a little breeze coming from the south, and the air smelling like crushed strawberries. Rex, his pelt sleek, and his nose joyfully to the ground, ran here and there, chasing some scent of his own. But he always came back to her afterwards, nudging at her hand with his velvet nose, happy beyond words that they were together again.

There wasn't much else she could ask for, Lily thought, as the road took a small twist and headed up into a wood of red-barked trees.

There was only one thing to ask for. Only...only one thing.

But this she was frightened to ask. This new road was so strange to her still. She had yet to find her confident footing on it.

Death seemed to understand this, and, serene as ever, walked along a little ahead of Lily and Rex, her long light cloak trailing in the reddish dust.

"Oh!" Death said smiling, looking back the way they came. "Look!"

When Lily looked where Death pointed, she saw a long thread unraveling from the edge of her own violet traveling cloak. "It must have been coming undone for miles!" Lily thought, because she could see a single purple thread winding back and back and back, disappearing down the hill into the glen now well behind them.

She hesitated. I know she hesitated. But the thread was tied to something back there, out of sight. To someone.

She stopped on the road, forehead furrowed. Rex, obedient as ever, stopped too.

"Death," she finally brought herself to say. "Death. I can't go on just yet. Wait a moment. Please."

Death looked at her speculatively, but said no more than "Allow me." And with a light gesture, Death plucked the thread up between her long, elegant fingers and held it to the light. Then she put it neatly between her even white teeth and, snap! She snapped it loose, just like that.

Lily shuddered. But then...then...

"All right," Death said vigorously. "Race you to the top of the hill!"

And Lily, feeling somehow lighter now, after Death had cut the violet thread, ran after her, Rex barking and jumping beside. That must have been the moment where she dropped the Key. Dropped it, unnoticed, from her pocket, the Rose-Gold Key, and left it there on the Road of the Dead, as she ran after Death. And as she ran, she forgot. The Key wasn't meant for her any longer. Now it would wait for someone else.

Death won the race, of course, because Death always does, but only by a hand's breadth, and then the three of them stopped, companions, at the top of the hill, on the other side of the wood.

The three of them sat there, looking down at the view below of the land and the sea, and a ship that waited for them at the end of the now narrow and dangerous road. It was midsummer. The day was very long, and they were able to sit there a long, long time before Death, with a sigh, stood up, dusted herself off, and, after helping Lily up, led the way down the steep cliffside path to the harbor.

A stiff wind blew as they went. She and Lily wrapped their cloaks around themselves more tightly for warmth.

§ § §

How do I know this? I know this because I've traveled the Road of the Dead myself, and met Death, who told me this part of the tale. "They never end, these tales," Death told me there, at the top of the path that led down to the harbor where Death's ship was docked, ready to set sail once again. "Your mother's story ends and yours begins. How can you tell where?"

She kissed me then, and turned me back on the path. It wasn't time for me to sail away with her. Not yet. Not then. I still had my own tale to tell.

§ § §

I was fifteen years old, and it was eight years after Will killed my mother, when my own story started.

"Kim," I said urgently, in a low tone so that the courtiers around us wouldn't hear. There were so many of them! And all of them having to be flattered and fed—oh, how I was sick of it that day. They would see me conferring, in my usual grave way, with Kim the Kind, who was known to be the Chief Counselor of State by Regal Decree, and some of them would write records of it, even though they had no idea what was said. Some of them would paint it as an historical scene, and some of them would write epic poetry about it. All of them would make careers from babbling thoughtlessly, without understanding what was, in truth, said. And this was the basis of the prestige of the upper classes, and the shaky foundation on which the economy of Arcadia was laid.

"Kim," I said again desperately that fatal day, "I really don't think I can stand this one more hour."

Kim the Kind looked at me with a worried face—one that had become increasingly worried in the last year, the year that I had reached my fifteenth birthday, and the courtiers had begun to talk of finding me a consort of a grandeur consonant with my high estate and that of Arcadia, whose sign and signal and banner I was, and blah blah blah. There was no one left in the world fit for their queen, these courtiers said to themselves in low, solemn tones around their electric fires—wood fires being for the lower classes, and for the Queen and her immediate Counselors, by royal decree. (In fact, after my mother's death, when I had inherited her room for my own, I loudly demanded a wood fire there, refusing any other kind—many books, poems, and musical compositions had been written about this strange freak of mine.) Arcadia's grandeur, since the days of Lily the Silent, who brought destruction to Megalopolis and renewed the springtime promise of her homeland, was unquestioned then.

There was no one left in the Four Corners, in the days after the Great Flood, no prince, to match my supposed eminence. And this was a problem the courtiers gnawed over as they gnawed over the bones of the endless supply of provisions that came from the Royal Pantry for their feasting, as was their right. No one could actually remember when this had become their right, but so many poems, articles, histories, songs, and dramatic presentations had been written about it that there was no one left to question why.

No one, that is, except me, Sophia, daughter of Lily the Silent and Conor Barr, who was to be known, much later, by people who didn't know any better, as Sophia the Wise.

So now I was Queen Sophia the First, like it or not, and, my somewhat too large nose twitching with suppressed disdain, I leaned over to Kim and cried out.

"They are a bunch of idiots, Aunt Kim, and I don't think I can bear to look at them one more day. Much less rule over them."

"Clare will be home soon, yer know, Soph, did you hear? Found a horse faster than the wind, they say, and she's bringing its foal home for you..."

"Nice try," I said. Kim sighed.

"No use is it, ever, trying to get you off something once you're on it," Kim complained—but there was, as always, a fond light in her eyes.

"No, indeed," I agreed as I climbed down off my throne. It was miles too big for me, and uncomfortable to boot, but the Court Sculptors would not allow it to be anything less than a perfect symbol of my supposed puissance. It was only later that I had the idea of the Central Court, with the Central Hearth, and a comfortable chair beside it for a throne. And anyway, I hated to contradict them and make them feel like fools.

"Not that they ever would," I said to Kim. "Feel like fools, I mean. I would like them so much more, if it would occur to them that they might look the tiniest bit stupid."

About this, Kim was forced to agree. Not the least tedious part of life at the Arcadian court was the great seriousness with which everyone took themselves. This importance was like a membrane, like an impenetrable cloak. We bleakly surveyed the courtiers as they milled about the enormous, marble-paved throne room, muttering importantly to themselves.

"Well," I said philosophically, wriggling down from the throne and adjusting my skirt with an irritable twitch. "I've had enough of this for today."

"Where you going then, love?"

"The usual," I said, and I'm sure my eyes brightened with anticipation. "I'm going to have my game of chess."

"With Will." Kim said. She gave a little snort, the way she had every day this last year, ever since, on my fifteenth birthday, I had announced my intention of a weekly visit to the Royal Prison in one of the two Royal Towers—the other holding the rooms of the queen herself, and her mother before her.

"With Will the Murderer," I said thoughtfully as I kissed my dear Kim on the cheek. "Yes."

"And he never says nothing 'bout that day?" Kim said wistfully. She hadn't understood my reasons—no one had—but she trusted her charge. Bless her.

"Nothing," I said cheerfully. "But then he wouldn't have a reason to, since I say nothing to him."

And even though no one would have believed it, it was true. For almost a year, I had visited Will the Murderer in his tower room. For all that time we played a weekly game of chess in silence. Sometimes Will won, sometimes it was my turn, and sometimes—and this was obscurely satisfying to both of us—it was a draw. But we never, in those days, exchanged a word.

Never, that is, until this very day of which we speak. Which was the real end of Lily the Silent's story, and the beginning of the tale of Sophia, called by some 'the Wise.'

§ § §

Why am I writing all this, telling it this way? Why don't I just leave it to Wilder, leave him his expiation, as he so grandly calls it—to sing the foundation myths of Arcadia and make up, on a daily basis, for his one great crime? Why don't I just get on with what everyone in Arcadia, with a few notable exceptions, thinks of as my real job? Which is, of course, Being Queen.

But what is Being Queen? That's the question I find I've asked myself for as long as I can remember. I'm convinced it's the question my mother bequeathed to me, the one she never found the answer to, and so passed it down.

I haven't found the answer. Sometimes I think I never will. For how many years do I have left? My adventures have been hard on me, and I know this old, familiar body took the brunt of my wanderings, of my curious inquiries into the nature of our world. I can't expect miracles from it. It's served me well enough as it is.

And what if I don't find the answer to the question: How is it best for us to live? If I can't discover the answer, I have to leave the question for someone else, the way my mother did, handing it down like an unlit torch from one to another, waiting for the day the light will come to it.

I think I've been waiting, all this winter while I pondered and wrote this small history down, for my goddaughter, for Shanti to be born. I think that's what started this, after all the years I spent locked in my study, refusing to do my royal duties, while I spent the afternoon poring over old manuscripts, gathering old stories, arguing and laughing over meanings with Wilder. It was when Devindra came to me, so happy to give me the news about her great-granddaughter Shiva Vale—that she and her husband, Walter Todhunter, were finally, after many barren years, going to have a child.

Devindra's great-great-grandchild. My...my goddaughter.

Of course this was more than usual cause for rejoicing. We all know Shiva and Walter have tried to have a child for many years, and there were so many reasons why they might never have succeeded. Those reasons go right to the heart of our present conundrum. Which is, I repeat, how is it best for us to live?

All through the months of waiting for Shanti, I have been writing this, the bits and pieces and scraps of what I know of my mother's history, which means the bits and pieces and scraps of who I am. And all of it, all of it, meant for Shanti.

For you, Shanti. If I can, if I may, I'll spend the next years telling you tale after tale, telling you bits I've forgotten to put in here, bits I haven't understood enough to put in here, bits I've begun to understand differently since I put them down here. I'll tell you what stories I can, in what time we have together.

But for now, there is this story, this tale of Lily the Silent, who was my mother and Arcadia's first queen. And of course, because tales never begin or end, not really, her story leads into mine.

§ § §

"Oh, Death!" Lily exclaimed from her comfortable seat on the deck of the white ship, Rex's head resting on her knee. "You give me so many gifts!"

Death, steering the ship so that it caught the breeze in its sails, just smiled her deep smile. She looked ahead. Very far away ahead.

On Lily's lap was a book wrapped in velvet and lace, and this had been Death's gift to her friend as they boarded the ship. "It's meant to pass the Time," Death explained, and Lily, half trembling, gave her cheek another timid kiss. "You can pick it up whenever you like, and then"—at this Death sighed and smiled another type of smile, this one more subtle than the ones that had gone before—"you can put it down again."

The day was warm, with a cool current running through it like a ribbon, and the sun was high over the sea. Death was so adept at sailing the tall, white ship that it was a pleasure to watch her, and this is what Lily and Rex did now.

After awhile, the sun dipped below the horizon; the stars came out, and a moon rose up so brightly that the sea shone under it, and you could even count the fish as they cavorted under the waves. "Look!" Lily said from where she leaned against the ship's rails, pointing the sights out to Rex (she had gotten up to get her cloak against the chill of the evening, and now, holding it closed at her chest, she was as warm as she had been under the bright gold of the sun). "Look, the Mermaids! Oh, I'm so glad!" For under the surface the Mermaids swam serenely alongside the ship, and among them Lily could see Phoebe riding the Manatee. Phoebe saluted her and the Manatee blew her a clumsy kiss. And Lily knew they would join her at the journey's end.

Now Lily after awhile remembered Death's gift, which lay on the deck beside her chair, and she went back to open it and read a little before she slept. Rex went with her and watched with interest as the pages began to turn.

Lily went through the book until she found the page she was looking for. There was a picture there of a wandering hermit, solitary and old, but determined to find the love that he had lost. "Will he be so much older than I am now when he finds me, Death?" she said sadly. "Will we even know each other then?"

Death didn't answer. But Lily was a queen, even in death, and she knew that to worry your heart over things that can't be fixed is foolish, in life, in death. It was enough to know that Conor would set out to find her some day.

She went back to the book, and turned another page.

"Look, Rex, there. There's Sophia, and her story. And it's part of ours, isn't it?" The Dog, nodding, agreed, and the two of them went on reading Sophia's story, absorbed. Death, who never slept, kept a stern eye on the goal far ahead.

§ § §

"The queen! The queen! My God, what has happened? Look at the queen!"

The courtiers of Arcadia ran to and fro like mice, squeaking in

241

dismay.

Clare the Rider, who had only just arrived, stood with Kim the Kind, both of them arrested by what they saw. Kim clutched at Clare's arm.

Queen Sophia the First, daughter of Lily the Silent and Conor Barr, stood at the top of the stairs to the tower where Will the Murderer was kept. She looked down at them all with an expression hard to read, a mixture of sadness and anger and relief all at once.

"She's young, but, ah, Clare, she's a deep one. She'll find a way out of this new mess, you wait and see!" That was what Kim the Kind said to Clare the Rider—or so the Arcadian historians later claimed.

For Sophia the First stood there, pretending to be as regal as ever, in spite of—or was it because of?—the new pair of scaly, horny, clawtoed, green and gray legs that replaced her formerly girlish ones. And in spite of—or was it because of?—the thick diamond-patterned tail that swirled out from under her dress and coiled around the floor in front of her.

"Well, you don't have to look at me like someone died or something," Sophia said in her severest voice as all the court looked up at her in horror. "It's only a murderer's curse. I mean, honestly. Garden variety, people! I felt sorry for him, okay? So I let him win. He seemed to take that badly."

At this her tail twitched and thumped, a proceeding she looked at with some interest, appearing to test how much control she had over this. Thumping it once, then twice, she was satisfied. "Hmm," she murmured. "Not bad. Not bad at all."

Another gasp of horror from the courtroom's floor recalled her to her audience and she said, "Well, who would have thought he had it in him, Will the Murderer? And me always thinking he didn't have much imagination to speak of. But to curse me into being half a lizard—well, it's not bad. It kind of gives me hope...." She gave another half smile, not saying what kind of hope she had. At this, Kim the Kind gave a cry and jumped forward—and not a moment too soon, because Sophia crumpled, fainting, to the floor. Kim was just in time to catch her before she hit the ground.

But then, in a flash, the fainting fit was gone, and Sophia, brushing Kim off her with the fondest of strokes to the cheek, jumped up onto her lizard feet and—at first clumsily, then with growing confidence— made her way down to the floor beneath, among the grieving, shrieking, whining court.

"All right," she said. "Enough moaning. Now I've got to start figuring out how to fix this thing. Clare! Call out the three best horses you have! The Lizard Princess might be a little heavy on her feet, but her brain's as good as it ever was."

"Yes, ma'am!" Clare said, and she was out of the throne room as swiftly as one of her own mares, and came back, as quick as you could say "happy/sad/happy/sad" three times without taking a breath, with a red mare, a black mare, and a gray. And before the stunned court could collect itself, Clare, Kim the Kind, and Sophia the Lizard Princess mounted (it was amazing in retrospect how Sophia so quickly learned how to manage that unwieldy tail and feet!), and went riding hard out the door.

"W-w-w-wait!" cried Michaeli, the Lord High Chancellor in a weak voice. "W-wait! St-st-stop! N-n-n-no!"

But Sophia the First, now the Lizard Princess, was gone with the wind and never once turned to look back until she became, so say the historians (but them you can't always believe), Sophia the Wise.

§ § §

"Ah," Lily said dreamily, as Sophia, Kim, and Clare rode away. "I wonder what will happen next?" Rex looked at her thoughtfully and, lying on the deck beside her, gave a contented grunt. Lily closed the book for now, and lay it down on its face. "For now," she said, "I think we'll just look at the sea."

"A good plan," Death said. "For we're almost there."

"Are we?" Lily said eagerly, jumping up. It was dawn now, and pink light was shining to the east, shimmering over the water. "Ah!" Lily said. "I can see it! I can see it! We're almost there!"

"Home," Death said.

"Home," Lily agreed, going to her side. "We're going home."

Death steered the tall white ship into a port in a clear blue bay. At the end of a wooden dock Maud stood, shading her eyes against the morning sun. And smiling.

"Is this the End, then, Death?" Lily asked, as she smiled back.

"No," Death said, smiling her own smile. "It's never the end."

"Oh," Lily said. "Good."

The ship docked, and Lily and Rex walked home, with Maud and Death herself, into a new day.

And in another world altogether, the Lizard Princess rode on her way to become (or, as she would always have it—and who knew better?—to try to become) Sophia the Wise.

But that is another story, for another place, and another Time.

THE END

A POSTSCRIPT FROM THE EDITOR:

In reading *Lily the Silent*, I have the funny feeling that some of its characters are familiar, even if different, from the first Arcadian fairy tale published by Exterminating Angel Press, *Snotty Saves the Day*. There's the Manatee. He has the bugged out eyes of Tuxton Ted in that first story, and he seems to know Lily from before they meet under the sea. On the Moon Itself, Lily sees, in her friend Phoebe, the Lemon Yellow Teddy Bear, Melia. Lily's name for her own daughter, Snowflake, is the same as that of the unicorn that led Snotty on his adventures. Then there's Livia. She brings up the unnerving image of Mr. Big.

Are these coincidence? Or something more?

I'm sure that something must account for this. Looking through other communications from Arcadia, I find a similar feel in the scientific treatise *On The Discovery of Biological Truths in Fairy Tales*, by the Arcadian scientist Dr. Alan Fallaize. Sure enough, in those Arcadian stories Fallaize recounts and analyzes, there are echoes of other characters. I've attached one of these tales, "The Girl with One Shoe," here. It's as if this is the story of Lily and Conor, told again in a different way, with a different, happier, end. Is this because both stories, one history, one fairy tale, reflect the same Arcadian values? Or is there something else, more mysterious, going on?

Am I just imagining things? Which would not be too surprising, given the circumstances.

Myself, I see evidence every day that Dr. Fallaize is right, and biological truths are contained in fairy tales. After all, aren't we all the water poured into the glass, drunk by the princess, pissed into the chamber pot, emptied into the cistern, flowing out to the sea, rising into the air, falling down as rain, poured into the glass again...?

Another question to talk over with Sophia, if I ever have the good fortune to see or hear from her again....

APPENDIX: An Arcadian Fairy Tale
From *On the Discovery of Biological Truth in Fairy Tales*,
by Dr. Alan Fallaize (Otterbridge University Press, year 61)

The Girl
With One Shoe

A young girl was taken as a concubine by an older, more powerful man. He was stocky and one of his ears stuck out farther than the other. But she loved him instantly, and in the true meaning of the word.

It was this man's habit to take and discard young women, who then could leave or stay, according to their choice, as servant to the next mistress. When it was her turn to be discarded, the girl stayed. She did this knowing well the pain that would come from knowing her True Love was sharing a bed with another woman.

He said he planned to marry this new woman. Still the girl stayed. He took away many of her clothes, and left her with only one shoe. Still she stayed. He moved all the rooms of the house, switching them so she could no longer find the place that was hers. But she knew it was a trick. Patient, still she stayed.

On the day of the wedding, she saw the man was old, grizzled, graying, and this made her feel more tenderly toward him even than before. But now she knew, by these signs, that time was running out, and unless she took charge and told him of his folly, it would be too late for happiness.

Accordingly, she told him: I am your Real Love. If you do not realize this, and send the other women on their way, and begin a true life with me, it will be too late, and you will miss your True Life and Happiness.

He looked at her and saw it was true. And he did as she said. And they had their True Life and were happy, so far as it is possible in this life to be.

ACKNOWLEDGMENTS

The discovery of Arcadia couldn't happen without the aid and comfort of so many differently talented people: Nate Dorward, John Sutherland, Molly Mikolowski and Nick Liberty at A Literary Light, everyone at Consortium Book Sales and Distribution, and at Constellation, too.

Alex, Gray, and Pearl provided constant support, companionship, and cups of perfectly brewed tea.

None of this could be done without Mike Madrid, who is not only responsible for the very elegant illustrations of *Lily the Silent*, but also for EAP's overall book design. He is always there to remind me to live in this century, with these readers, here, right now.

And to all the wonderful people who love and share books with us: our booksellers, our librarians, and, of course, most of all, readers everywhere, my warmest thanks. Where would ideas, new and old, be without you?

My thanks to all of you for being there, and for helping solve all the curious problems Arcadia provides. As everyone knows, it's great to have friends.

At EXTERMINATING ANGEL PRESS,
we're taking a new approach to our world.
A new way of looking at things.
New stories, new ways to live our lives.
We're dreaming how we want our lives and our world to be...

Also from
EXTERMINATING ANGEL PRESS

The Supergirls: *Fashion, Feminism, Fantasy,
and the History of Comic Book Heroines*
by Mike Madrid

Jam Today: *A Diary of Cooking With What You've Got*
by Tod Davies

Correcting Jesus: *2000 Years of Changing the Story*
by Brian Griffith

3 Dead Princes: *An Anarchist Fairy Tale*
by Danbert Nobacon
with illustrations by Alex Cox

Dirk Quigby's Guide to the Afterlife
by E. E. King

Snotty Saves the Day: *The History of Arcadia*
by Tod Davies
with illustrations by Gary Zaboly

This Is US: *The New All-American Family*
by David Marin

A Galaxy of Immortal Women:
The Yin Side of Chinese Civilization, by Brian Griffith

Park Songs: *A Poem/Play*, by David Budbill
with photos by R.C. Irwin

THE HISTORY OF ARCADIA series tells the story of a land that is literally formed by a story, by one person discovering and claiming who she really is . . . of the events that lead first to a deceptively happy world, then to an inevitably tragic outcome . . . and finally to a slow rebuilding of the world on foundations more deeply laid . . .

"Fascinating . . . A quirky, intelligent, and imaginative read for mid-teens and up." —*ForeWord Reviews*

"Awesome . . . There's plenty of humor in the book. . . . And the best is the truth—what Is, as the book calls it—Snotty discovers about himself. He doesn't just see the error of his old ways; he re-becomes an entirely different person. And that possibility, that ability—that we all might re-become what we were born to be—raises a wonder, a "sympathy with the idea of 'changing the world'" that beats louder than does a superficially bleeding heart."
—KRISTIN THIEL, *Nervous Breakdown*

"Ms. Davies blends folklore, fairy tales, fantasy, and even oral tradition—and does so brilliantly . . . *Snotty Saves the Day* is a book for mature or precocious teens, for fantasy and tale-within-a-tale lovers, and for thoughtful adults who seek the wonder and optimism so badly needed in today's times." —*New York Journal of Books*

"Like Susanna Clark's magnificent *Jonathan Strange & Mr. Norrell* . . . and many works by Nicholson Baker, *Snotty Saves the Day* features fictional footnotes that add another layer to the novel. . . . Davies touches on . . . very Big Ideas. But these themes are wrapped in wonders . . . What could have been simply "messagey" is a romp, and an original one at that. . . . Give it to a smart, precocious young person in your life, read it yourself, and see what kind of interesting conversation develops."
—DEB BAKER, Gibson's Bookstore (Concord, NH) @ *bookconscious*

"Blending the magic of fairy tales with the great existential mysteries, Tod Davies leads us into a phantasmagorical world that resurrects the complex lore of times past with vibrant narrative energy."
—MARIA TATAR, author of *The Annotated Brothers Grimm*

"An imaginative book that will make readers think twice."
—JACK ZIPES, author of *Why Fairy Tales Stick*

Available in print and electronic editions wherever books are sold

TOD DAVIES lives with her husband, the filmmaker Alex Cox, and their two dogs, in the alpine valley of Colestin, Oregon, and at the foot of the Rocky Mountains, in Boulder, Colorado. She is the author of the cooking memoir *Jam Today: A Diary of Cooking With What You've Got* and *Snotty Saves The Day*, the first book in *The History of Arcadia* series. Unsurprisingly, her attitude toward literature is the same as her attitude toward cooking—it's all about working with what you have to find new ways of looking at what you've got.

MIKE MADRID, a native San Franciscan, is the author of the *Supergirls: Fashion, Feminism, Fantasy, and The History of Comic Book Heroines*.